Thanks 4 the Support !.,

AMERICAN DREAM

Caremore Publications

Dedicated to the memories of Charlene G. White and Ermias 'Nipsey Hussle' Asghedon

Kevin Brown
Kevinbrownbooks.com

This Is What Made Me

"And last but most definitely not least, I bring to the stage, Lavon Jordan," shouted Felicia Taylor as she looked out into the packed auditorium.

I strolled out from behind the stage, cool as a fan, smooth as butter. If the crowd hadn't known any better I'd bet my last dollar that they thought I was some sort of male super model or something. Real shit.

Alright, ok, ok you got me, I'm lying my ass off, honestly I was dead focused on one thing, not embarrassing myself. As I carefully stepped, I took a brief glance out into the audience before taking a nice, long, slow breath, attempting to calm myself. It didn't work. The brutal image of me slipping, falling and sliding across the stage before somehow plummeting into the lap of some old ass church lady, knocking her wig and glasses off as she screamed in horror suddenly popped in my head.

"Oh shit," I said to myself before gaining my composure, closing my eyes and forcing myself to clear my head. "You got this, stop playing, you got this."

This was the final show of our three month Stage Play tour 'Us vs. them'. Can't lie, by far, this shit has definitely exceeded my expectations. See, initially we were only slated for a two weekend run in Atlanta. And even though it wasn't much, I was perfectly fine with that. Why wouldn't I be? It was my first real official paid acting gig. Yeah, I've been going hard, giving my all to this ol acting dream of mine for about 8 years, but up until now I could never seem to get my big break. Every time things seemed to be going my way something always came along to knock me on my ass. I swear, it never failed.

Thank God I always found the strength to keep going. If I wouldn't have, there's no way I'd be standing on this stage. Can't even lie, this feels good, real good. Safe to say, this here play was life changing.

After successfully reaching the edge of the stage, I proudly looked out into the crowd. Joy consumed my body as I took a bow. A tear drop hit the stage floor as I raised my head, peering back out to the hundreds of faces standing, clapping at the mere site of me. This was truly unbelievable.

Now hold on, before your mind gets to wandering, and you think I'm some ol soft cappuccino drinking, sunshade wearing, boujie wannabe Denzel, acting ass nigga, hell naw, never that, think again. I'm a real nigga, real as it gets, but for some damn reason I just been finding myself crying like a little ass bitch lately. I try to stop it, but it's uncontrollable. Shits crazy.

I gotta be honest though, ain't like all this crying emotional shit is new. I'm from the streets, I've been through a lot. So much that I can't even began to tell you about it. It's just too much. With that being said, of course I've cried my fair share of times over the years. But these tears, these tears today are different. These motherfuckers is happy tears. Up until a few months ago I swear I aint even know this kinda emotion existed.

No lie, I'm telling you, shit really just came outta nowhere. I remember it clear as day, I was riding down the street, leaving rehearsal, just thinking of how far I'd come, then suddenly I felt a lump in my chest. Being the man that I am, my first initial reaction was to fight the feeling, I shook it off, turned on some 21 savage and tried to thug it.

These emotions were too strong though, impossible to fight. Before long I gave in and in an instance tears burst from my eyes before speed racing their way to my cheeks, chin and shirt. It was wild. I drove, face drenched the entire ride to the crib.

I was only about five minutes away from home but still, that's a long ass time to be crying about some happy shit. By the time I'd finally arrived I'd wiped my eyes so much that I couldn't see a damn thing, shit was blurry as hell. I took a deep breath before pausing to say a quick prayer.

Whatsup God,

Man man man, wow, I'm finally headed to where I wanna be dog. You saw me at my worse and made sure I had the strength to keep trucking. If anybody knows, I know for a fact you know it was times when I felt like quitting this shit. My bad, my bad I didn't mean to cuss, but you know how we do. But yeah man, I'm so glad you kept sending me those signs I needed to keep going. If it weren't for you I don't know where I'd be. I swear I'll always trust in you. I'm sorry for ever doubting. I can't believe it's been three months. I was good with the little two weekends that I initially signed on for. But you came through again. I know it's only gonna go up from here, I can feel it. I can't wait to continue this journey. You the man Big God. I love you and I swear Ima tell everyone I can about you. My nigga.

After that little prayer I remember sparking my blunt, reclining my seat back and embracing the pure joy of simply being happy. Something I always craved, something I always prayed for. The road to success had suddenly cleared up for me. Seems like I'd been making wrong turns, ducking pot holes, and stuck in traffic forever. But my destination was clear ahead. I could smell it, damn near taste it.

And right now, at this second, standing on this stage, I knew I was closer than ever. As I continued to look out into the crowd I felt the need to personally look into the eyes of everyone in attendance. Of course that was impossible, but the ones I was able to make contact with, looked to me in admiration. I could try for centuries but it would be impossible for me to ever put my feelings into words.

If I could, I'd stand here forever, soaking the love in. Too bad I couldn't, the show must go on. So like the true professional I am, I waved to the crowd, mouthed the words "Thank you," before stepping back, joining my cast mates as our Director continued to thank the audience.

As I stood in alliance with my peers, I scanned the crowd searching for my girl, Alexis, hoping to catch her attention. Like we always say, we're connected, so of course it didn't take long for me to spot her out. I guess her brain didn't have service or something because she damn sure didn't connect back to me. I tried to somehow tap into her head so she'd notice that I was looking her way, but unfortunately it wasn't working. Her hazel eyes instead focused on Felecia, the Director.

Still, that didn't stop me from staring, she was looking too good. She was famous for always experimenting with new hair colors. Today it was lime green, yeah it may sound a tad bit on the wild side but she had a special knack for effortlessly pulling off any style she desired. I loved that about her. So different. She was unapologetically her, she couldn't care less about a negative opinion, which was another thing I loved, or should I say, admired. Yeah, admired may be a better word. I admired her, she was the shit and I made sure she knew it any chance I got.

It's crazy, even the things that I wasn't used to in other relationships and never thought I'd like, I found myself loving when she'd do it. Just for the simple fact it was her. She was everything I needed. In a way I kinda feel she's a big reason I'm standing on this stage. Just waking up next to her pushes me to do better. I'm going to give her the world one day, or at least die trying.

"Come on Von," said Mark, one of the shows other lead actors. I'd been so busy trying to get Alexis's attention that I hadn't even noticed it was time to exit the stage. "You still going out to eat with us?" he asked as we exited.

"Aw man I forgot all about that. Where'd you say we were going again? I promised my Ol Lady we'd head over to Papadeux to get some Seafood after the show."

"Papadeux? Man forget that, we're going to 'Big Daddy's Soul Kitchen'. You gotta come man. What's an after party without the shows leading man?"

"You're right about that. What would yall niggas do without me?" I asked, smiling.

"There you go," he said with a smirk. "So you're coming?"

"Man fuck it, hell yeah I'm coming. I can't miss the last night with yall crazy asses. We're family now. I just gotta let my girl know. I'm sure she'll be cool with it."

"Cool," he said as I attempted to walk towards the dressing room. "Where you going?" he asked.

"What do you mean?" I followed. "I'm going to get dressed."

"It's the final show, we gotta go meet the fans, shake some hands, kiss some babies, you gotta get used to this type shit. You're about to be a star," he answered, enthused.

"Damn. I forgot all about that shit," I replied smiling as I walked off.

Man I really gotta stop smoking weed. My memories shot. Actually, scratch that, hell am I thinking, I needed weed more than ever right now. I love my job, I really do. But the thought of talking to fans sometimes makes me nauseous. Don't get me wrong, yeah I appreciate the support. I wouldn't even have had a job if it weren't for them. I'm completely aware of that. But after a while, a nigga just gets tired of being asked the same questions over and fucking over. 'What are you doing next?' 'Where are you from?' Blah blah blah.

Oh yeah and if I have to hear about one more person who feels that they were 'Put on this earth to be an Actor' and need a few pointers I'm gonna go crazy. Man, oh my God. I hate that shit. I always want to scream out, 'No motherfucker I don't have any advice for you. You probably suck anyway, not to mention you're old, and ugly, and you look like you can't read. Fuck outta here.'

Of course I never say any of that. I just answer their questions as vaguely as I can as I struggle to squeeze out a smile. Shits tiresome though. But like always God was with me. I found a small escape, there was a little deserted corner no one seemed to be occupying. I could hideout as I text Alexis to find out where she was. Sure I know eventually someone will notice me but I should be good for at least a few minutes, hopefully.

'Hey bae. I'm in the lobby in the right corner. Where are you I have to ask you something?' I text.

I stood facing the wall peering off into my phone trying to not be seen before I felt a light tap on my shoulder. "Shit," I muttered to myself as I turned around, forcing one of my classic faux smiles. "Erika," I said, shockingly.

"Hey Von," she replied, soft spoken.

To my surprise, it wasn't a fan at all, it was Erika. She was a friend of mine from back home in Norfolk, Virginia. Real pretty girl, a sweetheart, with dimples as deep as a Malcolm X speech.

And before you get to thinking we got something going on, think again. She was just an old friend. Nothing more, nothing less. Yeah, I'll admit I had a slight crush on her back in high school, but that means nothing, everybody did. Aint like she ever paid us any mind. She'd never be caught dead with one of us, immature, pants saggin, knotty headed thugs. Hell no, Erika was the type to always have some boyfriend at another school, from the suburbs or something. She didn't think guys at my school were on her level. I must admit, she was right.

"Whatsup Erika," I said before leaning in to give her a hug. "I damn sure wasn't expecting to see you here."

"Are you crazy?" she replied joyfully. "What kinda friend would I be if I didn't make an appearance?" she asked as we embraced. "I wanted to surprise you. I can't believe you're an Actor now. I always knew you'd be someone special. I just knew it," she followed, stepping back, faced filled with glee.

"I'ma keep it real," I replied with a smile. "Normally when people say shit like that I kinda disregard it. A lot of people been trying to weasel their way into my life ever since my little success or whatever, but I know you aint lying. You're the only one who always told me that the streets aint love me and that I needed to leave them motherfuckers alone."

4

"Duh, I just knew it was something about you. And that's not the truth. I wasn't the only one to tell you that. Mike did too. That guy really loves you Von. He always knew you had so much more to offer the world than selling drugs and doing whatever else it was you were out there doing."

"Yeah, you're right," I replied.

Mike was my cousin. Damn near my brother. For the first 15 years of my life we were inseparable. Went everywhere together, talked on the phone every day and even spent the night at each other's cribs every weekend. But once high school kicked in, we kinda went different routes. Yeah we still hung occasionally but usually the only time we were together was when I needed him. I was a major fuck up back in those days.

I can't even begin to explain all the hundreds of times he's bailed me outta trouble. My nigga was sent straight from heaven or some shit. He was the only reason I even knew Erika. A girl like her usually wouldn't have been caught dead with a nigga like me. But she was one of Mike's best friends. They both was smart as hell so I guess they met in their little advanced classes or some shit like that. Up until that point I aint even know guys and girls could even be best friends. Shit was pretty weird to me at first.

But yeah, I'm pretty sure they single handily saved my life. See, my Mom died in a car accident back when I was 14 and my Dad went crazy the next week. No lie. Dude just snapped at the funeral. Yeah everybody was hurt but he went extra crazy, blacked out and just started swinging on people, nigga even ran over to me and started choking life from me.

"You did it, you did it," he screamed devilishly as he looked down to me.

I struggled to mumble the words, "I don't know what you're talking about," as I stared into his lifeless eyes. I swear I could feel the devil's scorching hot breath as my Father spoke.

"Motherfucker, you know what you did, you know what the fuck you did," he continued to scream as my Uncles and Aunts drug him off of me.

I stood to my feet, dusted off my suit and stared out as they dragged him, kicking and screaming out of the church. Sadly, he'd never be the same. Dr.'s said he had PTSD. He'd been to the war over in Desert Storm when I was a newborn back in 91.

I'm guessing he must've killed a few people, seen his homies die or maybe even saw kid's die, honestly I really don't know. He never mentioned it. All I know is whatever he saw over there in that damn war, triggered the moment he saw my Mom in a casket, leaving him forever changed. He's been certified legally crazy ever since. They got him locked up in some insane asylum back home.

So yeah, basically I lost my Mom and Dad in the same week. Luckily my Mom's Mother Grandma Glo lived in the city and graciously took me in. My baby, the sweetest woman in the world, we clung to one another. At that point she was all I really had.

5

Yeah I had a few Aunts and Uncles, they were cool, but they all had their own lives to live. Grandma Glo didn't though. Well at least I couldn't tell. She gave me the feeling that I was her life, and she was most definitely mine. She loved me like I was her own and I loved her back. She always called me her favorite Grandson, of course I was her only Grandson but hey, a win is a win.

Can't say I always returned her love though. I put her through it from the moment my suitcase hit the carpet. Back in my teens I was what most would call a Juvenile Delinquent. While the majority of kids parents have to come see the Principal when their child was acting up, my Grandma instead had to see the judge. I was in the back of police Cars so much you'd think I thought it was a taxi or something.

After losing my parents I didn't really have the drive or motivation to do anything constructive. Never had any goals for the future and none of the niggas I was hanging with at the time did either. We were sort of just living. We looked at people like Erika and Mike as squares. Who the fuck goes home and does homework when it was so much bullshit to get into in the streets? I know, stupid. But I was a kid, a lost kid.

But yeah like I was saying, Erika and Mike saved my life. By the age of 18 I was neck deep in the streets and had found myself beefing with a straight up lunatic, a nigga named Harris. I'm not gonna go into too much detail on how we got to beefing and what not but I'll just say it got pretty violent.

It all came to a head the night me and my nigga Charles was chilling in front of my crib sitting in my car. Out of nowhere I felt a dark presence over me. I looked up, it was Harris. In shock, my heart dropped as he lowered his hoody and I looked down the barrow of his gun, I'll never forget, it was a big ass chrome revolver.

Scared shitless I frantically cranked my car, attempting to escape. I was too late, after flashing a smile only Satan could love, he let loose, delivering bullet after bullet as glass shattered all around me. Luckily I managed to skate off unharmed.

Too bad luck wasn't on Charles's side. After pulling over a few blocks away I looked over to him, only to discover him slumped, head resting on his passenger side window as blood oozed from the side of his head.

Naturally I was feeling real down after that. Borderline suicidal. Life seemed meaningless. It was around that time that I really started to try and pray. My Grandma always told me I should. I never listened but things were beginning to become too much for me to deal with alone. I needed help.

Whatsup God,

Yo, man I don't even know what to say. I don't even know you. All I know is I fucking miss Charles and that I wanna kill Harris. My grandma told me that in one of your commandments or something you said 'thou shalt not kill' or something like that. But man what the fu-. I mean what am I supposed to do? I need some answers. I can't figure this out on my own. Whatsup God? If you real, like everybody say you is, you gotta help me. I'm losing it. If something don't happen soon to make me understand or feel better I'm gonna smoke me somebody or I'm killing myself. Simple as that. Come on God. I need you. Help a nigga out.

Bruh, I swear as soon as I opened my eyes after that prayer, my phone rung. It was Mike telling me to come ride with him and Erika. I agreed and he pulled up about 15 minutes later. Wasting no time, as soon as I hopped in the car his first words were "You know you're gonna die next."

"What?" I exclaimed, fist balled, ready to swing. I was feeling way too sensitive to hear some shit like that.

"He's right Von," followed Erika as she looked back at me from the passenger seat." Life aint a game. You should be able to see that. You've been going to jail for years now. What do you think is next?"

"Man-," I said brushing it off.

"Bro she's right. I know you hear my Pops and his old ass friends saying the streets only lead you to two places. Dead or in jail. They aint lying. How many old street niggas you know still living and successful?"

"Plenty," I replied stubbornly.

"Name one," followed Erika.

"Man-," I replied, unable to think of any.

"I'm serious Von, and even if you could name one. I guarantee they've done a bid or two," added Mike. "I guarantee it."

"Exactly," followed Erika.

"Von, our lives our precious, you can't waste a second," continued Mike. "You've already wasted some man. Come on bro this aint even you. I knew you all my life. I know what you've went through. I can't even sit here and try to act like I can relate. I can't. I know. But I also know the route you're going isn't the answer dog."

"Yeah Von. And I may have not known you all my life. But you're different," said Erika. "I can tell, it's something you have that the guys you hang around don't, I see it in your eyes."

"Yeah bro, you gotta leave the streets alone. I don't wanna lose you. You're like a brother to me."

"Man I hear yall," I replied after taking a deep breath. "But yall not seeing shit from my point of view. Yall graduated, freshman in college. I aint even got a damn G.E.D. or a damn plan. Fuck am I supposed to do out here? Work at Mickey D's or something? Fuck that. I can't fade it."

"Well bro, I can't sit here and act like I got all the answers. I don't. But I'll do anything to help out. Whatever it is that you need. I got you. But you gotta get out the streets. You just got to. Aint no love out there."

"Yeah, Von, we're the ones who love you," followed Erika.

That was damn near 9 years ago. I gotta admit, I stayed in the streets for about another month or so. But their voices kept popping up in my head every time I wanted to do something stupid. Eventually, with a little more prayer, and guidance from the two of them, I went and got my G.E.D. and even enrolled in community college. I'd found a small plan but more importantly I found out who my true friends were and that God really does answer prayers.

"Man you got me over here reminiscing and shit, how long you in town?" I asked as Erika and I continued to stand in the corner. "And oh yeah, I'm just now realizing that I aint officially thank you and Mike for doing everything you did for me back in the day. That shit meant the world to a nigga, real shit."

"Aww you're still a sweetheart. Thanks, you were my buddy, I only did what was right. And yeah, unfortunately I'm only here for a couple more hours. I only flew in to catch the show. I've gotta fly out to London for a month."

"London? Oh shit, excuse me, I don't even know why I thought you would have some free time to kick it with little ol me. I must've forgot who the hell I was talking to."

"Yeah, you know how I do," she said as we laughed. "But no seriously I wish I wasn't even going. But hey, I gotta pay the bills, this is the life that I chose."

"I can dig it. Well whenever you're back in 'The A', lunch on me. "

"Cool, I'm going to hold you to that. As you know I'll be back in a couple months."

"Really? For what?"

"Mike's wedding fool."

"Aw shit, I forgot all about it."

"How is it that both you guys move to Atlanta around the same time and don't manage to speak?"

"Oh naw, I never said we don't speak, I talked to him the other day, he just doesn't really mention the Wedding."

"Men," she said as she shook her head. "I guess something like finding the love of your life and finally becoming one with a person is something that easily slips you guys mind."

"Yeah, yeah, yeah," I said as we chuckled. "So what's up with your love life? You too busy traveling the world to have a man?"

8

"Unfortunately yeah. It sucks," she responded, rolling her eyes. "I mean I guess I do have time but all the guys I've been meeting have been irky. Either their too short or too broke or too selfish, or just too much into themselves. I'm kinda starting to lose all hope."

"Naw it's plenty of men out here, you just gotta open your eyes, he might be right in front of you."

"Oh really."

"And no I'm not talking about myself. You shot me down enough times back in the day. Besides, I'm a faithful man now," I said as I playfully lifted my nose to the ceiling.

"What? You faithful? I never thought I'd see the day."

"Shit, me either," I replied, laughing. "But when you keep making the same mistakes over and over, after a while you realize you gotta make some changes."

"Amen," she said, as she clapped softly. "Let me find out it actually is some good men left out here," she followed with a smile.

"Hey," interrupted Alexis as she cut in between us. "I've been looking all over for your ass."

"Hey Bae. You didn't get my text? I told you where I was," I replied.

"No. I didn't," she answered as I looked down to my phone. Like always I had forgotten to hit the send button.

"My bad baby," I said as I showed her my phone screen.

"Ok. I guess something must've caught your attention," she replied, side eyeing, Erika. "Go get dressed I'm hungry as hell."

"Hold on bae. I gotta introduce you to Erika. We grew up together, I know you've heard me talk about her before."

"It's so nice to meet you," said Erika as she held out her hand "Any girl who can turn this man around is one hell of a woman."

"Thanks," said Alexis, ignoring Erika's hand, smirking, blandly. "Come on. I'm starving," she continued, focusing her attention to me.

"Ok babe. Well it was nice seeing you Erika."

"Sure was. Great job tonight. I guess I'll see you two at the wedding. I can't wait to get on that dance floor and act a fool. I haven't partied with my Day 1's in so long."

"Hell yeah, and wait till you see Alexis's moves," I said looking over. "Ciara or Megan Thee Stallion aint got shit on her."

"Thank God, because I'd hate for you guys kids to come out with your two left feet like you."

We both laughed as Alexis struggled out a giggle.

"After all these years you're still a hater," I replied.

"Well it was nice meeting you Alexis," Erika said once again.

"Thanks," replied Alexis as Erika strutted away.

"What time are our reservations?" Alexis asked.

"Oh yeah that's what I wanted to talk to you about Bae. All the cast mates are heading out to eat together. They don't want me to miss it."

"Cast mates? You've been with them for the past three months. I really wanted some alone time."

"I know baby but what can I do? I'm kinda the star, I can't be a no show."

"Ok, I guess," she said rolling her eyes. "I'll be waiting in the car," she added as she walked off.

"Hey Babe," I yelled as she turned around. "I'll miss you," I said, giving her a wink.

She didn't feel the same. I could already tell she felt some type of way about Erika but fuck all of that, she should know by now that I'm not going anywhere. I hate when she does that. Besides, I'm used to her little attitudes, in a weird way it actually kinda turns me on.

I headed over to the dressing room before I was quickly reminded of where I was. I guess everyone was waiting for me to finish my convo with Erika or something because suddenly I had what seemed like millions of faces smiling, walking over to me.

"1,2,3, ShowTime," I said to myself before throwing on my game face along with my signature smile.

Man it took forever to get outta that building. I couldn't escape the attention. If I was a single man I'd have a ball. The women were basically throwing themselves at me. I heard it all, how sexy I was, what they'd do to me, and some even said that they loved me. Damn, if I'm getting this kinda attention now I can't even imagine how it is for real stars. But hey, guess I'm going to have to get used to it. This is my new life.

After undressing, I looked at my phone for the time, I'd had Alexis waiting for damn near an hour. Which resulted in 5 unread text messages from her. I didn't even open them. Fuck that. What for? I already knew she was pissed. Honestly, I really don't give a damn. Whenever it's time for us to go out on a date or something she takes an eternity but she doesn't seem to be able to wait five minutes for me. Women.

I jogged out to the car and hopped in the driver's seat of Alexis's Nissan Altima. I drove off and after about 5 minutes of silence she finally spoke.

"I told you I was hungry right?"

"Yeah."

"So why the fuck would you take so long to come out?"

"Hold on, chill out Bae, that shit is a part of my job, fans were talking to me."

"So what are you telling me? Them little fans you think you got are more important than me or something?"

"Huh?" I replied, confused. "What are you even talking about? You know they aint more important that you. You already know you mean everything to me, stop acting like that."

"I'm not acting like anything. All I know is that if you were hungry and I had you waiting for forever, I would have at least made sure I bought you out a snack from the vending machine or something."

"A snack? That's what you mad about? You want me to stop at the store for you?"

"No. We're almost at the damn restaurant now," she replied, arms folded.

"My bad Bae," I followed, taking a deep breath. "I'm sorry. I just wasn't thinking."

"I mean damn," she continued. "How many times are you going to kick the same old I'm sorry speech? How old are you? We've been together damn near three years, I shouldn't have to tell you what to do in a relationship, you're a grown ass man."

"What are you even talking about?" I followed, annoyed, attempting to hold in my frustration. "I'm hungry too and I didn't even bring myself anything. You act like we're not on our way to a damn restaurant."

"Just leave me alone," she said, motioning with her hand for me to stop speaking. "I don't even wanna talk about it anymore. You always got a fucking excuse," she replied before crossing her arms back, staring straight ahead.

"Oh my God man."

I cut up the radio. I love Alexis to death but she sure knows how to get under a nigga skin.

Whatsup God,

Let us have a good time in here. This is my last time being with the cast members and I just want to enjoy myself. Can you take Alexis's attitude down just a notch? I tried but you and I both know she's crazy.

We arrived at the restaurant right on time, everyone was just sitting down. Boy, it smelled amazing inside. If my Grandma hadn't passed away last year I'd swear she was back in the kitchen slaving over the stove. Smelled just like Thanksgiving at her crib. If it's one thing I can say I love about Atlanta, it's the food and "Big Daddy's Soul Kitchen' has to be one of the best spots in town.

"You alright bae?" I asked as Alexis looked over the menu.

"Yeah, just trying to find something worth ordering. I wasn't really in the mood to be eating this shit."

"Oh yeah, I'm sorry, I know you had your mouth set on Seafood," I said as I studied the menu. "They got fried catfish. That's seafood," I added as she rolled her eyes.

Everyone small talked amongst us as Alexis and I sat, awkwardly twiddling our thumbs. Not that I didn't wanna mingle with my crew, it's just that I didn't wanna have too much damn fun while Alexis was mad. Yeah, I know it sounds crazy but I don't even have time to hear her mouth later.

"Excuse me," said Felicia, the Director as she stood to her feet before tapping her spoon on her glass. "First of all I want to take this time to thank the entire cast and crew for a wonderful show. Magnificent. When I sat down to write this story I never dreamed that it would be this magical. I mean, wow," she continued as we clapped and shouted. "Everything was perfect. To start with only a weekend and then secure an entire three months traveling around the east coast. It just goes to show how great we as a collective are," she said as everyone cheered and applauded once again. "Hold on, hold on, I haven't even gotten to the good part yet. I've been keeping my lips tight, I didn't know if everything would work out but we have just been approached to take the show national. We'll be traveling the country for an entire year!" she shouted as everyone turned up.

Everyone except me, well and of course little Ms. Attitude. But Alexis was just trippin, I actually had a legit reason for my lack of excitement. The thing is, yeah I know traveling with the Play sounds like everything I'd been praying for. To have an acting job for a full year, a job where I'm the lead, would have been a dream come true in the past. It's just that something in my heart was telling me it wasn't the right move for me.

Over the last three months I'd been approached by some major folk in the industry. Folk who promised to help get me into film and T.V., my true dreams. Going on a yearlong journey could possibly be a conflict of interest. Sure I'd be secure for a year or so but I don't wanna be secure, I wanna take my talents to the next level. Taking the safe route may be easier, but my heart never seems to want to go the easy route.

For the remainder of the diner Alexis and I remained to our self. You could feel the delight in the air. In my heart I felt like a snake for ditching them. I pride myself on being Loyal. We had become family over the past months. My brain struggled to find a way to break the news to them.

After thinking and thinking, I was having no luck, I needed assistance. I figured I'd just ask Alexis for some advice once we got in the car. She's a business owner so I know she'd had to let people down a time or two.

After about another hour, we said our goodbyes, exited the restaurant and headed to our vehicles.

"Yo Bae," I said as we drove off.

"Whatsup," she answered, head in her phone.

"I'm not too sure about going on this tour."

"Good, I was thinking the same thing. I aint got time to be lonely for a whole year. I did three months but that's it. Maybe for a movie or something but not for no damn Play."

"I wasn't really talking about that," I replied. "Yeah, I'd miss you too but what I'm really concerned about is all the opportunities I'll be missing. You know I gotta lot of big gigs coming up. I don't wanna miss out."

"Well don't go," she said bluntly.

"You don't have an opinion?"

"You're grown, you gotta make your own choices. But what I do have an opinion on is that fat ass director Felicia. I hate the way that bitch always looking at me."

"Huh? Felicia's cool as hell. I wouldn't even be here without her."

"I don't give a fuck. I just don't like the bitch. Every time I come around she's always tryna to be better than me."

"Tryna be better than you? When? How?"

"That hoe always tryna make it be known that she's the director and she's special and shit," continued Alexis, irritated. Bitch we all know you wrote the damn Play. How many times you gotta say it."

"I don't know about all that, I never got that vibe from her."

"Of course you don't. You never see anything."

"Hell you mean by that?"

"Exactly what I said."

"Alright, give me an example then."

"No, it's ok."

"No. I want to know, give an example."

"Ok," she said looking over to me. "So earlier tonight when you were talking to your little friend."

"My little friend? Who? What little friend?"

"Nigga don't play fuckin dumb now," she barked, staring me down. "You know exactly who the fuck I'm talking about. That little big eyed bitch, Ebony or whatever the fuck her name is. You know, the hoe you supposed to have grown up with or whatever."

"Erika? What the fuck did she do?"

"Not just her, both of you motherfuckers. First of all I would have never talked to a man for that long before checking to see where you were."

"Naw, I told you I thought I'd texted you. Besides she flew all the way out here just to see me. What was I supposed to do? Not talk to her at all?"

"Oh yeah and that's another thing. Why the fuck is that bitch flying way out here to see you? Seems kinda suspect to me."

"Suspect? How?" I questioned, passionately. "Erika's a good ass friend of mine. I told your ass all about her a million times."

"I don't remember," she replied as she stared straight ahead once again. "Just don't be mad when I'm smiling all in some guy I went to high school withs face."

"I won't be. I trust you."

"Yeah you trust everybody. That's your problem."

"Yo you tripping."

"How? Because I want you to act like a grown ass 27 year old man?" she answered, finally looking back over to me.

"How the fuck don't I act like a grown man? I pay bills, come home every night, fuck you good. What the fuck else do you want from me?"

"Nothing, nothing," she stuttered, annoyed. "I don't want anything that you don't have to offer."

"Oh my God. Man you really trippin."

"Naw my nigga, you trippin," she said as we locked eyes for a split second.

That was my worse mistake I could possibly make in that moment. In the amount of time it took to look over to her, a car came flying outta nowhere, smacking our hood spinning us around in a circle before we came to a screeching halt, landing inches away from the interstate median.

"You ok, Baby?" I frantically, yelled.

"Yes, you ok," she replied, timidly.

"Yeah I'm good," I said as we both felt over our bodies.

"Oh my God, I'm so sorry baby. I don't wanna argue anymore," said Alexis.

"I'm sorry too baby. I love you."

"I love you more baby," she replied as we leaned over for a kiss.

"You guys ok?" asked a white man standing outside the car as he swung open my driver side door, causing shattered glass to fall hard to the ground.

"Yeah," I said as we both stumbled out side to our feet. Together we studied the car. One word. Fucked. Looking over to one another it was clear that we were blessed to still be alive. The car was totaled.

Within minute's ambulance and Police units rushed to the scene as we sat cuddled next to one another on the ground. Can't lie at the moment neither of us were seriously hurt, but we're both from the hood. With that being said, it should come as no surprise that we both agreed to act as if we were dying. If it's one thing I know, it's that when you get in an accident, you go to the hospital no matter what. My experience has taught me that there's a pretty good chance you could be getting seriously paid.

"You two ok?" asked one of the Paramedics who hopped out of the ambulance.

"Not really," I replied as Alexis and I both laid back on the ground, staring up at the night sky.

"Get the stretcher, get the stretcher," yelled another Paramedic.

Who would have thought my acting skills would be needed for a second time tonight. We both groaned and moaned as we were carted into the ambulance. As they asked us question after question, we answered, low in a whisper as if we were utilizing every ounce of strength in us to speak. Classic.

Once we arrived at the hospital they carted us off to different rooms. I laid back, thinking of everything I was going to tell the Dr. when suddenly two fat ass Police Officers marched in.

"Mr. Jordan," said the Hispanic fat one.

"Yes officer," I replied.

"How ya feeling?"

"I'm in a little pain but I'm sure I'll be fine. Is there a problem?"

"Were you aware that your license was suspended?"

"Huh?"

"Yeah. You're Lavon Jordan aren't you?" replied the White fat officer.

15

"Yeah but this has to be some type of mistake."

"Afraid not," the White one answered. "According to our records your license was suspended last week due to failure to pay a parking ticket. We're gonna have to take you down. It's against Georgia law to operate a motor vehicle without a license."

"What?" I shouted. "How yall just gonna come in here and say some bullshit like that?"

"Calm down sir," added the Hispanic Officer. "We're just doing our job."

"We're going to allow the Dr. to get you right but afterwards you're gonna have to come with us," stated the White officer.

"What the fuck!" I shouted before slamming my head to the back of my pillow.

I'm Mad

It had been so long since I'd sat in the back of one of these stinking ass, rock hard seated, cages they call Patrol Cars. I'd forgot the feeling. Aint take long for the shit to come right back to me though. In an instant my anxiety kicked in forcing me to exhale, taking a deep breath as a cold sweat chilled my body. I gotta be the dumbest. The stupidest. Fed up with myself I stared out the window. Watching my freedom slowly escape me.

Colorful memories of everything I'd done in the past to land me here ping ponged through my brain. Gotta admit this is light. There were times I sat, cuffed wondering if I'd ever see the light of day again. Stressed, searching for an escape, thinking of a masterplan, telling myself each and every time that this would be my last trip to hell. Sadly, so far, I've been wrong every time.

Fuck! I was doing so damn good. How in the hell did I end up back where I started? Shit. It's been years. Dumb ass Georgia. Yeah I love it here. But damn. Stupid ass laws. How the hell do you send someone to jail for driving on a suspended license? I mean damn, I didn't even know it was suspended. Cut a nigga some slack. I bet if I was white they wouldn't arrest me. I should sue their ass. I don't know what for. But fuck them. Stupid asses.

"Anything you wanna listen to while you're back there?" asked the Hispanic officer as he glanced at me through the rearview mirror.

"I'm good," I replied staring back. "I'm just ready to get inside, talk to the magistrate, get me a bond and get the fuck out."

"Well I hope you got some serious cash. They don't play about driving on a suspended down here," he followed.

"I got it," I shot back.

"Cool, I suggest you go get your license as soon as you get out. I know you don't want to have to keep spending thousands of dollars."

"Thousands?" I asked, surprised. "I'm sure it won't be that much."

"Oh no buddy I'm sure it will. I saw that your license was outta state. No bondsman in the city will take ten percent. You're gonna have to fork over the full ticket. They consider you a flight risk around these parts," added the White Officer.

"Flight risk? What? The full bond? And how much will that be?" I spat.

"Depends on how the magistrate is feeling," he replied.

"Yeah. Usually, anywhere between $1000-$2000 bucks," added the Hispanic officer.

"That's crazy? You gotta be kiddin me dog. For driving on a suspended?"

"Hey what can I say? Welcome to Georgia," he answered.

"Did you catch that game last night?" asked the White Officer to his partner.

Boy I'll tell ya. How the fuck do these niggas have the audacity to sit up there talking about a damn game? No fuckin respect. They don't give a damn about what the fuck I'm going through. Shit, if I was a Policeman I'll shut the fuck up the whole damn ride. It's the least they could do. Let a nigga think in peace.

Shit man. Maybe thinking was the wrong thing to do. I sat back and realized, I wasn't even driving my damn car. It was Alexis's. It's totaled. With me not having a license that means I wasn't insured. No insurance can sometimes equal no fucking insurance money. Fuck! Alexis is gonna kick my black ass.

Truthfully, I don't even want to see her, I already know she's gonna be pissed. Matter of fact, pissed aint even the word. She gon be Mad as a motherfucker, livid, her ass might even try to fight me or launch a shoe at me or something. Controlling her anger wasn't really one of her strong points. This shit can get bad, real bad. Kinda makes me wanna stay in jail. Probably be better than hearing her mouth. I can hear her now.

"How didn't you know your license was suspended?"

"You too old to be making these types of decisions."

"How did you forget to pay the damn ticket?"

And the fucked up part about it is I don't even have any answers. Shit, I been busy. How the hell was I supposed to think about a damn ticket with everything I got going on? Sometimes I can't even remember what day it is or if I remembered to eat breakfast. Still I know if I say that, that's gonna really piss her off.

I mean, I guess it is pretty stupid to say. My dumbass. I'm getting too old for this shit. Look at me, a little simple speeding ticket got me possibly spending thousands of dollars when I could've only spent 80. I guess maybe I do deserve everything she's gonna say. I wish it was a way I could have her a new car by the time I was released.

Fuck am I thinking, she'd still have something to say. Crazy ass.

"We're here," said the Hispanic officer excitedly, as he looked back to me smiling.

I wanted to say 'Bitch we aint at Disney World'. But I held my tongue.

We drove to the back of the Police Precinct and parked before the officers exited the vehicles and came around to my door.

They opened up and I scooted my way out of the seat.

"Yo can yall loosen these damn cuffs? Shits killing me." I said as I stood face to face with the officers.

18

"You'll have them off soon enough, hold tight," said the Hispanic officer as they escorted me into the building.

I stared at the ground as I walked, still in disbelief of how my night had drastically shifted.

We stepped inside. I never been to Atlanta's jail or any jail outside of Virginia but one things for sure, the feeling that consumes me is universal.

Whatsup God,

Man can you please make this as easy as possible? I just wanna get in and get out. Yeah yeah, I know it was my fault but I need to be cut a break. Please, I don't know what you can do. But I just need your help. Come on man, help a nigga out.

As time dragged I went through all the regular jail procedures.

"Take your laces out."

"Give me your jewelry."

"Empty your pockets."

Finally it was time to sit in front of the magistrate. If you've never been arrested you may not know exactly what they do. To put it in a nutshell their basically the bond God. In this moment, the person I sat in front of held my fate in their hands. They had the power to control if I went home for free, if I'd be forced to spend thousands or in the worst case they could see that I be granted no bond at all.

Hopefully everything works in my favor. I'd hate to sit down and be in front of some miserable motherfucker whose only joy in life comes from forcing niggas like myself to waste days or even months in jail for the pettiest of crimes.

I sat down, picked up a corded phone and stared into a small T.V. screen.

"Mr. Lavon Jordan," said the older female magistrate as she appeared on the screen. "I see you've been charged with driving on a suspended license," she added as she looked over a sheet of paper in front of her.

"Yes ma'am."

"Looks like you've been having problems keeping your license since you were 18."

"Unfortunately."

"Wow. And you seem to have a pretty extensive criminal record," she replied as she lowered her glasses, staring at a small laptop to the left of her.

"Yes but I haven't' been convicted of any crimes in almost 7 years, mostly everything happened when I was a juvenile, I was just charged as an adult a few times," I pleaded.

"I see, I see," she said as she continued to look over her computer screen. "Well in that case. I will set your bail at $1300."

"Ma'am," I replied, voice crackling. "Don't you think $1300 is kinda steep? I mean think about it, I didn't even know my license was suspended."

"Negligence of the law is no excuse," she answered sternly.

"I understand but I wasn't really negligent of the law. Can I explain?"

"I'm sure it won't make a difference but you may."

"Ok. My mail still gets sent to Virginia because I forgot to change my home address to Georgia. I had no idea my license was suspended. Plus, I'm going to have to buy my girl another car. I don't really have that kinda money to be spending. Is there any way I can get a P.R. bond? We do that all the time in Virginia. I can just sign a sheet of paper saying I'm coming back on my court date. Please, you can trust me. I'm just a young struggling Actor trying to make it."

"Oh an Actor. That's where I know you from. I knew I recognized you from 'Us vs. Them', you did an excellent job," she said with a bright smile.

"Thank you. So are you going to be able to help me out?" I asked, looking for sympathy.

"Nope. This is Atlanta honey. I come across bigger stars than you daily. And I treat them all the same. Sorry. But good luck on your career. You're really talented," she said as the Television screen went black, leaving my jaw hanging to the floor.

Next thing I know two Sheriffs are dragging me to some holding cell. They tossed me in with some light skin tall ass nigga. From the looks of him he was about my age, maybe a little older, shit maybe younger, I can't really tell with light skin niggas sometimes. But yeah, it was obvious he was a regular. He just had that 'come to jail a lot' demeanor. That comfortable, not a care in the world vibe.

"Whatsup Mane," he said as I sat down across from him.

"Whatsup."

"Boy yu luk mad as hell. Luk like yu ready to fie on somebody ass."

"Yeah."

"Yu'll be aite. I heard dem bitch ass Sheruffs talkin. They got yu in herre fuh sum bullshit traffic charge right?"

"Yeah. That's exactly what they got me in here for. Some bullshit," I said as I shook my head.

"Shit, leas yu know yu prolly gettin out tonigh. I ain leavin this mo'fucka no time soon and I ain even did shit."

"Oh really," said a tall black C.O. as he casually walked up.

"Hell na. I really didn. Punk ass Twelve jus always hatin on a nugga."

"You must come here a lot," I followed.

"Every other fuckin week," said an equally tall, but lighter C.O. as he tossed some drunk white man into the cell along with us.

"Hell yeah too damn much," said the dark-skinned Officer as he stood behind the other C.O. "And every time you come in this motherfucker you always saying you aint do shit."

"I didn fur real dis time though. I swea to God."

"Kermit, you say that every damn week. I told you your probation officer won't gonna keep playing with your ass," said the lighter one.

"Bruh, U'm dead ass serious. I ain do shit fur real dis time. I swea."

"So why you here Kermit?" asked the darker one.

"Yeah Kermit, I aint got shit but time. Let me here it. This should be funny," followed the lighter one as the two officers continued to stand outside of the cell.

"Aite gud, caus its kinda long story."

"Well get to it, we waiting," added the lighter one.

"Aite U'ma start yall frum the beginning. It all started when I was chillin down the block from my crib one night. Aite, so I'm drankin, having a good ass time wit sum of the homies in the hood. Nothin much we just relaxin til it starts to get late. It wun't no special day or nothing like that, jus a regula ol Tuesday or Wednesday, so ventually nuggas start headin to the crib. So I say fuck it, U'ma go too, like I said, it won't nothin really goin on out there. So I dap the little remainin people still outside up and make my way down the street, and what do you know, guess who I see, mo'fuckin Tisha."

"You say her name like we supposed to know her or something," said the darker officer.

"My bad, Tisha is dis bih I grew up wit. Ol crazy ass bih, love to get high. Can't een lie, back in the day the bih was bad as hell. No cap. Well, I don know if I can really say the bih was bad as hell. But fuck it, the bih did have a big phat ol ass, and back when we was kids that's all that mattered. Shit, still is fur real fur real. But yuh, like I wa sayin, the bih a damn full blown pill head now. She'll take anything, Xans, Percs, Adderall, any mo'fuckin thang. Feigned the fuck out, certified yung junky. And we all know junkie's gotta get they fix and without a job they usually gotta find another way tu get sum muney. Hers was trickin."

"You won't lying this story is long as hell. Yall sure yall care?" asked the lighter C.O. as he looked around to us all.

"I don't. I really don't," answered the darker one.

"Well mo'fucka. Yall shouldn have asked. Where was I? Oh I kno. Ok so I catch up to her."

"Wha up Tisha, beautifu night huh?"

"Boy what yu want some pussy or somethin?" she replied.

"Bih got straight to the point jus lik I lik it," continued Kermit.

"You a nasty motherfucker," added the darker C.O.

"Yo. You gon lemme tell my story or what?" shot back Kermit.

"Ok. Carry on."

"Well yuh, so I was like, 'I don even want the pussy baby. I jus need sum head'."

"How much yu got?" she asked.

"How much it usually cost?" I replied.

"See, I dont usually do that type shit. I dont be knowin prices and shit. And I guess she knew that. Because she tried to finesse me," said Kermit as he looked around to us all before continuing the story.

"$100," she said.

"$100? Bih is you crazy," I screamed. "Bih do yu know wha the fuck I can do with $100?"

"Nigga I ain no cheap hoe," she replied.

"So me bein the nugga I am. I pause, look her up and down. Bih had on baby phat and sum fake ass, dirty ass Uggs, leanin over and shit. I don't usually do that type of shit but common sense was tellin me that this bih was a baldhead lie, she was indeed a cheap hoe. Prolly the cheapest. Realizin this, I shot her my number, fuck it."

"Hoe I got $10."

Without even thinking bout it, this bih said, "Ok," quicker than a mo'fucker.

"Now I ain gon lie that kinda shocked me. Shit wa jus too easy. Had me kinda reconsiderin, thinkin like damn, do I even want sum head that's only $10. Like what kinda bullshit could this bih possibly have that was floatin in her mouf? But I ain gon lie. A nugga was horny as a mo'fucker and my girl had gone out that night. So I jus went wit the flow."

"Cool."

"So where we goin?" she asked.

"Man I dont know. Where you usually go?"

"That's not really my job to find the location," Tisha followed.

"Well where do most nuggas take yu?"

"It depend. Sometime house, car, sometime we get a room at a hotel."

"Now I ain have no hotel money nor did I have a car. Shit, that was the reason I was walkin in the first place. But I did have a crib. Now I know yall probably wonderin how was I gonna pull dis off since I live with my Ol Lady."

"Naw I was actually thinking when this motherfucker was gon be done with this dumb ass story," added the lighter C.O..

"Fuc yu. Well for the people who was wonderin why would I take a prostitute to my crib I shared with my ol lady," he said as he looked around. "I didnt. Well not exactly. I got one of them big ol fenced in back yards. Big ass gate. Can't nobody see shit back there. So that's where I decide to take her. I was gon sit down on my lil deck and let her go to work. So yuh, we walkin and talkin. Next thang I know the mo'fuckin Police pulled up on us."

"Hold on I aint know you was in here for buying some pussy," said the Darker C.O..

"Can I tell my story mo'fucka?" Kermit replied, annoyed. "I'm not. Jus lemme explain. So yuh, like I was sayin before I was so rudely interrupted, Twelve pulled up."

"Hey what are you doing?" he asked as he hopped out of his Patrol unit. "Yall bouta go have some sex or you selling her some dope or something? I know it's one of the two, don't bullshit me."

"Neither one officer. We just some good old childhood friends," I replied with a smile.

"I knew he won goin for that bullshit though. It was worf a try but this bih is a well known hoe, a head monster, the freak of all freaks. Mo'fuckin Police probably sneak and get head from her ass from time to time, thats how he probably knew I was up to somethin. Crooked mo'fuckas."

"Yeah right," the bitch ass Police officer said. "But since I'm feeling good, I'm not going to bother you."

"Thanks officer," I replied.

"So me and the bih attempt to keep on strollin."

"Hold on motherfucker," the officer blurted. "I aint stupid, I never said yall could walk together. You go this way and you go that way," he said pointing in two different directions.

"Now I ain gon lie. In my head I was happy then a mo'fucka he let us go. I had a lil bud in my pocket and I ain have time to be showin up to this mo'fuckin jail for a half a gram of damn weed. But still, as I walked my horniness start to kick in like a mo'fucker. A nigga dick was rock hard. Shit got me fie hot mad. Dumb ass Police fucked my damn plan up. So I sat on my front steps hopin she would walk past. And just like clockwork, five minutes lata, the bih did. I look out to see if any of my nosey ass neighbors was out, I couldn risk lettin any of them snitch ass mo'fuckas see what the fuck I had goin on. So I look left, then look right, the coast was clear. I nod for her to go on back. I walk back bout a minute lata after I made sure once again that nobody saw what the fuck wa goin on," Kermit said as he looked around as if he was still in his neighborhood. "So we got back there and I swea she aint waste a mo'fuckin second, she yank my mo'fuckin pants down and went straight to work. Bih damn near suck my damn socks off. Head was a fuckin missile. That was like a month ago."

"Man what the fuck is you talking about?" asked the lighter C.O. "What the fuck is the point of this dumb as story? I'm getting lost."

"Dog, I told you it was a long ass story. Chill out. Ok so listen, aite, that was bout a month ago. Fast forward to tonight, me and my girl was bout to throw somethin on the grill. We go to the mo'fuckin backyard and what do you kno. This bitch Tisha out there butt naked wit sum random ass white fat mo'fucka. His big ass was taggin her ass frum the back, rabbit style, her titties bouncin, his titties bouncin, funk everywhere. So my girl get mad as a mo'fucker, and instantly get tuh whuppin Tisha ass. Bih was going crazy, left jab, right hook, uppercut, stomp. She was goin ham. I tried to get the dude but he was outta there, white boy was fast as fuck. So I just stood over top of my girl cheerin her on as she got this bih Tisha on the ground."

"Bih why the fuck is you in my back yard fucking?" my girl screamed.

"U'm sorry, Kermit took me hea a lil while ago and I though it was cool."

"Thats when all hell broke loose. Man my bih turn around, looked at me with a look in her eye Ive neva seen. A nugga knew he was in trouble. Bih start growlin like a pit or somethin, like a damn monsta. Swea she started foamin at the mouf and erthang. Had a nugga heart poundin like she had a pistol or some shit, damn near pissed on myself."

"You're a funny dude," said the darker officer as he laughed.

"So me, not being a fool, I dip, hit the forty on her as, straight out the front gate. But what I didn kno was that my bih was related to 'The Flash' or sum shit, she was faster than a sonbih. Bih caught me by my colla, luckily I had on one of them cheap ass fruit of the loom tee shirts, shirt ripped clean in half. Had it been a Hanes tee shirt she woulda' caught my ass."

"Man this story is retarded, I still don't see the fucking point," said the lighter officer.

"Mane how many times I gotta tell you to hold on. I'm gettin to it. So like I said, I escape and U'm runnin and shit, bouta be clean down the road, when suddenly my dumbass neighbor clothes line tackle me."

"Your neighbor? For what?" asked the lighter C.O..

"Mane who the fuck knows? I told you they some ol nosey, in the way ass mo'fuckas. Nugga came outta nowhere. And once I was on the ground the nugga sat on top of me. I look up and I see a big ass sandal comin toward my face. It was my bih. Luckily I'm quick, I block the shit, but not before she stomped on every damn bone in my body. Bih went coo coo, no cap. Cussin me out, calling me every name in the book. I'm tellin yu this shit was goin on foreva. I was kinda happy when the mo'fuckin police showed up. Too bad they was on some bullshit. Yall know how them niggas is."

"Yeah, yeah," replied the lighter Officer.

"U'm sittin there all bruise and battered and they steady askin who fault it was. Now at first, me or my girl aint wanna talk, we ain tell them bih ass niggas shit, but all that shit change when they said…"

"We didn't come out here for nothing, somebody's going to jail."

"And me bein the man I am. I told them mo'fuckas to take her ass. Shit, U'ma innocent man. Plus I'm on probation. I ain got time fur that shit."

The officers started laughing.

"You're a true class act," said the darker one.

"I guess, but that shit ain work either, her lil stupid ass told them mo'fuckas I had weed in my pocket. And hea I am now."

"And you still think it wasn't your fault?" said the lighter one, continuing to laugh.

"Hell naw I aint do shit wrong."

"I can't believe I actually sat here and listened to that pointless ass story," added the darker officer.

"Fuck yall. Ain like yall got some shit to do. All yall do is sit round and get fat. Lazy mo'fuckas."

"You think its easy dealing with stupid motherfuckers like you every day?" asked the lighter officer.

"Yo can I get my phone call," I interrupted, I'd had had enough.

"See, yall ain even give the man his phone call," Kermit said, pointing to me. "Too busy worry bout the wrong thang."

"Fuck you," said the darker officer as he unlocked the cell and escorted me to the phone next to some angry dread head tattoo faced ass nigga. It was obvious he was on the phone with his girl.

"You went through my phone? Baby I dont even talk to her no more" he said before pausing. "I don't know why she sent me naked pics. So you not gon bail me out? But bih it's my money," he yelled. "If I don't come home how the hell you gon pay the rent? Oh you got a new nugga? If I find out a new nugga anywhere round my kids you dead. On God," he screamed. "Yeah bih fuc you too. I dont care who you tell. Cant none of your punk ass brothers or cousins beat my ass," he said as he slammed the phone to the receiver.

25

Wow. Gotta admit, hearing all that made me kinda hesitant, aint no telling what Alexis is about to say to me.

Whatsup God,

Yo yo, ay Big God I need your help again. Let me say the right things to Alexis. I need to get out of here.

I picked up the phone and dialed. The little operator said whatever bullshit they always said on these jail calls and then asked me my name. "Baby its Von," I said before finally we were connected.

"Hello," she said.

"Whatsup Bae, did you hear what happened?"

"Hell yeah," she spat. "The damn Dr.'s told me all about it. Did you know you didn't have a license?"

"No. But I know it's all my fault."

"Ya damn right it is," she barked. Who the fuck else fault is it? Now your stupid ass got me out here with no damn car. You know damn well my insurance aint gonna cover shit since you aint have no license. My car is gone. Totaled. Hell am I gonna do?"

"Chill baby, chill, you can have mine till I get you another one. I got some money stashed in the crib."

"Money stashed in the crib? Don't you have a bank account? You're a fucking actor. Why would you have money stashed in the crib? You think you're still a street nigga or something?"

"Baby, that's beside the point. Listen, I need you to get $1300 out of there and get me up outta here."

"$1300?" she shouted. "Well what the fuck did you do besides drive because I aint never heard of no damn bail that high for something minor like that."

"Baby just bring the money. I'll explain it all once you get here."

"$1300 and buying a new fuckin car. You see what being so damn forgetful gets you? Forget every damn thing. But I see you don't forget them damn lines that fat ass bitch Felicia tell your ass to say."

"Alexis, you coming or not?"

"I mean, what other choice do I have?"

"Well the money's in my Adidas box under my dirty clothes in the closet."

"Ok."

"I love y-" I started to say before the phone hung up. "Dumbass," I said under my breath as I walked back over to the cell and stood. "Yo can yall let me back in," I said, never making eye contact with anyone.

"My pleasure," said the Darker C.O. as he walked over.

I stepped back inside, immediately dropping my head. I'm so fucking stupid. I gotta get the fuck outta here. Feels like the walls are caving in on me. Alexis gotta bring her ass, the longer she takes the more of a chance I got of them sending my ass upstairs to the real cells. No, I'm not scared or nothing. I just aint got time for all that shit. I don't even want those negative vibes around me. Too many mad ass niggas. Aint no telling what they'll do. Like I said, no I aint scared but who wanna be around all that shit? I'm damn near thirty.

Not just that, in order to go up there you gotta get butt ass naked, squat, cough and all that bullshit. I aint no fucking animal, that's just too much for me. Fuck that. But as the minutes sped by and I witnessed more and more guys being sent up, it looks as if I may not have a choice.

Thinking back, there was a time when I fit right in perfectly in jail. Safe to say, those times are long gone. At this very moment there are over 7 different conversations going on, everyone yelling through the bars and I still haven't found one that I could remotely relate to. Damn, my life did a whole 360, who would've thought. Times like this it's only one person who understands me.

Whatsup God,

Yo you remember I was one of these niggas? Yeah, I know you do. Boy was I really this wild? Never mind. No need to answer. I know I was. Ay God, why did you even save me in the first place? I guess I know. Seems like you gotta bigger plan for me or something. I hope so. Well, not hope, I already know you do. Remember the first time I was in jail? Yo I was scared as a motherfucker. But you always kept me safe. I aint even ever been in a jail fight. Actually, if I think about it, you always kept me safe through everything in life. You may have let me bump my head a few times but you always saw me through. Guess I can't even be mad that I'm here. It could have been worse, shit somebody could have died. Maybe I should be thanking you for this. I don't really know the reason but I'm sure it's one. I know this aint really got nothing to do with nothing, but dog, I just want to be happy today and every day for the rest of my life and it sucks because I thought I was on my way to that. Guess I still got a few things to work on. Lord. Please send me a blessing today. Please.

In the next hour I got finger printed and even took my mugshot picture. I thought for sure I was going upstairs.

"Jordan," said the lighter C.O. "You made bail," he finally said.

I stood up and nodded to the other inmates.

"Ay bruh," said Kermit to me. "You mind goin to see my gurl and tellin her I'm sorry?"

"Shawty shut your dumb ass up," interrupted an inmate who'd been placed in our cell.

"Yuh bruh. I'm just a nigga out here tryna do right and take care of my seeds."

"But hold on. So you mean to tell me that you don't like your baby mama at all? Like not even a little bit?"

"Hell naw I don't," Rell blurted before thinking. "I mean, yuh, I guess I somewhat like her, but bruh I ain even the same nugga I was when I met her. Met her damn near ten years ago. I was a lil nugga. I changed, she didnt, she ain got no goal, no nothing. I want me a boss ass bih. Need me a bih like Beyoncé or somethin."

"Damn bro I aint never really know you felt like that. That's crazy."

"Shit ain crazy. Don't no nigga really want his Baby Mama. Shit, if we did we'd marry em. We just tryna have as least drama as we can. That's why I dont understand why the hell you stickin round ova there when yall ain even got no damn kids."

"Yet," I blurted. "We talk about it from time to time. On the real, I can't wait to have some. That unconditional love gotta be the shit. Kids are really a motherfucking blessing dog."

"What?" he exclaimed. "You sound crazy as hell. Fuck them kids. You trippin shawty. If I could I'd do shit a lot different. I'll at least wait till I was a lil olda or somethin."

"Damn, foreal?"

"Nugga damn right. Yu dont even fully know who the fuck yu is when you have em when youre young. Its hard as hell teachin a lil nigga some shit yu dont even really know yet."

"Ok, ok, I see what you're saying."

"Yuh bruh, if it's one thang I learned from working as a furniture mover back in the day, its that white rich mo'fuckers wait late as hell to have kids. Them nuggas be damn near fifty."

"True, true," I replied.

"Yep. By that time their seasoned, they know who the fuck they are and most of the time theyre already established for the rest of their life. But us on the otha hand, our dumb ass poppin babies out in our Teens and Twenty's talkin bout 'I'ma still be young when lil John John turn 18,' Rell said in a mocking tone. "In my head I'm thinking 'So Motherfucker. Ain like yu gon be able to really live, you just gave up the best years of your life to your Ungrateful ass children and now yu lost out here tryna find out who the fuck yu really is, when yu 18 years behind."

"Yo ass got a theory for everything. Can't cap though, you be having some good ass points. Shit, foreal foreal, niggas having babies young as hell is probably the main reasons all these damn single mamas out here."

"Hell yuh bruh, these young ass Daddy's ain stickin aroun if they dont have to, we just too dumb to realize we needa stop having them lil bad mo'fuckas so early," Rell continued. "Shit, the Mamas would leave too, they ol bitter asses just don't be havin a choice."

"Unless they got a Grandma to take them to or something."

"Exactly. But ay, I can say this though, it is one good thing coming out of all them girls taking care of them kids by they damn self."

"What?"

"These single Mamas out here bossin the fuck up, no cap." he replied as he looked over to me. "Every week theyre popping up with a new business."

"Yeah, females are some strong ass creatures. That's one of the reasons I love Alexis."

"Aw man here we go."

"Naw man I'm serious, just here me out bro."

"Ok. What the hell you gotta say?"

"Man she believed in me when nobody else did. Bro, would you believe I didn't even tell anybody I was around that I wanted to be an actor. It took me years to let people know."

"So you mean to tell me you ain tell nobody? Ever?"

"I mean I guess I did when I first found out that's what I wanted to do. But bro, I swear everybody I told all looked down on me and said I wouldn't make it. How the fuck could little ol me from Norfolk, Virginia, make it in Hollywood. But fuck that, I still believed and grinded for years," I said looking over to him. "Bro I even moved to New York without a place to stay, broke as hell, just walking on faith. Shit was hard as a bitch. Getting rejection after rejection. It seemed like I had no one in the world who truly believed in me, until I met Alexis."

"See, now that you put it like that, I guess I kinda understand. How the hell you meet her cra-, I mean her ass anyway."

"Man I was back home in V.A.," I said, reminiscing. "I'd been back from New York for about a year. Shit was getting rough. And even though I said I wouldn't go back to the streets I still ended up selling weed."

"You was out hea hustlin? Let me find out your ol Michael B. Jordan face ass use to be a Trap Star."

"Nigga hell yeah, I was booming too, getting hella money. Then one day, Alexis was visiting Virginia and I guess somebody gave her my number and said I had some good smoke. So she hit me up to cop a sack or whatever. When she pulled up I was like damn, she fine as hell. Then she started talking and shit. So I asked her where she was from. Said she was from Atlanta or whatever. After that we just got to kickin it. I aint sell another sack all night. Yo, we talked about everything in life for hours, we just clicked naturally, it was like love at first sight or something."

"Love at first sight," he replied, laughing. "Oh this nugga a real actor, shit got you living in a fantasy world."

"Naw man I'm serious, it really was. She felt it too. We got a lot in common. Both got parents who passed away. And man when she was telling me about her hustle, the fact that she takes care of her own shit and works for herself-."

"She does nails right?" Rell said, cutting me off.

"Yep. But the way she does it is what got me. It's creative as hell man. Being a mobile nail tech, getting her own money and controlling her own life. I'm an artist. I'm big on creativity dawg."

"I can dig it."

"Yeah man, and when I told her what I did and how bad I wanted to be an actor she asked me why the fuck was I in boring ass Virginia selling weed. She said Atlanta was the new Black Hollywood and I could come stay with her."

"Damn jus like dat?"

"Just like that. She told me God told her to do it. So I quit everything I was doing right then and there. That shit was almost three years ago. And she just been riding with me ever since."

"What you think yall Bonnie and Clyde or somethin?" Rell asked, amused.

"Naw man, I'm just saying, she's a real chick, really held a nigga down. Dog, I came here broke as hell, I even had to work at Checkers."

"Damn so you use to be one of them niggas coming home smelling like burger grease and old milk shakes?"

"Hell yeah man. Here she is a boss ass bitch and her nigga flipping Burgers at Checkers. But she aint mind. She cooked for me, cleaned, she did a lot, all while never really making me feel like I was less than her."

"Yeah, that's cool and all, but answer me this. Was her ass always so mo'fuckin mean?"

"I can't even lie, hell yeah. But honestly man, it aint as bad as it seems. Sometimes she's the sweetest girl in the world. We be having a ball together, talking about our dreams, the past, just everything man."

"Alright, Mr. Lover Man, I got one more question. Take your time before you answer."

"Ok, whatsup?"

"Yu feel like the gud outweighs the bad?"

"Yeah," I replied before thinking for a second. "Well, most of the time. I just wish she'd stop being so damn jealous. Ever since I been getting the attention from the Play she won't stop bringing up hoes and shit. She thinks I'ma leave her or something."

"Shit, you might. A man's only as faithful as his options."

"Man fuck that shit, Ima loyal dude. I know when someone has my back. I aint gonna do her dirty. I couldn't even imagine being rich and famous without her. I don't wanna be with somebody who doesn't know my struggle."

"Nigga is you bouta cry," he asked, laughing once again as he looked over to me. "Oh hell naw. We endin this convo right mo'fuckin now."

"Nigga fuck you, aint nobody crying," I shot back.

"Yeah whateva. But for real bruh we getting a lil too deep in here," he said as he turned up some music. "U'm too mo'fuckin hi for all this emotional, ventin ass shit. You know these damn Percocets make a nugga sensitive."

"My bad, my bad," I replied.

"It's cool," he said as he looked down at his phone. "Ay my car plug just hit me, he say how much you tryna spend?"

"I got bout 3 racks to play with."

"You or yall?"

"What you mean?" I asked.

"You or yall? Is she helpin yu pay or you frontin the whole ticket?"

"I'm kicking off by myself. Shit, I'm the one that was driving, not her."

"What?" Rell exclaimed. "Bruh yall a team. I heard everythang you just told me but fuck all that. She betta go half. You cant be round here kissin ass and payin all the bills. Where the fuck is her money goin? Dont be a sucka bruh."

"Bro I told you she's an entrepreneur she got investments and shit."

"Man fuck all that. Her ass blowin that money. You eva think that she just saw you as a come up?"

"Come up? Hell no. I told you she had more than me when I came out here."

"So nugga. These Atlanta bih's is scandalous. Bruh, it's obvious you gon be somebody one day. Nugga, you sitting over there lookin like a fuckin model. Ol Pretty ass nigga. Even I know you gon be somebody. You got the classic story. Grindin, broke for years, then you pop. We all seen this shit play out a million times. Just go watch any Behind The Music or Unsung or somethin. She might have saw you as an investment."

"Man hell naw. Alexis aint even like that."

"Ok, if you say so. Just throwin it out there. I wouldnt be a real partna if I didn'," he said as he pulled into a Wal-Mart parking lot. "Yo let me run in the store right quick. I gotta pick up somethin from the pharmacy," he said before exiting the car.

"Cool."

I sat, damn near pissing on myself, why hadn't I went inside with him. After a few minutes, no longer able to hold it, I yanked his key from the ignition before racing inside. I hadn't used the bathroom since I'd been at the hospital.

Once inside, I did my business, washed my hands and walked out.

"Suspect is wearing a blue hoody and joggers," I overheard from a Police Officer's walky talky as I stepped out of the restroom. He and another officer were walking towards the pharmacy and had described Rell perfectly.

"Bro run," I yelled down to the Pharmacy where Rell was standing as the two officers looked back to me before looking over to Rell.

Without wasting a second Rell beat his feet. We both got the hell on, fast. I had no idea why in the hell we were running but what I did know was that my street senses were tingling. If my nigga run, I run, hood rules, simple as that.

In no time we both arrived at his whip, damn near outta breath, we hopped in, I through him the keys and we skated out of the parking lot, leaving the police in our dust.

"Bro what the fuck going on?" I asked, attempting to catch my breath as he weaved in and out of traffic like a pro.

"Oh it ain nothin. The bih at the counter musta told them that wasnt my name on the prescription. Don't worry, we gud."

"What? I'm lost."

"My bad, I forgot to tell yu. I got a fake prescription book that my Baby Mama stole from her Dr. He mustve reported it stolen or somethin. I told you, we gud though. I'm bout to take you to the dealership."

"Ay bro," I said laughing. "You the smoothest criminal I ever seen in my life. Nigga damn near lost his freedom 2 seconds ago and you chilling like aint nothing wrong."

"Anotha effect of being high off these damn Percocets," he said laughing as we speeded through the city.

Can't lie, a nigga was having flashbacks. Something about escaping the long arm of the law just does something to my spirit. It's like an adrenaline rush, better than sex. Forget busting a nut, you ever snatched your freedom back from the Cops? Motherfucking priceless. Niggas don't get to outsmart them often but when we do, it's special. Police vs. Us. It's like a sport, and no matter how long you're out the game, the love never goes away. Fuck the Police!

In no time we arrived at his homies shop.

"Yo just pick out the whip you want. I'll do all the talkin," Rell said as we parked.

"Bet."

"And before we cop this whip. You sure Alexis is gon be cool with this?"

"Hell yeah, why wouldn't she be?"

"Bruh I ain tryna act like I know yo ol lady betta than you. But something tells me she's the type of woman who likes to make her own decision."

"Fuck that. She getting a damn surprise today," I replied.

"Oh shit, lemme find out runnin from Twelve gotcha lettin ya nuts hang."

"Yeah nigga," I said as I grabbed my crotch, smiling.

We strolled up to the door. With each step I took, it became more evident that by no means was this your typical, every day friendly car dealership. Grade A marijuana oozed out of the building invading my nostrils as what sounded like 100 men competed to see who could laugh and yell the loudest.

Rell knocked as I anxiously awaited what was inside. I had to see this shit for myself.

"Who is it?" yelled a strong voice from behind the door.

"It's Rell mo'fuckin G."

The door opened. "Rell Mo'fuckin G. What it is pimp," said a large black man draped in gold jewelry.

"Shit I can't call it," he said as we walked in. "This my partner Von, Von this Moe, he the owna of this hea fine establishment."

"Whatsup Lil Bruh," said Moe, extending his hand for dap.

"Whatsup." I replied, as we slapped hands. I looked around. It was like a motherfucking Trap House in this bitch, niggas smoking, shooting dice, watching Sports Center. I aint never seen nothing like it. I mean who actually runs a business like this. But shit, I guess it's working.

"Yo Rell, you got that for me?" asked Moe.

"Aw man, lemme tell yu what the fuck just happened," Rell explained. "I go to get the pills and the bih behind the counter called Twelve on me. I had to get low, skated on them folk."

"Damn my boy. I was countin on ya. I'm ready to get hi. I been sober as a bih all damn day, you know I need me a mo'fuckin perc."

"My bad my nugga. I got some Xanax if you want some."

"Xanax? Hell naw nugga. Last time I popped one of dem bih's I woke up on my front porch wit one sock on and no shoe, no wallet, no shirt and a big ass knot on my head. Fuck that shit."

37

"Well fuck it, I got some bread to put in your pocket, that'll make you feel better."

"You right about that. I just got a whole new fleet too. Walk with me," he said as he motioned for us to follow him.

I squeezed past all the homies before we finally got to the back lot. Rell was right, bro had everything I could think of.

"Damn bro you comin up aint you?" said Rell as he looked around.

"Yuh my nigga. I think I really found my niche. Damn sure betta than sittin in the trap paranoid all day. At least this shit legal. And I'm helpin mo'fuckers."

"Fo sho, fo sho," replied Rell, nodding.

"But yuh bruh, look around for a second, I think I just seen my Baby Mama pullin up," Moe said before darting off.

"Cool, cool," said Rell. "See somethin yu think she gon like?" he asked, looking over to me.

"I see a couple," I replied as I scanned the lot. "Yo you sure these whips legit?" I asked, skeptical.

"Hell yuh bruh. Yu my boy so I'ma tell yu, Moe got the plug for the Police auction. You know all the cars dope boys be havin when they get locked up?"

"Yeah," I replied.

"Well they get sold for dirt cheap, and Moe flips em."

"Oh damn that's lit," I said, excitedly. "What about that one over there?" I asked as I pointed.

"The Nissan Altima?"

"Yeah."

"Ain that the same exact whip she just had?"

"Yep."

"Smart," Rell replied.

We waited for Moe to come back before giving it a test drive. Can't lie, shit ran like a pearl. We drove around for a while before heading back to the lot. Once we got there I did all the regular checks niggas like me who don't know shit about cars do. Looked at the tires, checked the oil, and blasted the radio. All of it looked on point to me. Plus Rell said she was a go. That's all the confirmation I need. I cashed before making my way back home.

The closer I got to the crib, the more nervous I became, not just because I was driving once again with no license, I had more important shit on my mind.

38

Whatsup God,

Yo yo, ay make sure Alexis likes this whip. I aint got time to hear her mouth.

"Hey Bae," I said as I walked into the crib.

"Where you been, I cooked?" she asked. I could tell she was in a better mood. Weed and alone time usually does that for her.

"I went out to get you a car."

"You got one?" she asked, enthused.

"Yep. Its outside."

No shoes, no socks, no headscarf, no problem, she ran out the crib ASAP.

"Aw baby. Thank you, thank you. I love it," she said excitedly as she rushed over to check out the interior.

"You don't mind that it's the same car you already had?"

"No. Of course not. I'm actually happy you went and did this shit all on your own. It's kinda sexy," she said as she planted a kiss on my lips.

"Not as sexy as you," I said as I held out 3 cheesecake cookies from subway. I bought her some home every night. They were her favorite. Even on days when I know she's pissed at me I can always squeeze out a smile when I whip em out. "Here baby," I said.

"Thanks bae," she replied, grateful. "I already rolled up a couple blunts for us."

"Cool."

We shot back in the crib. I kicked off my shoes, relaxed and got comfortable as we smoked, ate and watched T.V. Cant front, a nigga lives for times like these. I massaged her feet as I thought about everything Rell and I had talked about earlier.

Safe to say I'm still standing on everything I said. At the end of the day, all the attitude, all the complaining is 100 percent worth it. Sitting here with her gives me an at ease feeling that no other human on this earth can seem to do. Together, no one matters but the two of us. Just me and my Bae. Any stress the world brings me are non-existent when I'm in her presence. She may be a headache. But she's my headache and she worth it. At least to me.

"Give me a kiss," I said as she turned to the evening news.

"Suspects on the loose. If anyone knows these two men Call 1-888-lock-u-up," said the newscaster as the backside of Rell and I were seen plastered on the television.

I looked over to Alexis, nervously.

"You gotta be the stupidest motherfucker in the world," she said as she swerved away from my kiss.

Damn.

She stormed out of the room. How could I even be mad at her for being angry? Fuck it though, she'll get over it. Honestly, she need to just look on the bright side, at least she got a car. That's her problem, always worried about the wrong shit. I'm just glad neither me nor Rell's faces were clear. No one would ever know it was us. Shit, Alexis wouldn't have even known if it weren't for the fact that I still had on the same clothes as I did in the video.

Going Thru Some Thangs

"Thank you," I said as two delivery drivers exited my crib. They had just delivered a new fucking refrigerator. A fucking refrigerator. I don't know if you know how much those motherfuckers cost. But them bitches aint cheap. On top of that I just had to go half with Alexis on a motherfucking hot water heater last week.

It's been almost a month since the last day of the Play and I swear with each day I been getting broker and broker. I'm talking dead broke. It's like I just can't stop spending money. Always got some bullshit to kick off for. It's crazy, if it aint one thing it's another. Shits pretty miserable if you ask me. Thank God I go to court today for my driving on a Suspended License charge. I dropped $500 to pay off my fine and the dumb ass late fee they applied so I'd be able to get my license reinstated. If everything goes as planned I should be getting my $1300 I kicked for the bond back. At least that's how things work back home in Virginia, you come to court with your license and the judge drops the case. I pray it works in my favor. Lord knows I need it. That's the only reason I even agreed to pay for the new fridge.

Truthfully, aint like I had too much of a choice. Alexis doesn't really have any extra cash, she's been investing all of her money into her new Nail shop/Bus. From the looks of things it's gonna be dope as hell, she got it for the low off of Craigslist and she's been spending the majority of her days upgrading it. It's gonna have TV's, seats that massages the clients as she does their nails and a whole bunch of other fly ass shit.

Soon as it gets up and running she's hitting the road. She already has a pretty big social media following, so she's gonna do little pop up shops inside the bus all over the country. Dope right? What kinda girl thinks of shit like that? One of the many reasons I love her ass. I can just see it now, News Reporters and social media are all gonna have a ball with the story. A young black female entrepreneur out in the streets, getting it on her own. Their gonna eat it up.

Can't lie though the pressures of getting it together is kinda getting the best of her. She aint verbally said it but I know she aint really been feeling me lately. How do I know? Simple, she aint been calling me Bae. I aint no genius but I know whenever she calls me by my Government name, somethings up.

And not just that, it's worse, a lot worse, this bit-, I mean Alexis, stopped doing the one thing that raises my spirits when times are getting hard, the one thing that brings sunshine to my cloudy days. SHE STOPPED SUCKING DICK!

Yeah, we fuck, but that aint nothing, it aint the same, she got needs too, the way I see it, she's basically just using me for a nut and that's cool I guess. But not sucking dick, oh hell naw. I'll never be cool with that, never. To me it's a lot deeper than it seems. See, I never hid from Alexis how much I loved head, I let her know every chance I could get how much it means to me, I even went to the sex store and bought her all types of freaky little gadgets to make the whole process pleasurable to her. Not to mention I eat her up a wall every chance I get. So, for her not to be returning the favor means she don't give a fuck about my happiness, simple as that.

41

I don't' mean to keep going on about it but that shit really been pissing me off. I love head, I wake up in the morning thinking about it, brush my teeth thinking about it, think about it in the shower. I aint gonna keep going on and on but I know you get the point. How the fuck is she just gonna stop all of a sudden. Especially when she was doing it consistently at one point. Got me all addicted, and then just gonna stop? Oh hell naw, fuck naw. As many bills as I pay around this motherfucker, as many motherfucking subway cookies I buy, all them doors I hold open.

Yeah I said it, holding motherfuking doors. May not seem like much, but up until her I aint never did no shit like that. I mean yeah I hold doors for women who are walking in a building at the same time as me, who doesn't. But what I do for Alexis is different, I actually open her car door for her each and every time she gets in or out if I'm around. How many niggas do that in this day and age? I damn sure don't know any. It's gotten to the point where she doesn't even get out of the car if she pulls up to the house and I'm already there, she just sits in the whip waiting for me to come out and open it.

You telling me shit like that don't deserve a little head? Not even a lot, just a little, I mean damn, she can at least suck the tip, lick the shit, something. I mean damn, what the fuck. Aint like I'm asking for it every night. Of course I'd love to get it every night, but aint like I'm expecting it.

I just don't get it, hell, I'll even take once a week. I know that aint too much to ask for. Especially when I gotta sit in the house and listen to her complain all day every day. Man, not having a job and constantly being around her can get annoying as fuck, fast. I swear all I hear all day is.

"Why is the toilet seat up?"

"Didn't I tell you to close the shower curtain when you get out?"

"Who taught you how to cut grass, it's not even, even?"

No bullshit, outta everything, her bitching about the grass really pisses me the fuck off. First of all I'm allergic to the shit. I really aint even supposed to be doing it. I gotta pop Claritin allergy pills, wear a mask and drink Emergen-C juice just to even go out there. Before living with her I aint never cut no grass in my life. Ever. She should be thankful that I even do the shit. But all she says is, "If you can't do it right, I can just call one of these little kids in the neighborhood to do it for you. I'm pretty sure they can do it just as good if not better."

All jokes to the side, I wanna cuss her ass out every time she say that dumb ass shit. But I chill. See, I'm a changed man. I gotta be honest, back in the day, in all my past relationships, I was the worse boyfriend ever. I cheated, came in late and straight disrespected women. Shit, I gotta keep it all the way real, I even put my hands on my ex's a few times.

Now before you go judging me, let me at least say this. I aint proud at all about it. Honestly it's one of my biggest regrets. But in my defense I was young and dumb. All the guys I grew up with hit their girls so I thought that was how you handled women. Aint like I'd seen too many healthy relationships growing up. Yeah, yeah I know it doesn't make it any better. But hey, at least I'm a changed man.

So yeah, anyway, that's kinda why I let her say some of the things she says to me. I'm just tryna try something different. My goal is to be the best man I can be. If this relationship doesn't work I want to know that I gave it my all. Can't lie, this good guy shit is hard, but I just feel like it's gonna be a lot easier once I finally get us in the position that we deserve to be in.

I drove to court in a pretty good mood. Even turned on some Chance The Rapper, he's the closest thing I got to Gospel on my playlist. Listening to him had me more confident than ever that I was getting my money back. As his lyrics 'Are you ready for your blessing' blasted through my stereo, I answered as if he was talking to me. "Damn right I'm ready. I'm ready for my blessing!" I missed my money and couldn't wait to get it back.

My mood kinda shifted once I actually walked inside the courtroom. Ever since a kid it always put an uneasy feeling inside of me. You don't know what vulnerable is until your fait lies in another motherfuckers hands.

Boy, aint no worse feeling than being found guilty and having that Sherriff walk behind you, cuffs out. You look around for options but there's nowhere to run, nowhere to hide, you're trapped, staring at your lawyer with the 'help me face' as he kinda just shrugs his shoulders.

Whatsup God,

Please let me get outta here safe. I know its only Traffic court. But you never know... you never know.

I walked slowly to my seat. The courtroom was packed. Looking around all I could see were faces that looked like mine preparing to fight for their lives. Ok, Ok, maybe fighting for our lives is a bit of a stretch, it's only traffic court. But niggas was definitely fighting for their freedom.

I sat down and watched as niggas were cuffed and taken to the back, the dark side, aka hell on earth. Some people walk back there for a week but others walk back and never see the light of day again. Suddenly I felt my body start to tremble.

"Three months."

"Four months."

"12 months."

This Judge wasn't playing any games. Niggas was going through it. Then it was my turn. I took a deep breath as I walked up.

Whatsup God,

I hope you heard me Lord. You know I got stuff to do. Please let this work out for me. Let her have some compassion. She's a black lady, make her understand me Lord. I aint even know my license was suspended. You know that.

43

"Lavon Jordan."

"Hello Your Honor."

"Hello," she replied, dryly. "Ok. I see, you're here for a Driving on a Suspended license. How do you plead?" she asked as she read over her sheet of paper, never looking up at me.

"Um. I'm not really sure. See, I'm from Virginia---."

"Guilty or not guilty," she followed, finally looking over to me.

"Not guilty."

"Did you have a license at the time of your offence?"

"No but-."

"Ok. Then you are guilty."

"Your honor can I say one thing."

"Go ahead," she replied, annoyed.

"I had no idea that my license was suspended. And I recently paid my fine and my reinstatement for another license."

"That's all fine and dandy. But if you did not have it on the day of your arrest it really means nothing."

"But-."

"But nothing. I sentence you to one year probation and a $1500 fine. Your bail will be used. Therefore you will only owe $200."

"Your honor," I pleaded. "I know you don't really care. But I need that money, for real. I don't mind paying the fine but can I make payments instead of you all using my bond money? I was really counting on getting it back today."

"Sorry but rules are rules. That's how we do things around here."

"But your honor I really need it. Please work with me. I really need it."

"Sorry, we really need drivers to obey the laws of the road. Next case," she said as she looked away from me.

I stormed out of court. Heated.

Whatsup God,

Help me Lord. I know I don't need to be this angry. Keep me calm Lord. Just let me know everything will be ok. Give me a sign or something. Man, life aint fair and you know it. Just help me out my nigga. You know I'ma good person. I just need a break right quick.

I drove off before receiving a phone call.

"Hey Von," said Alexis.

"Whatsup?" I replied back.

"Court didn't go so well?" she asked.

"Nope. But I don't really wanna talk about it."

"Aww Von, I'm sorry. Well you're not going to jail are you?"

"No," I replied.

"Well hey, at least you're free."

"Yeah, you're right."

"Ok, well I guess I'll talk to you when you get home. Love you."

"Love you too."

I hung up the phone before immediately receiving a call from Kyle Upshaw. He was the guy I'd met at one of our shows who said he had a role for me in his upcoming flick. It was a small Independent Film but who cares, I'd be getting exposure, and better than that, I'd be getting a check. Not to mention the fact that Kyle's pretty connected to the industry so I got a good feeling it could be picked up by Netflix or maybe even theatres or something.

"Yo whatsup Kyle."

"What sup Lavon? How you?"

"Can't complain. What's happening?"

"Same ol, same ol. You busy?"

"Nope. I was actually just on my way home," I replied.

"You mind stopping through the office for a second?"

"Yeah, I can do that."

"You remember the address?"

"Yep."

"Cool," he said.

"Bet, I'll see you in about 20-25 minutes."

Whatsup God,

Man I need this. Let him tell me some good news. I know I can kill this role. I need as many people as possible to see it. I need this to be my big break. I need this Lord, I'm ready, please, I'm ready.

Only took about 25 minutes to get to his office. Actually I'm not too sure if Office is the correct word. It's really just a big old ass house in the middle of the Westside of Atlanta they'd been using. Still, it has everything a film office would need, green room, computers, cameras. I love it. It's Raw, with an authentic vibe. Felt family orientated.

I can't wait to help him build from the ground up. I gotta feeling this is gonna be legendary and I'm willing to do anything to assist. I even have some movie ideas of my own that I want to run across them.

"Whatsup Kyle," I said as I entered the house.

"How you doing Von? It's so nice to see you," he replied as we embraced.

"Likewise, likewise. Whatchu doing, creating some more magic?" I asked.

"You know me too well," he said as he motioned for me to follow him to his office.

"Come on, you're a creative just like myself I know you always got something up your sleeve," I replied as I took a look at Kyle's attire. Not that it matters but Kyle's gay and he wasn't afraid to show it. He definitely looked the part, flamboyant is an understatement. Luckily living in Atlanta has opened my eyes. There was a time in the past where I was uncomfortable around Gays but nowadays I just see them like I see everyone else. I'd be a liar if I said I didn't feel kinda uncomfortable when they'd make little slick remarks but Kyles not like that. It's strictly business.

"Yep," Kyle replied as we entered his office. "And by the way. I caught the last show you guys did. Marvelous job, you were even better than I'd remembered. I don't want to disrespect all the time you've been putting in by saying this, but you make it look effortless, you're a natural. It's in you. You're going to be a huge star."

"Thanks," I replied as we both took a seat around his desk. "I can't wait to get to work. I been going over the script daily. I basically know the whole thing by heart. Shit, I even got the other actor's lines memorized. I really want to get into the role. I want to know everything that's going on. I want to know what everyone else is thinking so it can better help me know how to react. Ya know what I'm saying?"

"Wow. That's awesome that's some real dedication."

"I wanna be the best. This is what I wake up for. I actually had a chance to continue the Play but I knew what we had planned. I couldn't. This just feels right."

"Wow," said Kyle, as he took in a deep breath.

"What's wrong?"

"I'm afraid I got bad news," he replied.

"What? We won't be able to start on time?"

"Not exactly."

"Whatsup, what's going on?"

"We lost the funding for the movie."

"Huh?'" I blurted.

"I'm sorry Lavon," Kyle said, sadly. "It's effecting me too. But the company we were going through pulled out. We were the second film they were financing and the first film was a total flop. They lost a shitload of money and they don't feel they can take the risk right now."

"Damn," I replied, desperately attempting to hide my disappointment.

"I know man."

"We can't start a go fund me or a fund raiser or something? This is a big movie. We can't just give up like that."

"Yeah I'd love to keep going. But we gotta be honest. Things like that take time. I don't wanna give you any false hope. But what I can do is get you an audition with my buddy Mike Rollings. It's nothing in stone but I think he'd be able to work with you."

"Really?" I asked, attempting to find a glimmer of hope. "When?"

"It's soon. I have to get all of the information for you."

"Ay man. Just let me know. I'd love anything right about now, anything."

"Will do. So I take it that your spots been filled for the Play you were in?"

"Yeah. Their already on the road," I replied as we both shook our heads.

"Again Von, I'm so sorry."

"It's cool. They say everything happens for a reason right," I replied.

"Yep, you're right. That's a great attitude to have."

"Yeah man. Well I'm gonna get up outta hea," I said, standing to my feet.

"Ok," he replied, standing up along with me. "And I'll be calling you soon to let you know about the audition."

"Great. Thanks man," I said as I extended my hand for a handshake before I exited.

I plopped down in the driver's seat of my car, wishing I could somehow sink down into my seat, disappearing forever. How the fuck did this happen? Why the fuck did this happen? The feeling of not being in control is one that I hate. What the fuck did he mean the funding didn't come through? Was there ever any damn funding? Was all this shit a fucking lie? And if he did have funding, did he already know things went bad weeks before and just didn't tell me? Was he trying to sabotage me? So much was running through my head.

Whatsup God,

Calm me down Lord. I need to calm down. This is crazy. I just knew I'd be getting a check next week. Come on dog why is everything going wrong? What's the reason? I asked you for a sign and this is what you're giving me? Why is everything going wrong, come on man, let me know, let me know. I'm trying to be calm. I been taking deep breaths, reading, doing everything I can to get where I wanna be. Why is it so hard for me? I don't know what to do. I want to believe that he has an audition but I just don't know. I don't know anything, nothing at all.

"Everything ok?" asked Kyle as he knocked on my driver side window, startling me.

"Yeah," I said as I cranked up my car, pulling off.

Whatsup God

I need you Lord. Just give me some strength man. I don't know how much more I can take. I'm getting too old to be broke. Just help me man. Please, I'm beggin you, help me, please.

I drove down the street in silence before pulling up to a Subway to get Alexis her cookies. It was hard for me to even order, I could hardly speak, I was completely lost for words. I'm not even sure I gave the cashier the correct change, I just through some cash in his hands, snatched my cookies and hopped back in the whip, in route for the crib.

Whatsup God,

Boost my spirits for me. You know Alexis can always tell when something's wrong. I aint even in the mood to be talking about it. You know I like to be quiet during times like this. Aint like nobody truly cares. Well maybe she does. But it aint like I can really explain to her how I feel. I can't even understand my own self most days. How can I expect anyone else to?

"Come on Von, get your shit together," I said to myself as I unlocked the front door.

"Hey Von," Alexis said as I walked into the house.

"Hey Bae," I smiled as I held up the cookies before heading to the kitchen to place them on the stove.

"Thanks. You ok?" she asked, concerned.

"Yeah," I replied as I attempted to walk away.

"Nigga why you lying? You know I can always tell when somethings wrong," she said as she stood in my way, causing me to side step her.

I sat down on the couch. "I'm good."

"Ok, I guess. Well I made something to eat. "

"I'm ok right now," I replied as she plopped down next to me.

"Well you know what to do once you're hungry. You came in right on time. This is the Kalief Browder story," she said as she pointed up to the T.V.

"Cool," I replied.

We cuddled up and tuned it. Well I did, Alexis fell asleep damn near 5 minutes into it as usual. Shit got crazy. Dude's life was tragic. As the show went on I found it harder and harder not to burst in to tears, by the end, it was impossible, water shot from my eyes.

I don't know if I've ever seen something so sad in my damn life. Nigga went through hell only to be left so weak that he killed himself. Shit had me thinking, like why the fuck did he deserve that shit? Maybe he'd done something that no one knows about and God was punishing him. I don't know. Or maybe some people are just put on this earth to struggle.

At that moment anxiety consumed my body. What if I'm one of the people who were put here to struggle? Unsolvable problems suddenly began to flood my brain, overpowering any ounce of positivity I had left.

I couldn't believe the damn movie had been canceled. How dare they? Damn. You'd think I'd be used to disappointment by now. But I'm not, every time hurts just like the last. I'm exhausted, giving up never seemed so tempting.

Why the fuck did I even want to be an actor in the first place? My dumb ass. If I would have put this kinda time and dedication into anything else I'd probably be the C.E.O. of a company or something by now. But look at me, damn near thirty and broke. Why the fuck can't I live how I want? Why can't I just be fuckin happy? It's people who don't work nearly as hard as I do and are ten times happier than me.

Life was eating me alive. I turned off the T.V. and started to look through my phone. Social media was worst. I never considered myself a jealous nigga. But right now I am. Look at these motherfuckers, smiling, happy as hell, not a care in the world. Why the fuck can't I look like that?

I couldn't take it anymore. I tossed my phone across the room.

Whatsup God,

Yo why you got me feeling like this? I can't take it. I miss being excited about life. I don't know what to do man. You got me sitting here waiting for a blessing. This shit is the closest thing to sitting in jail with no release date. I aint got nobody to talk to. Nobody. Aint like I'm picky I'll talk to anybody right now. Maybe I needa go talk to some Pastor or something. Actually what the fuck am I thinking, they aint gonna understand me either. Nobody does. Ay man let me ask you something. How come the people who supposed to be the closest to knowing God like Pastors and Deacons don't understand a person like me chasing a dream? They always got the stupidest advice. You'd think they'd understand the concept of walking on faith, but they don't. They understand the thought of it but have never truly put in the work. It's crazy. I need somebody man, please send me somebody. I feel defeated Lord, defeated and alone. But still in my heart I know something has to be brewing. It just has to. I dedicated my whole life to this. I know you can't possibly have me going out sad like this. I know you got my back, I just know it. I need you to come through for me. I need you man.

The longer I sat I swear it felt as if the walls were caving in on me. Paranoid, my eyeballs frantically bounced around the room, the silence became intimidating as sweat squirted and leaked down my face. My heart pumped at a sprinters pace as it became hotter and hotter, causing me to strip down into my underwear as I paced around the room unable to hold back the tears. Becoming weak, I dropped down to my knees defeated, the Devil himself seemed to be wrapping his scorching hot arms around my body, nearly suffocating me. Gasping for air, I crawled over to Alexis, I needed help.

"Alexis, Alexis, wake up. I need you," I said as I shook her from my knees.

"Whatsup Bae," she replied, startled.

"I'm fucked up, I aint doing ok."

"What's wrong?"

"Everything," I said as my face fell into her lap.

"Huh, what's wrong Baby?" she asked as she gently rubbed my scalp.

"My life, everything, shit just starting to spin outta control," I answered, sobbing.

"Ok Bae, calm down, just talk to me, I'm here."

"I swear ever since that accident everything just been going wrong man," I replied, finally looking up to her, embarrassed.

"Baby it's just a little court fine."

"That's not it. The funding for the movie didn't come through. It's dead, over."

"Really?" she asked as she pulled me closer, resting my head on her breast.

"Yep."

"It's ok, it's ok," she added as she continued to console me. "We're gonna figure something out. Have you thought of any other options so far?"

"I mean Kyle said it was another audition soon that he thinks I can get," I said as I backed away, wiping my tears as I sat next to her on the couch. "But the way my lucks been set up. I don't know what's gonna happen," I added, dropping my head.

"Baby it's gonna be ok," she said as she gently placed her hand at the bottom up my chin, raising it to the sky.

"Yeah you say that shit now," I replied, staring eye to eye. "But I'm getting broker by the day. Bills are coming in faster than I don't know what. I'm kinda losing faith. I mean I guess I'm not that concerned about my dreams actually coming true. I've been given enough signs to know they will. It's just not knowing how long the struggle will last makes me sad as hell," I continued, shaking my head. "I mean who really wants to knowingly walk through a storm after they've already walked through countless others. I might just have to go look for a job or something, I don't know," I said, shaking my head.

"No. No. You don't have to get no fuckin job. Fuck that. Don't worry about any bills. Get yourself together," she replied, hand on my chin as she stared into my eyes." I can handle everything. Trust me. Just figure out what you're gonna do. I got your back."

"Really?"

"Hell yeah. I believe in you Bae. I know you're gonna get over this. God has something special for you. Besides, we can't act like you've exhausted all of your options. Hell, you might even need to try to be an Instagram comedian, you're pretty funny, maybe that's where you'll really get discovered. Who knows?"

"Damn, you're right. I'm trippin. Thanks Bae. That means a lot," I replied, as we both smiled at one another.

"What did you think I would say? Von, you're the greatest man I've ever met. I want you to win and I'm gonna do anything in my power to see you do it."

"Damn," I replied, relieved. "And to think, I was over here damn near going crazy. I didn't know what to do. I didn't even know how to break the bad news to you."

"I should smack your ass," she replied playfully. "You should never be afraid to tell me anything. We're a team, stop trippin. Don't think the things that you've done go unnoticed. You add more value to my life than you'll ever know," she continued, before leaning in for a kiss. "Let's ride out," she said.

"Where you wanna go?" I asked.

"I got an idea. I'm gonna go hop in the shower. Roll up a few blunts while I'm in there," Alexis replied.

About an hour later we headed out. We passed blunts as we zoned out listening to 90's RnB, both of our favorites. As I sat thinking of my next move, I looked over to Alexis, can't lie, knowing she had my back lifted a huge weight from off of my shoulders. Still, at the end of the day, I'm a man, and I don't feel like a man if I'm not taking care of my responsibilities. I gotta make a way.

It's crazy, I always thought I didn't need a Plan B. Always heard that a Plan B is like planning on not conquering my Plan A. I mean how can you truly give something your all if you know if it doesn't work you have the opportunity to do something else. If you really want something you gotta go all in. But shit, at times like this I sure as hell wish I had a damn back up plan. I was taught to follow my heart, but right now I feel like I followed it only to be led to a cliff, and I'm falling face first with no parachute.

Needing comfort, I reached over to Alexis and grabbed her by the hand, squeezing tightly. Slightly blushing, she looked over to me and smiled leaving my body tingling. Her eyes were like the sun, she brightened my day and warmed my heart. In all my years on earth she's the only one who's ever had the power to relax me in such a way. I don't care who doesn't understand it, she's my everything. I'd be lost without her. Shit, I'm lost with her, so I can only imagine a life where she's absent. And although she doesn't really admit it, I know she feels the same way.

"Lake Lanier," I said as I read a sign we were approaching. "Hell is this?"

"It's my favorite Lake. Being that you grew up 20 minutes from Virginia Beach I know you'd appreciate the water," she said as she looked ahead. There was a huge lake, surrounded by gigantic trees, housing thousands of sturdy leaves. "Even though this isn't a beach, I was hoping you could find some sorta comfort here being that you're away from home. Maybe this will get you feeling like yourself again. Besides, it's beautiful," she said, peering out into the world.

"It is," I agreed as we parked under a tall tree.

"Yep and as you can see we're all alone."

"Just how I like it," I replied as we exited the car.

She popped open her trunk before walking over to it.

"And I bought us a little wine so we can really relax," she said as she held up a bottle of Moscato and a couple Styrofoam cups.

"Damn. I didn't even see you bring that out."

"Somethings aren't meant for you to see," she said with a wink.

"Well aint you so romantic," I said as we kissed.

I grabbed the bottle, blanket and her hand as we walked over to a small dock, it was completely dark, minus the light shining down from the stars sparkling over our heads. I laid a blanket down before we sat cuddled up, staring up at the dark night.

We sat sipping wine, passing a blunt for what seemed like hours without speaking a word. Even if this was only temporary, I enjoyed the luxury of peace.

"What you thinking about?" I asked looking over to Alexis.

"A lot," she replied.

"Like what?"

"You really wanna know?" she asked softly, looking deep into my eyes.

"Yeah, I do."

"Well, take a guess," she said.

"I think I got a pretty good idea. Your Mom?"

"Jackpot. I knew you'd get it right," she said, smiling.

"Of course. I was thinking about mine too," I said as I looked up to the sky. "Do you really think their up there?"

"Up Where? Like in the sky or in heaven?" she asked.

"I mean, I guess both," I said as I gathered my words. "Do you really believe Heaven exists?"

"I hope so," she replied.

"Yeah me too," I said as I paused continuing to look up to the sky. "Ya know, sometimes I wonder what the qualifications are to go. Honestly, sometimes I find myself questioning the bible. Something in me just won't let me believe God is so damn judgmental."

"It's crazy, I've been feeling the same way. I don't think any of us truly know what exactly to believe. Shit kinda sucks."

"Hell yeah. In my heart I want to believe it's a God but he just confuses me. It's like if he loves me so much why let me suffer? Like why would he have to take our Moms away?" I asked still looking up to the sky.

"Yeah like what the fuck could they have possibly done to deserve to die?" she asked.

"I know they say everything happens for a reason but what could be the reason that they didn't deserve to live anymore?"

"I just don't get it," Alexis followed.

"It's something I just can't stop thinking about. I can't even lie, sometimes crazy shit runs through my mind."

"Like what?" Alexis asked.

"I don't know why but sometimes I wonder if the reason they died was because of something they did that we don't know."

"What do you mean? Like they did something to deserve it. Like Karma or something?" she asked.

"Yeah."

"Hell no," Alexis replied quickly. "It's crazy, I was just thinking about that. But I know it aint true. It can't be. My Mom was an Angel."

"I never said I thought they actually did something bad. All I'm tryna say is that everything crosses my mind. It's so fucking confusing. Not to mention everything reminds me of her. I can't even walk into a grocery store without seeing some lady with the same lipstick she wore or smelling like her perfume."

"Or hear someone yelling 'Get your butt back over here' when their kids are running in the grocery store," mocked Alexis.

"Hell yeah. I used to hate shit like that," I replied, laughing. "But boy what I'd do to hear her voice one more time."

"Who you telling. I'd die to feel her touch right now, actually I don't even need to feel her touch, maybe her presence would just be enough. I guess I just really wanna know if she's ok, or just to make sure she knows I'm ok. I was her baby man," Alexis said, shaking her head.

"That's crazy."

"What?" replied Alexis as she looked over to me.

"You think just like me," I added.

"Really? Why don't you ever say anything?" she asked.

"I don't know, I guess I just kinda stopped talking about her a while ago. For some reason it seems like it makes people feel uncomfortable or something. Besides, I aint looking for no pity party."

"Yeah, I know the feeling." she said. "But maybe we should start talking to each other about it."

"That's cool. I'd like that," I replied.

"Can I ask you something serious?" Alexis asked.

"Of course."

"Ok. Don't judge me but-," she said before taking a brief pause." Do you ever think about joining them?"

"What do you mean?"

"Nothing, never mind," Alexis replied.

"Naw baby what do you mean?" I asked, concerned.

"I mean do you ever miss her so much that you feel like just ending it down here and going wherever they are?" she replied, looking me in the eyes.

"Like killing yourself?"

"Maybe," she answered, never taking her eyes off of me.

Turning my head, looking out into the water, I sat thinking for a second. I wanted so bad to tell her that I'd been having the same feelings. But naw, I know I have to be strong. This shit just came out of nowhere. She always seemed to have everything under control. I'm shocked.

"Why though?" I asked.

"I guess I just get tired of having to be so tough. Having to do so much. Besides, sometimes I fear even if I don't kill myself I'll die from a broken heart."

"Damn," I replied, searching for the right things to say. "I'm sorry Baby."

"No. No. You actually make my life easier. A lot easier. I've been dealing with this shit for years. My Mom's been gone a while. I just sometimes want someone to baby me and tell me it's gonna be ok. I don't know, it's like sometimes I feel like I'll never be truly happy."

"Damn Bae. It's my fault," I replied, grabbing her, holding her tight. "I'm gonna make you happy. I have to. You're my woman. I'll baby you. I'll do whatever. I just have to go harder. I got us. I'm gonna help you take a load off your shoulders. Everything's gonna work out big time. I feel it in my gut. I don't want you to ever feel like not being here. Just give me a second."

"I'm sorry Baby. Blame the alcohol, I'm kinda tipsy. I don't want you feeling like you don't do enough. You're appreciated," she said as she kissed me on the cheek. "It's just me. I gotta find a way to get over this feeling. I have to, it takes over my life and turns me into someone I hate."

"Well I'm gonna help you. Besides, if something happens to you I don't know what I'd do. When my Mom died I basically lost my Dad the same week and with my Grandma gone, you're really all I got. I'll never leave you. I can't lose you. I love your lil stupid ass."

"And I love your lil irritating ass more," Alexis replied as we held on to one another.

I sat, soaking it all in. I always thought Alexis had it all figured out. Who would have guessed it was all a front. I thought I knew her so well. How had I had missed it? Gotta admit, in a way, it kinda made me feel better to know that I wasn't alone with my dark feelings. I believe we're closer now. I gotta make sure she's straight. My heart hurts for her. That's my baby.

For the remainder of the night we sat still, together. I held her until the sun started to peek through the clouds. At that moment we were one. God wants it this way, he put us together and I know he'll keep our union strong. I was made for her and she was made for me.

Too Much

After two long drawn out weeks of struggling and tryna stay strong Kyle made due on his word to get me an audition. I had been going over my lines nonstop around the clock and today was the day.

If you ask me, I'm pretty sure I got it down pat. I read the script so many times I'm starting to see that shit in my dreams. Not only that but I've also been watching movies, reading books and basically anything else I could do to help prepare.

No bullshit, I even tried meditation. Gotta admit, I aint know what the fuck I was doing, not a clue. Fuck it though, I dived right in, I was willing to do whatever I had to do to get this damn role. So I turned off the lights, sat in the middle of the floor Indian style, closed my eyes and attempted to clear my mind. Not too sure if I was doing it right, the whole time I couldn't stop thinking about not thinking. Actually I know I didn't do it right, that shit aint help a damn thing. But hey, fuck it, at least I tried.

It's so much pressure on me. All I know is that I can't fuck up. This is my shot. Maybe my only shot. This could make me or break me. My chance of changing my life could be depending on this very moment. As the seconds get closer, the more anxious I became. I sat in my car, staring at my reflection in the rearview, I'm looking pretty good if I do say so myself. Rell had given me a fresh edge up last night and I even did a couple pushups just to make sure my arms were on swole. Looking good and feeling good. I'm ready to show these folk what I got. I stepped out, confident as ever, head to the sky as I made my way into the building.

Man, all that confident, 'I can do it' shit all but wore off once I finally entered the studio. My nerves seemed to be having a dance battle throughout my body. It was so many actors. All of them in their own zone going over lines, talking to themselves, some of them were even looking pretty weird, humming and chanting and shit.

Still, as I gazed around to all of the many faces, I didn't see not one like mine. It was clear, these niggas can't fuck with me. I'm the best. The greatest.

"You got this," I said under my breath as I signed in and awaited my name to be called.

As all of the Actors continued to practice I decided to holla at my main man.

Whatsup God,

YoYo, you know a nigga need you today. I need you to help me stay on point. Keep me strong in there man. I need to be able to pull out all of the stops. I'm serious, I need you to even keep cole outta my throat. This is my shot. This gotta be perfect. I know everything is riding on this. I know this is a test. And I'm ready to pass it. Just be patient with me. I learned a lot. I got this. I'm ready to go to the next level. Please let me get this part, please Lord.

I sat eyes closed, still trying to figure out this meditation thing.

"Lavon Jordan," screamed a woman from the audition room.

I stood to my feet.

Whatsup God,

Help me.

"Hello Mr. Jordan," said a chubby black man. I could tell right away he and Kyle had a lot in common. "I'm Steve and that's Pam and Liza. This right here is Amanda," he said as he pointed over to a young black girl. "She will Act alongside of you as 'Tia'. As you know 'American Rap Star' will be a huge film. I want you to give it your all."

"Gotcha," I replied, nodding my head, focused.

He sat back down as all three stared at me.

"Action," he said.

I jumped into character as Amanda stepped in front of me.

"Come on Tia. I said I was sorry," I bolted.

"Boy do you know how many times you've said sorry? You embarrassed me for the last fucking time. Got bitches out here talking behind my back and shit. Fuck you."

"Baby I'm sorry. I don't even know why I do what I do," I said. "Well I guess I do. But no funny shit it's like I can't even really explain it."

"Nigga whatever," Tia replied, arms crossed. "You can't explain it cause you don't have a reason. You're just stupid as hell. And I aint got time for no stupid ass nigga. I'm abouta get me a smart nigga. Someone with some common sense, who appreciates me. Watch."

"What?" I blurted.

"Yeah nigga you won't the only one getting attention today. You're trippin if you think I'm about to sit around here playing dumb. Boy, you must don't know," she said, shaking her head.

"Man Tia I'm sorry. I can't lose you though. No funny shit."

"Boy whatever. I'm done. I heard all of this shit before," she said as she spoke using her neck. "I'm too young and too bomb to be wasting my time. You said what you got to say. Now I'm going in the house. Pick up all this shit before you leave," she said turning around.

"No. No," I said before grabbing her by the arm. "You all I got foreal Tia. And you probably gonna be the best I'm ever going to get. I don't really know how to do this love shit. Aint nobody never loved me before. See, you can go in the house and leave me and you

know for a fact your Mama love you more than anything in this world. I don't got nobody to love me. You the only one. You leave me and I'm alone out here. Dolo. No funny shit."

We ran our lines for about fifteen minutes before Steve cut us off and said, "Great Job," nonchalantly as the other two lady's sat continuing to be silent.

I tried to look over to them but I was stuck. As sweat dripped onto the floor my eyes remained locked with the actress. For a minute it was as if we were the only ones standing in the room. Now I've had some great performances in my day but this was different. At that moment there was no way possible you could convince me that I wasn't really my character and she wasn't my girl. This was different, different but magical at the same time.

"Guys," Steve screamed, snapping us out of our trance. "Snap out of it, you guys did a great job."

That was all the confirmation I needed. We said our goodbyes, shook hands and I could tell by the way Steve looked in my eyes, this part was mine and he knew it. I walked out head high, triumphant. Strolling past the rest of the so called actors I smiled, yeah I might be a little older than what the part calls for but I know I can pull it off, it's funny, they had no idea that they were wasting their time.

I hopped in the whip.

Whatsup God,

Lord, Lord, Lord. If that wasn't enough to get the part I don't know what I will have to do. But man, please just make sure the Directors and producers find it in their hearts to choose me. Did you see me? I killed it. It's like I could feel the words. Like I wrote them or something. This part was meant for me and if no one knows it, I do. It's crazy how much I could relate. Help me lord. Help me.

I opened my eyes and drove in silence until the phone rang. I picked up and it was Kyle Upshaw.

"Lavon!" he shouted.

"Whatsup Kyle. I just left the audition."

"You don't have to tell me. Steve called as soon as you left. They say you smoked it! They're even considering stopping auditions all together. What did you do in there?"

"Really? I was just being myself. I can really relate to the role."

"Man. I think you're on to something. They should be giving you a call within the next two weeks. But I'm telling you outta my mouth. You got it man. Just go home and be patient. Get as much alone time with your girl as possible because in a few months you're gonna be swamped with work. Congrats."

"Thanks man."

I hung up the phone.

Whatsup God,

You did it a-motherfucking-gain. Aw man why do I continue to doubt you when you always make a way for a nigga? Damn. I don't even know what to do right now. Yeah! Yo this is amazing. I wanna cry. For some reason I really feel like you bouta bless a nigga. I'm really starting to understand things. At least I think so. Well my body does feel less stressed. That's weird. You know I been stressed to the max. At this moment I'm not as worried as I once was. Hopefully that's a sign. I truly feel I have something to offer the world. I'm not sure exactly what that is but I feel at this moment I'm ready. I don't know everything but the things I do feel I know, I feel strongly about and I believe the sky is the limit. I guess that's why I never lose faith and stop talking to you. Well I guess almost never. I know I truly can't get to where I desire without you. Actually I'm not even too sure if I'd even want to go. Guess that's the main reason I really need you. Basically to make me happy. So I guess me not being in control is a good thing. Because I would have no idea where to start. Maybe Father really does know best.

I stopped at Subways before racing home. I couldn't wait to tell Alexis what was going on. I can't lie, it's been a little shaky walking around not knowing how I'm gonna eat. Especially considering everything she'd told me at the Lake that night. I just wanna make her smile.

"Whatsup bae. I think I may have the part," I said as I stepped in the crib.

"That's cool but what about playing your mo'fuckin part in this house and kicking me some damn money. The fucking lights got turned off," she shouted. "I had to pay the damn crackhead down the street to cut them back on."

"Huh? Alexis, you know damn well I aint got no money."

"How am I supposed to know that?"

"What? Are you serious right now? You're the one who told me to focus on my craft and wait it out. How was I supposed to make money?"

"Well you never told me you were flat broke. I thought you had a little bit saved or something."

"Saved? Did you forget about everything I've payed since not having a job, Cable, lights, new refrigerator, hot water heater."

"Nigga I was helping too. You were only going half."

"First of all, no the fuck I wasn't. Did I go half when I bought you a car?"

"Hold on motherfucker," she replied with her hand placed on her hip. "Don't act like you went out here and bought me a motherfucking Benz or something. Besides, aint you the motherfucker who crashed the damn car? Mr. Driving on suspended license."

"Man you know that won't my motherfucking fault," I spat.

"First of all who you cussing at? Secondly, yes the fuck it was motherfucker."

"You crazy as hell man, I can't believe you."

"Ya damn right I'm crazy, crazy for relying on your dumb ass. Nigga I can't believe you. Just sitting around here broke, barely tryna make moves."

"What? I was just talking about getting a job. I was ready to get a motherfucking job," I yelled. "You told me to keep going."

"Motherfucker I thought you would at least do something."

"You aint see me practicing my damn lines? Dedicating whole damn days to that shit. What the fuck you think that is?"

"I think you lazy as hell," she said as she began to walk away from me.

"Lazy?" I shouted as I walked behind her. "I can't believe your ass."

"Nigga I can't believe you either," she said turning around, as we stared face to face. "Even the bums in the street wash a couple cars a day for some extra money."

"Damn that's what we doing, comparing each other to bums on the street?"

"Naw motherfucker, that's what I'm doing. I don't know what the fuck you doing. Actually I'm trippin, I aint even got time to talk to you. I gotta make something shake since I guess nobody else in this house knows how to," she said before storming off.

"What?" I yelled as the front door slammed shut.

How? How? Just how the fuck could she say some dumbass shit like that. Excuse me for doing my fucking best to make shit right for us. I aint ask her for shit that I wouldn't have did for her.

I paced around the house, livid, before going to our weed drawer. I needed to smoke, bad.

"Fucking bitch," I yelled, infuriated. She had took all of it. Now granted, she did buy it, but still, it was plenty of times I bought the weed and just gave it to her. She smoked more than me anyway. Can't believe she got me in the house alone, angry with no motherfucking weed. Fuck that. She got me fucked up. So I did what I had to do, dipped out the crib and knocked on my nigga Rell G's spot. I knew he'd have my back.

One of the best things about Rell is the fact that I don't have to buy weed when I'm around him. It was free. Not saying he was just going to pass me a big ass bag to take home, I'm just saying he smokes so much that all I gotta do is hang with him for five minutes and a blunt would be passed to me. Facts.

"Whatsup Jaz. Rell in the crib?" I asked as his girl stood at the door way.

"Sup Von. Yuh his ass in hea," she said before walking away and screaming, "Rell!"

I sat on the porch and waited.

"Sup Shawty," said Rell as he walked out of the house.

"Yo," I said looking up to him.

"Hea fool," he said as he passed me a blunt he was already smoking. "I already know yu need it, yu can have it."

"Damn. How you know?" I asked as I hit the blunt.

"I just saw your Ol Lady speed off down the street. The way her ass was drivin I figured yall had got into it or somethin. No offence but dawg I don't know how yo ass do it."

"Me either man, me either, it's getting crazy bro."

"What's gon on?"

"Too damn much," I replied as I hit the blunt once again. "Ok, so you know I've been going hard for my audition and what not."

"Yuh."

"Well it was today."

"Oh damn. How was it?"

"Dog, I smoked it," I replied as I hit the blunt once more. "But you think her ass gave a damn?"

"Hell naw."

"Of course she didn't. But you know what she had the nerve to say when I got in the crib and told her about it?"

"Some irrelevant ass shit that ain got nothin to do wit actin," he replied as he shook his head.

"Yeah bro. She in that bitch screaming about bills. How the fuck is she mad because she got to pay a few things by herself when she's the one who told me she was fucking cool with it," I complained, hitting the blunt again.

"Typical. See, yo first mistake was believin her when she said she was cool wit yu takin some time to get your shit togetha. Bih's is famous for sayin some bullshit that sound gud."

"Aint that the fucking truth."

"Hell yuh. Bruh, your brain and gut will tell you if a bih aint right for yu. Niggas just ignore all the mo'fuckin signs. See man, in life you gotta learn to have your brain, gut and heart workin in sync to really get where yu wanna go. If not, a bih will bring you down so low that you find yourself lookin up to her when she talk."

"That's some real shit bro," I replied, hitting the blunt. "You like a ghetto guru or some shit."

"I ain sayin all that, I just understand these broads. Most of em ain built for the journey, they jus want you to swing back and scoop em when you reach yo destination."

"Man," I said shaking my head. "This love shit complicated as hell."

"Harda than Chinese arithmetic. I swea love so mo'fuckin powerful it'll have you forgettin that your bitch is a hoe."

"Chill man I never said all that," I replied, after hitting the blunt again.

"Naw bruh, jus hear me out. I'm not talkin bout you, I'm just talkin in general."

"Oh Ok."

"Jus thank about all yo girls from the past, not jus Alexis. Jus thank, you can meet a bih, she look like a hoe, talk like a hoe, dress like a hoe, and you end up fuckin the bih jus like a hoe as soon as you meet her. But for some strange reason you like the hoe. Yall start spendin time togetha, laughin, eatin, just creating a good ass bond. Now suddenly you try to forget how you met this hoe because you love her."

"Yo, why the fuck all of your scenarios so funny?" I asked, laughing.

"Nigga ain nobody tryna be funny. This real life shit, I been through it. U'm not even sayin its anythang wrong with hoes. U'm jus sayin if you meet her and she a hoe, why the fuck would you thank yo dick is whats gon change her. Thats just plain ol dumb."

"So what exactly are you saying bro? I'm lost as hell."

"Cheat nigga!" he shouted.

"What?" I asked. "Bro what the fuck are you talking about? I was with you at first but now you're trippin," I added as I hit the blunt again.

"Bruh, all U'm saying is that love will have you doin some of the stupidest shit, and you wont even realize it until its too late. Thats why I say, just cheat just in case."

"Naw nigga I aint going for that. What if you cheating and she aint even doing nothing. Now you just fucked up some good shit."

"Nigga fuck all that. Cheat! Its the only way to keep thangs even, I ain tryna hea none of that sucka ass shit you talkin. I'm speakin frum experience."

"Naw nigga don't try to put me in your category. Aint my fault these hoes got you bitter," I replied as I hit the blunt.

"Bitter?" he barked. "Nigga yu trippin, ain nobody bitter, I still love hoes, U'm just not stupid like yo lil green ass. Hell, my Baby Mama was a hoe," he said as he pointed towards his house.

"What?" I replied laughing. "And you cool with that?"

"Fuck yeah, I'll take a hoe who knows herself before I take some lost bih reading Steve Harvey books to find out when she posed to throw a nigga some pussy."

"Man," I replied. "I don't know about all that. I still think Alexis is a good girl. I just think things need to be tightened up. I gotta figure some things out."

"Yu gotta figure thangs out? Bruh I'ma keep it real. Alexis lucky as hell."

"You might be right. But shit, I'm lucky too."

"Hell naw bruh. Least not like her ass is, jus hear me out," he replied as he gathered his thoughts. "Bruh, yu a young nigga with a plan. Yu got this life shit figured out. All the rest of us just existin, basically tryna get where yo ass already at. When you really thank bout it, most thangs humans do on a daily basis is pretty meaningless. If you ask me she should be grateful to have a nugga like you."

"Yeah, that's sounds good," I replied sarcastically, hitting the blunt.

"Nigga fuck sounding gud. That shit need to be yo reality. I swea every time you step foot in that mo'fuckin crib she posed to drop down to her knees and suck some dick."

"Yeah right, nigga Bill Gates probably don't even get that type of treatment."

"So nigga, that don't make the shit right. These females needa reality check. They see these rich ass mo'fuckers on TV and shit and don't realize they was once broke too. Don't shit come over night. And if that shit do, it probably ain gon last."

"Now that's a fact."

"Nigga erthang U'm sayin is facts. Like I said, these bih's gotta learn to handle a man when he down. They think holdin shit down for a week or two is somethin special. They got the game fucked up."

"Yeah I gotta admit, you're right. I just wish shit would change. A nigga really is broke as hell. Got me really thinking about going to get a nine to five right quick or something"

"9-5? Fuck that, that's the fastest way to stay broke. I could neva."

"Yeah I feel you but you're different, you don't care how you get your money and that's cool. But I can't do that, if it aint within the law I can't fuck with it. Fuck crime, been there, done that."

"Fuck crime, been there done that," he said, playfully mocking me. "Yuh, yuh, fuck all that. Fuck the law. What the fuck is the law anyway? Whoever made them mo'fuckers was probably breakin em the second they wrote em. No cap. I don't give a fuck if shit is legal or not I'ma find me a way to get rich out hea, fuck that. And I know exactly what the first thang I'ma do when I get my mo'fuckin money."

"What?"

"Tell a nigga to shut his broke ass up," Rell exclaimed.

"What?" I replied, with a laugh. "Man you been doing that," I added as I hit the blunt once again.

"Yeah but I want it to really come from the soul, I want a nigga to feel that shit in his chest," Rell replied.

"Man you crazy as hell," I said laughing. "Well as soon as you get that money I might need a loan."

"Bruh you trippin, you gon have your own cash by then. But for right now I think I might be able to get you some paper today, maybe a couple grand or somethin."

"How?"

"Deese mo'fuckers," he replied as he whipped out a few random credit cards from his pocket.

"Credit Cards?" I asked.

"Not jus credit cards, 'Somebody' else's credit card," Rell replied with a smirk. "I think I may have the answers to your prayers."

"So exactly what are we gonna do with those?"

"You trust me right?"

"Yeah nigga," I replied. "But I still wanna know what you gonna do with them."

"Ok, so yeah, you see I gotta few credit cards. Don't ask me how I got em, that aint important. But what is important is the fact that I think I may be able to get us some money."

"Again I ask, how nigga?" I asked curiously.

"You down?"

"Bro, can you at least just tell me whats going on."

"Ok, ok, so I got this lil bih who work at Verizon," he said as he nodded his head, smiling.

"What the fuck do that mean?"

"Damn I forgot who I was talking to, you don't know shit," he replied, shaking his head. "She not gonna ask for any I.D. for the purchase. Bruh, all we gotta do is swipe these cards, buy some Apple watches, phones and Mac Books and take it to my man Benny ova at 'Electronic Goods', sell them and bam, we up a couple racks."

"That simple?"

"Dat simple," he replied. "I just need you to go in the stores and do it. Her pussy ass co-workers already know me. You wit it?"

I thought for a second before replying, "Yeah bro, I'm with it."

"My nigga," he replied enthused. "You got your phone though?"

"Yeah," I replied, holding it up.

"Good, I need to use it to call my Verizon Bih up. I thank somebody stole mine."

"Bro aint nobody steal your damn phone. You lose that motherfucker every week."

"Man I know, you're right. Shit sad, I'd lose my head if it wont attached to my body. But to be honest I hate havin a phone sometimes."

"Nigga why?"

"I don't like mo'fuckas bein able to reach me anytime they want. I hate my girl having full access to me. All of a sudden U'm gettin random I love you text and shit."

"I love those. What's wrong with that?" I asked as I hit the blunt one last time, before tossing it to the ground.

"What's wrong with that?" he shouted. "Nigga what aint wrong with that. Shit a fuckin mood killa. Ain nothin worse than chillin with the homies, laughin, jokin, drankin and what not, only to be interrupted by an 'I love you text'. Bih leave me alone, it's a time and a place for erthang, fuck all that lovey dovey shit."

Rell told more stories as we laughed all the way to the bank, literally. Everything went smooth, too smooth. His girl at Verizon let me swipe for everything he wanted. We racked up. Can't lie, the thought that this could be wrong did cross my brain. I mean I guess it is pretty fucked up to use someone else's card. But fuck that. I need this shit. I been putting good energy out into the world for years now and to tell the truth I aint really seen too much good come from it. My good karma gotta be stacked up by now or something. I know I'm good for at least one fuck up. It's only right.

"Bro this our lucky motherfucking day. We got $10,000. $5,000 a piece," Rell said as he hopped back in the car after selling all the merchandise.

"Oh shit," I replied.

"We gotta celebrate."

"Whatsup. What you got in mind?" I asked.

"Well-," Rell replied hesitant.

"Well what, nigga whatsup?"

"I mean, I got some hoes. You down?" he asked, looking over to me.

"Hell yeah," I replied without thinking.

"Now I ain makin you," he said as he looked over to me. "But I'm tellin you these some real freak hoes."

"Nigga, I said yes. Why are you telling me they some freak hoes like that's supposed to be a bad thing or something?"

"Bruh, I neva said it was a bad thang, U'm jus lettin you know what you gettin yoself into."

"Rell, I know I've been a square ever since you met me but trust me nigga, I know all about freaks."

"Yuh right."

"Nigga I'm serious."

"Aite, so what's the freakiest shit a bitch ever did to you?" he quizzed.

"Nigga I don't know off the top of my head, you put me on the spot."

"See, just by you sayin that, I know you don't know about no freaks. Real freaks leave a mark on you that lasts a life time."

"Alright whatever. So what's the freakiest shit a bitch did to you then?" I asked.

"Man shit, I got millions of story's, but U'ma jus tell you what one of the hoes who we're about to meet up with did."

"Alright. What did she do?" I asked, intrigued.

"Bih fucked around and raped me," Rell replied as he pulled off.

"Raped you?" I exclaimed. "Hell naw. Nigga that aint freaky, that's a fucking crime."

"Yup, yu jus proved my point, yu dont know freaky."

"Hold on," I replied. "So you serious? You mean to tell me a chick actually raped your ugly ass," I said, laughing.

"Damn right. Ain shit funny, this shit serious," he replied, struggling to hold back his own laughter. "I'm scarred for life."

"Ok, ok, my bad, my bad," I said, attempting to control my own amusement. "How in the hell did that happen?"

"Bruh shit was crazy. So boom, I got pissy drunk with her one night. We in the hotel fuckin like rabbits, I'm beating her back in, bitch squirtin and creamin all over a nigga. U'm tellin yu, we had to have fucked at least six times. After a while, my dick was on noodle, I was done, I ain have shit else to give the bih. But she won't having it."

"So the bitch raped you?"

"Man hell yeah!" he shouted.

"How the fuck you let a girl do that?" I replied. "I'm listening," I added, attentively.

"Aite, so we had a big ass suite at the embassy," he replied. "My homeboy work there and get it for the low or what not. But anyway, I was butt ass neked, fakin sleep on the couch, whole time I'm still peekin at her ass. She lookin crazy as hell, like she really goin through it, bih pacin, lookin back at me and shit. Then finally she did it."

"Did what?" I asked, curiously. "I gotta hear this."

"Bruh, the bih came over to me and just started rubbin on me, kissin all over my neck and shit. I'm still bein strong though, eye's closed like a mo'fucker, U'm even throwin out a couple fake snores jus so she could really get the picture."

"Man," I said, laughing. "I can see that shit in my head. You funny as hell."

"Chill bruh, lemme tell the story."

"My bad, my bad."

"Ok, where was I? Oh yeah, ok, so once she seen that won't workin, she dropped down to her knees and started suckin a nigga off. Mind you, I told you my dick was on noodle, soft as a bih but once she started suckin, man my shit shot right on up."

"Nigga that don't sound like rape."

"You shittin me, jus cause my wood was hard dont mean I was with it. I told you, I was exhausted, so I continued fake sleepin."

"I know she was mad."

"Mad asa mo'fucker."

67

"So I guess that's when she raped you."

"Nope, she tried to hop on top of me but er time she stopped suckin I went soft. Not to mention the way I was positioned on the couch she couldn' really do what she wanted. So yeah, she gettin madda and madda, then finally I feel her grab me by the wrist. All of a sudden I feel this bih yankin on me."

"Yanking on you?"

"Yuh nigga, yanking on me. Bih had the nerve to drag my neked ass off the couch down to the damn flo. I'm layin down lookin bout dumb as hell. I know I must've looked dead. But that ain stop the bih."

"Her ass seems determined."

"Determined ain the word, more like possessed."

"That's wild."

"Hell yuh, and I ain even done. Bih tried to suck it again, only this time I was able to keep it soft. That shit made her even madda."

"Hell she do next?" I asked curiously.

"Bih did the unthinkable. Bih had the nerve to reach in my mouf, grab my mo'fuckin tongue and pulled that bitch out."

"Oh hell naw, you gots to be lying."

"Nigga if U'm lyin I'm flyin," he said, raising his right hand as he drove. "So yuh, I ain gon lie I was kinda curious to what the fuk she wa bouta do, so I kept that mo'fucka out and squinted my eyes only to look up and see ass droppin down on me. The bih was tryna ride my face."

"Bro that's crazy as hell," I shouted, as I grew weaker and weaker from laughter. "What you do next?"

"I bit that hoe mo'fuckin coochie. Bih started screaming like a mo'fucker. I don't play that shit."

"Yo," I yelled laughing. "You a funny ass nigga."

"Ain shit funny. U'm serious. But look, I still ain done, that shit turned the bih on even more."

"So how the hell you get outta fuckin her?"

"I didnt nigga. That shit turned my ass on too. U'ma real freak. The question is, is you? Sure you down with kickin it with dese hoes? Like I said, they sum real freaks. This shit ain for no lil bitty boys."

"Bro like I said, I'm down. Besides this seems like exactly what Alexis wants and I'ma give her what she asks for."

"Bet. I couldnt agree more. This shit gon take your mind off of things. Life too short to be walkin round stressed and shit."

"Hell yeah you right bro."

"Nugga I know I am. Now lemme call dese hoes up. I cant wait for you to meet em. Lemme see yo phone."

I was torn. A part of me wanted to go get some hoes, I can't lie. I mean, if you want to get technical, I kinda deserved them. Besides, I wanted to be around somebody who actually acted as if they liked me. Someone who didn't make me feel like a burden to be around. It's only so long a nigga can take the feeling of always being in the way.

Still, I had a funny feeling in my gut. Yeah, I'm backed up, Alexis had been pretty stingy with the pussy lately. It's just that something told me this wasn't the right thing to do. Too bad it was too late, I'd already committed, I'm too far in. He was already on the phone with them. Fuck it.

"They say meet em at the Jamaica festival downtown. They can get us in for the free."

"Foreal?"

"Hell yuh. We bouta pipe that shit up," he replied, excitedly as he tossed me back my phone.

We shot down to the Festival listening to Young Crazy. I sat rapping along, trying to hide the fact that I was more nervous than a bitch. The closer we got the more I felt like I was a teen going on his first date or something. I even blew my breath into my hand to check for funk, I won't tryna scare the bitch off soon as I spoke.

As we drove, for the first time in a while I started to really imagine life without Alexis. A stress free one. Yeah maybe I'd be without a home cooked meal at night but that was just a risk I'm willing to take. Honestly, I might not even be without one, I'm a handsome dude. I'm sure I can get me a girl to do things for me.

Suddenly I started to think about the pros and cons of being with her. What does Alexis actually do for me that I can't find out here in these streets? I sat pondering, nothing seemed to come to mind. Maybe she was holding me back. Maybe I need to cheat, I'm feigning to experience being in control again. I can't tell you the last time I've had that feeling.

Then it hit me, Alexis owns the crib we stay in. If I get caught I could end up homeless. Wow, I never really gave too much thought on all the stuff I myself own in this world. After, a second I realized the exact reason why I'd never thought about what I owned. It's simple, that's because I don't own shit. Not a motherfucking thing, nothing, no house, no money, shit, not even a car. I make payments on that shit every month.

No wonder Alexis talks to me like she does. I'm a fucking loser. Suddenly the sky seemed to darken as my mood shifted. I felt low. Usually I push emotions to the back of my head as soon as any inkling of negativity surfaces. Thinking about certain things can ruin your whole day. Luckily Rell was there to snap me out of it.

"Those the hoes right there," he said as we parked our car in a large vacant lot.

"Damn!" I replied, watching them as they strutted over to us.

No lie they was bad. He won't lying when he said they were strippers. It was evident. I aint gonna sit and act like they faces were all that but their bodies was stupid. Stupid big ass titties, and stupid big ass assess. I had to hurry and close my mouth before drool started to ooze out.

"Hey Rell," said the taller girl as we stepped outside to greet them.

"Sup shawty," Rell said as he exited the car. "Yo dis my nugga Von. He a actor and shit. Von this Moni and Jasmine. Two of the finest bih's from the East Side."

"Hey Von," said Jasmine.

"Oh shit, I know yo ass. You was in that play 'Us vs. Them'," added Moni, the shorter of the two girls.

"Yeah, that's me," I followed as I extended my hand.

"Damn nigga, you aint tell me I was gon be with a star and shit," she said to Rell.

"Yup," he replied. "And to think yall ain even wanna link up wit a nugga at first."

"That's only because you know how niggas is round hea. Yall love setting bitches up for the okeydoke," replied Jasmine.

"Hell yeah, can't trust Atlanta niggas for shit. They'll tell you their homeboy is the man and when he pulls up it's a damn midget with one leg or something," added Moni.

"Yep bitch. And the whole time they're just using the midget because he got a car," followed Jasmine.

"Hell naw that ain even my style. Yall know U'm official," rebutted Rell.

"Yeah we see now. But what's up. The festival aint even lit yet. Yall tryna go get some drinks until it get poppin?" asked Moni.

"Cool we can do that," replied Rell. "Hop in the whip."

The two hoes hopped in. Moni got in the back with me.

"So Von. Where you from. I can already tell you aint one of these fuck ass Atlanta niggas."

"Damn what the hell you mean by that?" asked Rell from the driver's seat.

"Damn nigga why you all in my business back here?" Moni asked. "But if you must know, Atlanta niggas got that 'Use a bitch' vibe written all over them."

"What?" exclaimed Rell.

"Nigga don't play dumb, you know all Atlanta niggas do is finesse women outta money."

"Hell naw I don't finesse shit," said Rell.

"Boy, lie again. Shit, this probably your Baby Mama whip we in right now."

"Hell naw that's big cap, I make all my own scratch I don't need my B.M. for shit," he said as he flashed a wad of cash.

"Oh shit, ok ok," added Jasmine.

"You got money like that to Von?" asked Moni.

"Naw I'm chilling," I replied.

"Nigga you an actor I know you paid," she followed.

"Naw I wouldn't say all that," I said.

"Man dont let that nugga lie to you," butted in Rell. "He got money and bouta have plenty more. He actually just got hired for a new movie this mornin. Thats why we called yall, we needed some pretty females to celebrate with us."

"Oh shit, a movie? Any big stars gonna be in it?" asked Moni.

"I don't know yet," I said. I felt bad that I was lying about receiving the role but I decided to just go with the flow.

"Man fuck a big star. My boy is the big star. You trippin shawty," added Rell.

"True, true. I like that. I aint never been with an actor before," she replied as she inched closer to me, placing her hand on my thigh. "That's sexy as hell. How do you be remembering all them damn lines and shit?"

"Well I practice a lot, but truthfully it just kinda comes naturally."

"Damn that's whatsup. I don't think I ever heard a nigga say he practiced for some shit," she added, nodding her head approvingly. "What made you even start acting? I aint gon lie you kinda remind me of an ex hood nigga or something."

"Shit, that's actually exactly what I am," I said, trying not to smile. "But as far as this acting shit, it's just my passion. I couldn't escape it, I feel like it's why I'm on this earth."

"Oh my God. I knew I met yo ass for a damn reason. I need some help," Moni continued.

"What kinda help?" I asked as she inched even closer.

"I know I got this big ol ass but I feel like it aint just meant for the pole no more. This mo'fucka needs to be on the big screen."

"Right bitch," agreed Jasmine, as she looked back, slapping fives with Moni.

Once we arrived to the bar we split up into pairs, ordered shots and began to get wasted. We was having a ball, not a care in the world and honestly it felt damn good to have a chick down on me like that.

"You look like you got a fat dick," blurted Moni as she seductively looked into my eyes.

"Maybe I do," I replied with a smirk.

"You do," she said as she grabbed my crotch.

"I like that," I said. "You're a little freak aint you."

"Yep. I can't help it I was born this way."

"Yo whatsup with yall Atlanta people? Why all yall think yall so freaky?" I asked with a smile.

"Well I don't know about the other people from Atlanta but I'm dead ass serious. I really was born this way."

"That's crazy. I aint even know that was possible."

"What? Are you serious? This freak shit runs in my blood. I can remember being nasty since I was about four years old."

"Four?"

"Yep, that's when I first started watching porn."

"Porn?" I shouted. You gotta be cappin. I don't believe you. Who the fuck watches porn at four?"

"Me nigga," she replied playfully. "Who gonna lie about some shit like that?"

"Ok, ok, I guess you're right. But why? How? Who the fuck you even get some porn from?"

"Ok," she said. "I'll tell you but first we gotta take another shot."

"Cool," I replied as we both through back double shots of Patron.

"Wooo," we both screamed as the liquor hit our chest.

"Ok where was I?" she said as she placed her shot glass on the counter.

"You were about to tell me how you started watching porn at 4."

"Oh yeah, well ok, It all started when I was looking for my purple Barney VHS. I couldn't find that shit anywhere. It was my favorite one, I damn near watched it every day. So after looking all over the damn crib I finally went into my Moms room and looked through her drawers. That's when I found a tape."

"So you found a tape hidden in your Mom's drawer and thought it was Barney?" I asked, laughing. "Was it even Purple?"

"No," she replied, sharing my laughter. "But again I was only four, I thought it had changed colors or something, I aint know. Ok, so back to the story. So I pop the VHS in."

"Hold on one more time, where was everybody else? Why in the fuck were you 4 years old looking for shit? Why you aint ask an adult?"

"Nigga I'm from the hood. I don't know where the fuck everybody was, they was probably sitting on the porch drinking or something. I don't know, that shit aint important. Can I get back to my story?"

"My bad my bad."

"Ok so I pop the tape in. First thing I see is a big ass black dick. No lie."

"I know you was bouta shit yourself."

"Hell naw. I was mesmerized, on some love at first site type shit. I had never seen anything so amazing, it was all veiny and strong."

"At four years old?"

"Hell yeah, I still remember every detail about it. It was a big tall bald black man and some light skin lady with hair all over her coochie. He was wearing her ass out, I'm talking straight pounding her ass."

"I'm still stuck on the four years old part."

"Yep four years old. I watched that shit every day for years every chance I could get until my Mom caught me and took it away."

"You got caught? How?"

"She just came in the house one day and I was laying across the couch watching it like it was a Disney Movie or something. I was mad as hell when she busted in. My favorite scene was coming up."

"Yo you crazy. What did she say?"

"She aint say shit, she whipped the black off my ass, I guess she was trying to beat the freak spirit up out of me or something."

"I'm assuming it didn't work."

"Hell naw. I was feigning for more. By now I was about 8 and I can still remember sitting in elementary school day dreaming about the nastiest shit."

"8 years old?"

"Yep, 8. But daydreaming was just the beginning. Soon I started doing some wild shit."

"Wild like what?"

"Promise not to judge me," she said as she held out her pinky.

"Ok. I promise," I replied, as we locked fingers.

"Ok, see back then we had this dog named Kane."

"What kinda dog?"

"A pit, but he was nice, he wouldn't bust a damn grape in a fruit fight. But yeah, like I was saying, one day I just got so horny I couldn't take it, I needed something, I didn't quite know what I needed, but I knew I needed it," she said before pausing.

"Come on Moni, you got me interested, whatsup."

"I never really told anybody any of this, shits pretty embarrassing."

"How can I judge something you did as a child? What you do?" I asked.

"Ok, so I got some peanut butter, dabbed it on my private area and I guess you can use your imagination for the rest."

"He licked it?" I asked.

"Yep," she replied, staring straight in my eyes.

"Whoa!" I shouted.

"I thought you said you wasn't gonna judge me."

"I'm not, I'm not, that just took me through a loop. I won't ready for that. That's crazy."

"I know, I know but what's crazier is that I got caught doing that shit too."

"Damn, you aint go no luck. Your mamma again?"

"Nope. My lil dumb ass sister, and the little bitch had the nerve to blackmail me. I had to do her damn chores for a year for her not to tell."

"Smart little girl," I said jokingly. "So was that the end of your little freak stage?"

"Fuck no, I told you I was born this way, it's in me not on me, aint no changing."

"Wow. I don't know if I even want to know anymore."

"Too bad, I told you I've never told anybody any of this shit, you bouta get all of this tea today nigga."

"Fuck it, let me hear it," I replied as I motioned for the bartender to bring two more shots.

"Ok so again, after getting caught I was searching for another fix. I was cold turkey for a while, probably until 6th grade. That's when I started staying up late and we all know what used to come on late night back in the day."

"What?"

"Girls Gone Wild commercials nigga," she replied.

"Oh yeah I forgot all about that. So you liked girls too?"

"Read my lips," she said before speaking slowly, "I'm a freak," she said as she licked her lips. "But yes, I love girls, I used to sit up close to the T.V. just praying that one day they'd forget to put the censor over the titties."

"Yo, that's funny as hell, I used to do the same shit."

"Yeah man, they never did it though."

"Ol bitch ass niggas," I added, jokingly.

"Right, but with me being such a fucking horn dog, I just started ordering the shit my damn self. I even started ordering Pay-Per-View porn. I couldn't fight the temptation."

"So I'll assume you got caught again."

"Nope not me. My Mom's boyfriend did though. She thought it was him ordering up all that shit and she kicked his ass right on out."

"Damn did you feel bad?" I asked.

"Nope. I was a little sad though. His daughter lived with us too. I forgot to mention that around this time we'd started kinda exploring each other's bodies and shit. Every night we ended up licking and sucking on each other. I was mad as hell we was gonna have to stop."

"Freaky ass." I replied as the bartender brung us our shots.

"Yep and that wasn't even the worse part. What really had me mad was the fact that I was gonna miss out on hearing my Mom and her Boyfriend fucking at night."

"What?" I exclaimed, as we through back our shots. "This story's getting wilder by the second."

"I'm serious. I used to love that shit. I remember staying up late and putting my head to the wall. It was like music to my ears," she said blushing. "Boy, over the years I've heard so many people have sex. Have you?"

"Can't say that I have."

"You haven't'?" she asked surprised. "OMG you don't know what you're missing. Aint nothing like the sound of a big dick going in and out of some juicy ass pussy. Especially fat girls. They got the wettest pussy."

"Yall ready to go?" said Rell as he stumbled over, interrupting.

"Hell yeah, get me out of here I was damn near bouta tell this nigga my whole life story," said Moni.

Shit grew deeper as the night crept away, by the time we got to the festival Moni and I had grew inseparable. Anyone glancing over would have no choice but to assume we were madly in love. She was all over me, kissing me, poking her phat ass on me, whispering freaky ass shit in my ear, any other man would be having the time of their life.

Don't get me wrong, I was enjoying myself, it's just being all out in the public, cuffing with another bitch was beginning to scare the hell outta me. It was no telling who was watching. Thank God it started to pour down raining. I couldn't wait to get the fuck away.

"Aw man, I don't wanna leave yall," said Moni as we all hopped in Rell's car, soaking wet.

"Me either. Where yall going?" asked Jasmine.

"I don't know but I know we gotta get outta these clothes," answered Rell.

"That sounds like a good as idea. I wanna see that big ass dick anyway," said Jasmine as she rubbed her hand across Rell's chest.

"Bitch I was just thinking the same motherfucking thing," added Moni as she looked over to me, biting her lip.

Rell looked over to me, smirking. "Well lets go back to yo spot."

"Let's go," said Jasmine.

If I was nervous before, I gotta say I'm shitting bricks now, belly on overload, won't no butterflies in my stomach though, nope I had birds in my shit. Felt like my insides was gonna explode. I tried to relax but I couldn't, it wasn't working at all. I hadn't had sex with another girl in so long. Part of me wanted to, but another part of me was bitching out. I know I said I was ready but that was before shit was actually real. Fuck. I sat silent, leg shaking nervously the entire ride as they all drunkenly rapped along to the radio.

We got to the crib quick as hell. This shit had me even more uneasy. This bitch lived in the fucking hood. Trash all over the street, abandoned homes and there were people everywhere, just walking and riding bikes like it wasn't damn near midnight. I looked over to everyone else as we exited, they aint have a care in the world. I tried my hardest to do the same. I couldn't though, what if one of these niggas on the block was Alexis's family or something, you never know. Just in case, I lowered my head and stared at the ground as I followed them into the apartment.

Wasting no time, Rell and Jasmine shot upstairs to the shower, leaving Moni and I on the first floor. She stripped down while I opted to keep on my wet clothes. Truthfully I wanted to go sit in the car but considering Rell's the only one with a gun and there are what seems like hundreds of goons lurking by I stayed inside. Plus I aint wanna be too much of a square. Luckily she rolled up some more weed, hopefully that will take the edge off of things.

"Man I'm just so comfortable around you," said Moni.

"Yeah. I feel the same way," I followed.

"Really?

"Yeah," I lied.

"Good cause I gotta ask you a question."

"Whatsup?"

"Ok, so I don't want you to look at me like I'm crazy. Promise you won't," she said as she held out her pinky once again.

"Ok. I promise," I replied, as I used my ringer finger to lock with hers. "I didn't even look at you crazy when you told me all your freaky ass kid stories at the bar."

"Yeah you're right, you didn't. Ok, so here's the deal, I'm about to take a shower in a second, go freshen up for you," she said seductively. "But I'm feeling really relaxed right now and don't really feel like moving."

"Ok, so what are you saying?"

"Basically what I'm saying is I have to fart bad as hell and I don't feel like getting up and going to the bathroom. You mind if I let one lose?"

"Huh?" I asked, attempting to make sure I'd heard her correctly.

"Do you mind if I fart?" she repeated.

"Um," I replied slowly. "I guess not."

That was the last straw. This bitch farted. And it stunk, smelled like it had been sitting in a bottle for 3 years and someone had just popped the top. On top of that I was growing paranoid and the weed wasn't calming me down. After a while I couldn't take it anymore. I had to say something.

"Ay Rell let me holla at you outside for a second," I said as I looked up and discovered him stepping out of the bedroom.

"Bruh, I'm kinda in the middle of somethin," he replied as I saw Jasmine slide into the bedroom with nothing but a towel.

"Bro it'll just be a second," I added.

"Man, ok," he said as he through on his pants and shoes to come down, shirtless.

"I'll be right back," I said to Moni.

We stepped out the door and instantly a cold pistol was slammed to our dome.

"Get yall mo'fuckin ass on the damn ground," screamed a masked man as his partner handled Rell.

"Oh shit," I said as we both plopped down to the concrete. I could hear the sound of the front door shutting and locking.

"Yuh nigga, run that shit," said one of the goons as they reached down into our pockets. "Nigga stop Moving! I'll air this whole bitch out," he barked.

Whatsup God,

Man I aint even gonna fight this. I guess this is what I deserve. Shit, what the fuck am I even doing getting involved with illegal credit cards scams for anyway. I knew that dumbass shit was wrong when I did it. Now look at me, at some strange bitch crib getting robbed. All I ask is that you don't let these niggas kill us. It's gonna fuck Alexis up if the last place they find me at is here. I don't want her thinking I was a cheater the whole time. Please just keep me safe lord. I learned my lesson. I swear I'm bouta go on the straight path. Fuck this. Help me, please.

"You got erthang?" asked the second goon to his partner as completed their mission.

"Yeah bruh, I got erthang," he answered as he held our cash and a few more items as I looked up to him.

"Nigga, what the fuck you lookin at?" he barked before kicking me in my side.

"Let's be out," he said as they ran away from the crib.

We waited for them to leave our site before we bounced up.

"Bih, you got us robbed," screamed Rell as he banged on their door. "Open the fuck up."

"What are you talking bout?" Jasmine asked as she opened the door with Moni standing behind her. "What happened?

"What bih? You think I'm retarded?" he screamed as he stepped to her face. "How the hell else would they know to jus come ova hea for no damn reason. I should kill yo ass."

"With what mo'fucka. You left yo damn gun in hea."

"Bih," screamed Rell,

"Mo'fucka who the fuck you calling a bitch?" Moni said as she stepped between the two, pointing Rell's gun to his head. "I suggest you get the fuck outta here before your money, gun and shirt ain't the only thing you lose," she said, aggressively.

"Bro lets go," I said to Rell as I tugged his arm for us to leave.

We trotted down the steps as the door slammed shut.

"I'm mad as a bih" screamed Rell. "Man these niggas got my car keys and erthang."

"Fuck," I said back.

"I gotta find somebody with a phone."

"I left mine in the car under the seat before we came in. I think I left your door unlocked," I replied as we headed over.

"Ay baby," said Rell after retrieving my phone. "Ay can you come get me I done fucked around and got robbed. Nigga took erthang from me. I need you to brang the extra spare key."

"Mo'fucka I aint brangin you shit," I heard through the phones speaker. "You aint lose your mo'fuckin phone. I took the bitch."

"What?" screamed Rell.

"Yup hoe ass nigga. I went through yo lil triflin ass phone. You aint shit mo'fucka. Who the fuck is Rica, and you been fucking your ex?"

"Huh? No I haven't."

"Fuck nigga you think I'm stupid? You probably with some hoes right now. I hope your broke ass got some money because erthang you own is bouta go up in flames. You tried the wrong bih!"

"Oh hell naw!" he screamed. "Bih don touch my shit."

"Watch me," she said as she hung up the phone.

"Yo we gotta get on that damn bus," he said pointing across the street.

"Nigga we aint even got a bus pass or money."

"Shit," he replied. "You right. Man fuck it," Rell said as he looked over to two crack feigns riding bikes. "We bouta go take theirs."

Wasting no time, he darted over and punched them both off, leaving them lying flat on the ground confused. "Come on bro," he said as he hopped on one as I rushed over to the vacant bike.

We raced home.

"Yo come in the crib with me right quick," Rell said, as we finally made it to our neighborhood.

"For what?"

"You gotta tell Jaz it was you sending them hoes all the text she read."

"What? Bro, she aint stupid, she aint bouta believe that shit."

"Nigga, it's gon work, trust me, I jus need your help."

"Man ok," I agreed.

"Just wait out hea for a sec, U'ma come get you once I need you," he said before knocking on the door. "Baby," he yelled as the door opened and he stepped inside.

"Get down on the ground," yelled a voice from inside. It was the police. They had to have been waiting for him.

"What the fuck," I heard Rell yell.

"Yeah mo'fucka," screamed his girl as I heard what sounded like Rell being tossed to the ground. "You wanna cheat on me. Well let them nasty ass hoes take care of yo funky ass in jail. Yeah officer he the one who was in Wal-Mart tryna get them Percocet's," she screamed. "He always doing it. And he got some pills and a gun in the house too."

"Bih you tripping," Rell screamed.

Thank God, they hadn't noticed me. I snuck off, leaving the bike before realizing I'd been robbed for my keys too. "Fuck," I said to myself.

I went to every door and window hoping they would somehow be unlocked but of course they weren't. I was gonna have to bite the bullet. I rang the doorbell.

After about two or three minutes I heard the sound of the door unlocking. Not sure of what exactly to do once we were face to face, I decided to smile. In most cases it works for me.

"Hey baby," I said.

"Hey Baby? Motherfucker I should beat your ass. You been gone all day without even telling me where the fuck you was, not to mention it's a fucking holiday."

"Holiday? What holiday is it? Besides I thought you was mad at me. Aint like you texted or called me," I shot back.

"Motherfucker its Cinco de Mayo. A day where couples get together and get drunk. And look at me, by my damn self. Been waiting for your stupid ass all day, I aint call you because I was waiting on my apology that I never fucking got."

"Apology? And hold on, I didn't even realize it was Cinco de Mayo. Plus when the fuck did Cinco de Mayo suddenly become a couple's day? We aint Mexican. What the fuck is Cinco de mayo anyway?"

"Nigga don't play dumb."

"I'm not."

"Yeah you're right, I forgot you're just naturally this stupid."

"Baby. I really didn't know it was that serious."

She paused, staring at me. "Nigga what do you know?"

I couldn't think of anything to say. "I don't know."

"Dumbass nigga," she said before speed walking away.

My attempt to chase behind her as she darted upstairs was quickly halted when our bedroom door was slammed in my face, literally, it damn near broke my nose. Fuck it though, my day was long enough. I couldn't find the energy to argue, so I did what I always did in moments such as this, took off my damp clothes, got a blanket and curled up on the couch. Lately going to bed, escaping reality had become the highlight of my day.

Unable to sleep, I laid awake, eyes wide staring up at the ceiling. It seemed as if no matter what I did I was wrong. How could the day start off so promising and then take such a tragic dive like that. Story of my life.

I tossed and turned for hours wondering what was the exact moment where I went wrong. Where had I fucked up so bad that I deserved a life like this? So much on my damn my mind and I had no idea what to do. People talk all this 'put positive stuff out into the universe' bullshit. But I don't get it. When I say and do good shit I never get any good in return. But soon as I do some foul, fucked up shit, I get robbed immediately. I don't know, but it makes me think that this life shit is just a gamble. It's all a matter of luck. And right now it was clear to see what kinda luck I had, the worse. Sad but true.

<u>Devils</u>

Day one million and motherfucking eighty five. Life still in shambles. I miss everything that's good that's ever happened to me. I should have cherished the good times a little more. Life is so damn good when you're happy. I wish I was happy. Fuck. Feeling like this makes me question every decision I've made in the past that could have possibly led to this.

I wake up angry daily, confused, with no one in my corner who remotely understands me. So many thoughts swim through my head. I swear my brain is on overload. I know my destination but have no clear way of reaching it. Each day I find it harder and harder to pull myself out of bed. I'd remained myself and followed my heart and still nothing worked. How much rejection can a person take before they snap? I swear, to be an artist who can't fully express himself and create is as traumatic as an Eagle with broken wings.

Whatsup God,

Come on man. Give me a hint on what I should do. I need a fresh start and some fresh answers. I can't keep living like this. Please give me some answers or at least let me go to sleep. I'm restless. I feel like I've come to a dead end on my journey. Only options I see are to turn around or have faith in you. I'm doing everything I can to choose faith to get me over this hurdle. I need you man. I've been having some crazy ass thoughts. Can't lie, sometimes I feel like you and the Devil are the same person. I'm sorry, I know it sounds bad but hear me out. It feels as though the same person who gave me all of my joy is the same person who's watching me suffer. How do you watch me in so much pain and do nothing about it? I could never watch someone I love feel the way I feel. You trippin man, foreal Lord. Shit aint right. How do you watch me suffer to the point where I'm damn near bouta smoke myself and still not bring me joy? How man? How many times do you want me to prove my faith? Is there a lesson I'm supposed to be learning that I'm missing? If so, if I'm not learning it on my own why can't you just make it more clear to me or something? Damn. I'm exhausted. I just don't get it. Why the fuck do you keep testing me? Why do you want me to believe in you so much? You got low self-esteem or something? You need my love to make you feel better about yourself? What is it? I'm starting to question you dog. I've done all that I can or at least all that I have in me. If being successful comes with this much pain maybe I don't wanna be successful. And if I'm not successful in the field that in my heart I feel is destined for me, why can't I be happy doing something else? What the fuck! Make me understand, please. After I put all of this fucking work in you telling me I don't deserve some type of real success? Actually, just give me the strength to get through this. I know you can at least do that. Damn.

"You weak as hell," I said as I played PlayStation with Alexis's 12 year old nephew Cee Cee.

"Naw you just cheating," he replied.

He had been staying at our crib for about a week. His Pops, Alexis's brother had just been shot and was in the hospital in critical condition. Thankfully he's slowly progressing. While he's recovering we agreed to keep Cee Cee for a while. Shit was cool as hell. I fucked with the little motherfucker. It wasn't my first time being around him. I use to teach a little acting class on the weekends for kids and he was usually the only one who attended.

All that one on one time kinda gotta us tight, I liked having a little dude around who looked up to me. Not to mention with him around he kinda took some of the tension off of me and Alexis. Not all of it though, shit was still real around here. We were cool, sometimes. But other times she just walked on past me as if I didn't exist. I'm learning to deal with it. Kinda only been speaking when spoken to.

I'm telling you, shits tough, on top of that, the Producers of the film I'd auditioned for hadn't called me back yet. I don't know how long I can wait. Desperation is in full effect, I even tried to make funny little Instagram's videos like Alexis had suggested, EPIC FAIL, I suck, I'm an actor not a comedian.

That aint all I've been doing either, I've even been looking for little temp jobs on the side to make a little cash. Still no luck, not one company called me back, who would have thought I was too good for minimum wage.

Shit's been so real around here that somedays I leave the house early and go sit at the library or mall all day just so Alexis would think I was doing something productive. Seemed like more than ever our relationship was holding on by a thread. Things been going from bad to worse. I can feel her love slipping away from me. And what's crazy, I aint even mad at her, I'm pretty much useless, how could I blame her.

"You know you used the last roll of toilet paper?" said Alexis bursting into the room.

"Damn my bad."

"Yeah and we don't have no more toothpaste, dish detergent, bleach or napkins either."

"Oh damn. I'll go get some," I replied.

"And don't get none of that cheap ass shit you got last time."

"OK," I said as I stood up.

"Cool. I'm going too," said Cee Cee before standing to his feet.

"Boy, you are a child," Alexis replied sternly. "You ask before you just get the hell up. Fuck is wrong with your ass?"

"I'm sorry. Can I go Aunt Lex?"

"Yeah," she said reluctantly looking over to me. "I guess. But don't listen to shit Von says. He's childish and if you let him get you in trouble I'ma beat your ass."

"Ok," replied Cee Cee.

I stared for a second. Excuse my language, I rarely call women this anymore but this bitch tripping. I'm the same nigga who has put money in her nephew's pocket. The same nigga who she once trusted to spend entire days with him, alone. I may be down right now but I'ma strong nigga with a lotta of sense. It took everything in me not to say anything back. Just had to realize it wasn't worth it. She wasn't worth it. I took a deep breath.

Whatsup God,

Give me the strength to push forward. I don't know how long I can stay here. If I'm not supposed to be here give me a sign. It's getting to the point where I'm going crazy. I'd rather go crazy by myself than to have someone treat me like this. Either help us get through this or let me know that I need to move on. Please Lord.

"Come on," I said to Cee Cee as we headed out the door and hopped in the whip.

"Ay so Von, you really gonna have a role in a movie?" he asked as we cruised down the street.

"That's what I'm hoping for. I haven't officially gotten it yet but I should know pretty soon."

"Man that's so cool. I wanna play in movies too."

"Foreal? Why?"

"So I can get rich. Duh."

"See, that's where you messing up. Never choose a job because of the pay. I mean sure moneys important but you have to always have your eye on your true calling, your passion. No amount of money can bring you happiness. So you have to find something that brings you joy every day when you wake up. Something that makes your soul smile."

"I never knew that."

"I bet. Most people will tell you to get a job with good benefits and money but who wants to live a miserable life. No matter what people say, money don't bring you happiness, that's something I'm still tryna get a grasp of myself."

"Yeah I guess you're right. But what if I don't know what makes me happy?"

"Nigga sure you do. Everybody does. What do you do for fun?"

"Um," he replied, thinking. "I love Marvel Comics."

"Well maybe you can write comic books."

"I hate writing."

I laughed. "Ok ok, well at the end of the day you're only 12. But what I can tell you is that if you look for your passion, you'll eventually find it."

"How do you know?"

"Think about it like this, you ever lost a toy or something in the house?"

"Yeah. Plenty of times."

"Ok. So what usually happens if you look around the house nonstop for it?"

"I find it."

"Exactly. That's with anything in life, you look hard enough for something, and you'll eventually come across it."

"Wow that's cool."

"Yep but once you find it, it's up to you to go hard for it. You'll get out what you put in, in this world."

"So how much have you put in?"

"Years and years of practice."

"So shouldn't you be rich if you get what you put in?"

"Yeah, you'd think so. But that's another part of being successful. You have to learn to be patient. Patience is the key. Everything won't happen when you want it to but if you keep fighting and walking by faith it'll happen."

"Wow. That seems kinda hard Von."

"I can't lie. It is. But if it was easy everyone would be successful."

I cranked up the radio and we bobbed our heads silently before finally arriving at Wal-Mart. Once inside I noticed that everything Alexis had instructed me to buy was expensive as hell. Yeah I could afford it. But if I bought it I'd be flat broke.

With that being said I knew I had to take it old school, the five finger rule was in full effect. Self-check-out here I come. After retrieving all of the items, I stood in line calmly before it was my turn to ring up. Slowly, I rung up the dish detergent before ensuring no one was looking, once the coast was clear, I pretended to scan the other items before throwing everything else in the bag.

Boy I'm telling you, I was so nervous, scratch that, nervous aint even the word, petrified is what I was as I approached the exit. Maybe this is what Alexis was talking about when she told Cee Cee not to let me get him into any trouble. But fuck that. Fuck would she send me to the store for when she knew I was broke? I'll never do any shit like that to her. Not to mention she wanted me to get all this expensive ass shit. I mean what kinda sense did that make. If you ask me I think she wanted me to steal. Seems like she gets a kick outta seeing me put myself in fucked up situations.

Confidently I walked towards the exit, Cee Cee on the side of me. The door greeter and I locked eyes as I got closer. My heart pounded.

Whatsup God,

I know thou shalt not steal. But just let me get pass him. It was my last time. I promise. Well I think I promise, I don't know but just don't let me get caught while I'm with Cee Cee. Please.

"Have a nice day fellas," said the greeter.

I sighed a breath of relief as we headed to our vehicle.

We pulled back up to the crib. The moment I got there I noticed that the grass was tall as hell.

"You feel like cutting some grass?" I asked, looking over as we walked towards the front door.

"Sure. Aint like I really got anything else to do."

"Cool. You can do the front and I'll do the back."

"Alright go change clothes," I said as we walked into the crib.

"Change his clothes for what?" butted in Alexis from the couch.

"We're about to cut the grass."

"We're?" she shouted. "My nephew aint bouta do shit. If your ass don't wanna cut the damn grass than I'll just pay somebody. He don't even know what the fuck he's doing. You always tryna take the easy way out. You aint bouta use my motherfucking nephew," she barked.

"Ok. I'll cut it myself," I replied, defeated.

Again, I couldn't believe this bitch. She's the same one who just a couple months ago when I was traveling with the Play said that she would get Cee Cee to come over and cut the grass since I couldn't do it. That's where I even got the fucking idea of letting him help me. Dumb ass bitch. I took a deep breath before throwing on some old clothes and cutting it my damn self. How ironic is it that even though I'm dead broke and unemployed, living in a house with Alexis is still a full time job.

After finishing, for the remainder of the day I didn't say not one word to her, straight igg mode. Gotta admit, it was pretty peaceful, just chilling, all day Cee Cee and I did nothing but watch 'The Flash' on Netflix till we both fell asleep on the couch.

That was only before Alexis woke the both of us up, screaming to the top of her lungs the next morning. "Who ate all the fucking cereal?"

"I let Cee Cee get some last night while you were sleep," I replied, opening my eyes discovering Alexis standing a few feet away from me.

"What? Cereal is fucking breakfast."

"My bad I aint know it was that big of a deal."

"Again I ask, what the fuck do you know?"

Right then and there I knew this could quite possibly be my last night in this house. Fuck all this. Homeless shelter here I come.

"Oh my fucking God. The water is off," she screamed as she exited the kitchen.

"Yo why are you screaming?" I asked.

"Why am I screaming? Why am I screaming? My fucking water is off and I got a whole grown ass man living in my house."

"Then fucking pay the bill," I yelled, waking Cee Cee as I stood to my feet. "I paid that shit for months by myself. I did everything in this motherfucker. And you complaining about one little ass month. Fuck you. Always talking about 'My' house whenever you get mad. If it's your house pay 'Your' fucking bills."

"Fuck you. Broke ass nigga. Got me in here taking care of two damn kids."

"Two kids?"

"Yeah motherfucker, aint no difference between you two."

"Well you can make it one. I'm out, I hate you. I don't give a fuck about you," I replied as I stormed off.

"Hate me? What? I bet you never did give a fuck about me motherfucker," she said as tears burst from her eyes.

"You're right," I replied, turning around. "Fuck you."

"IIIIII!" she screamed as she ran up on me, fist closed.

Without thinking I grabbed her, slamming her down on the couch.

"Yo calm down. You tripping," I demanded.

"You don't care about me," she yelled as I tried to restrain her from kicking and punching. "You never did. Nobody does," she continued, as her face became soaked with tears.

"Yo what the fuck are you even talking about?" I asked, still, holding her as I looked over to Cee-Cee. He wasn't crying but it was clear as day he was effected.

"You leaving right? After everything? You gonna just leave after I sacrificed so much?" she screamed as I released her, backing away.

"After you sacrificed? Motherfucker you aint the only one," I said as I pointed to her. "All you do is think about your motherfuckin self. I'm done with this shit. I don't wanna be nowhere I'm not wanted."

"Fuck you," she screamed. "You leave and you're gonna be sorry."

"I'm already sorry. I'm sorry you wasted my fucking time. I'm sorry I met you, sorry I told you I love you. I'm sorry for everything."

"Fuck you," she barked once again.

"Naw fuck you," I yelled. "Don't you know there are a lot of women who would really appreciate me? And here you are acting like I'm the devil or something. You're fucking miserable, I swear."

"Ya damn right I am. And you're the fucking blame," she yelled before darting off.

"I don't give a damn. You deserve that shit," I added.

I barged into the restroom, slamming the door behind me. I was fully prepared to leave but I had to get myself together first. Don't ask me why I decided to come in here. Honestly, my brain isn't even functioning enough to give you an answer.

I laid down on the floor next to the toilet for an hour gazing up at the ceiling.

Whatsup God,

Yo what am I about to do? I been waiting for some answers but I just can't seem to get any from you. Whatsup Lord? I know I gotta go but where? Is this a sign to quit acting? Or maybe you wouldn't let me proceed with her in my life. Is she my downfall or something? Is that the case? Let me know something, damn. Whatsup? Should I have left a long time ago? Should I really leave now? Come on Lord. Help me. I'm completely lost, my mind is Blanc. I know some of this is my fault. I Know I aint been giving my all. But this broke shit is killing me, kinda causing me to resent her. You know how it is, shit, you made me, I feel like you put something in every man's DNA that makes us want to take care of a woman. So now that I can't its killing me, I feel weak, exhausted. I'm trying my fucking hardest! I'm out here feeling like a bitch, can't even dictate shit in my own crib. Only way I feel a tiny bit better is when I'm away from her. Seeing her constantly reminds me of how bad I'm doing. Being away from her, not having to think about my problems 24/7 sorta eases the pain of failure. I keep waiting for you man. On my lonely days, which happens to be every day I just sit back and think of.how I've come such a long way. I'm not perfect but I made a conscious effort to do the right thing in damn near every situation. Even if the wrong thing is easier. Most times it goes unnoticed and just about every time it went without reward. But in my head I figure it's only a matter of time before you bless me for my good deeds. But it never seems to happen. On days when I feel I'm trapped and there's no way out I just knew you would come swooping down to save me. Wrong, of course I always found a way but it usually came with a whole other struggle of its own. I never get my big break. Whatsup with that man? Help me. Again I'm asking from the bottom of my heart, with everything in me, help me, please. PLEASE.

I opened my eyes and looked over to the door. There was a letter on the floor. Initially I didn't want to read it but something drew me to it.

Dear Von,

You aint shit! I told you I was going through a lot and you never did shit to help me. Nothing. I have no one who truly loves me for me in this world. I thought it was you but I guess I was wrong. Fuck you! I hate you! You don't know what the fuck I've been through and you don't give a fuck. You ever been raped? Huh? I have. Multiple occasions. I still can remember my older cousins making me suck there penis when I was 8 years old. I had no idea what was going on but I knew it was wrong so I never told. I thought my family would be mad at me and punish me. I just carried it inside of me. I can't even look at my cousins to this day. I felt like shit at my Moms funeral. There she was in a casket and all I could do was think about them sitting behind me. I almost turned around to kill them too. But I stayed strong, like I always do. Even against my uncle. My Dad's twin brother. As you know my Dad died from Aids. And before that he had been in Prison all of my life. So after my Mom died I decided to go stay with his family in Philly. I knew nothing about them but felt I needed to get connected to my family. Everything was good. Until one day I woke up with my Dads twin brother on top of me. Imagine looking at a figure that was identical to your Dad on top of you over powering you. You can't imagine it, I know you can't, no one can. Yeah I left his house the next morning but I left my soul too. From that day forward I knew I was alone. I guess it was sorta a good thing because I eventually opened up my own business because I didn't trust anyone enough to even give me a check. Then I met you. I opened my heart to you. You seemed genuine and real. I would have did anything for you. But it seems as if all you care about is yourself. I told you I was hurting and you did nothing but worry about your own career. What about me? Why didn't I come first? I needed you! But it's ok. I'm out. I won't need anyone else where I'm going. I can't take this anymore. Just remember you did this to me. Fuck you and this world. People are always saying somebody should have told them they were feeling suicidal because they would have helped. Liars! You Motherfuckers knew I was struggling. My life just wasn't worth you sacrificing anything for and soon I'll be forgotten. But who cares, at least I won't be here. People say when you kill yourself it's selfish. How? Family will suffer for about a year or two. I've been suffering for years and the pain doesn't seem to be letting up. You told me you had my back forever and now you're leaving. Liar! I never left. I stayed, I talked shit, but I stayed. But fuck that. No one is leaving me anymore. I'm leaving first. Fuck you!

Hate, Alexis

Out of nowhere I heard a thud outside. Concerned, I creeped out to check things out. Slowly I opened the front door, only to discover Alexis's body hanging from a sheet, twitching and convulsing from the second floor window.

"Alexis!" I screamed, as I dropped down to my knees before hearing a screeching scream from behind me. With tears rushing down my face I took a look back, there was Cee Cee.

The world stopped.

Take My Pain Away

Funeral Day. I stood weak, staring down my reflection in the bathroom mirror, searching for something beyond my eyes, not sure what, but whatever it was I prayed it came equip with the courage I required to walk out into the unfiltered world. A place where I'd come face to face with Alexis for the final time.

Everything's changed. Over the past week I've experienced a constant never ending downward spiral, giving me firsthand experience in a living hell. A place I assumed I knew all about. I was wrong. Dead wrong. Now, something as simple as stepping out of the bed to use the restroom had suddenly become an almost impossible task. The soles of my feet burned as I stepped, leaving me deeply pained, forcing me down to my hands and knees, crawling desperately to my destination.

Day after day I realized exactly how clueless I'd been. I thought I was alone. Yeah right. I had no idea what true loneliness consisted of. I do now. Sleeping in the bed Alexis and I once shared is an unmatched pain. My eyes bleed as my hidden soul aches each and every time my body slightly touches her ice cold side of the bed.

Still, I can't bring myself to part ways. How can I? This is the closest I'll ever physically be to her. Her fragrance still softly floats through the damaged air. At times I feel she's still here, watching me. I can feel her. She's angry. There's a dark presence looming above me, mirroring my every move, breathing softly down my stiff neck. I'm telling you, it's gotta be her. I know it. I deserve this. There has to be some sorta punishment for my actions. She was right, I said I'd never leave and I lied. My deceptive words broke her, leaving her heart shattered in a million pieces. I'm a murderer.

Each day I feel less of a man than before. And no, I can't act as if no one has reached out. Actually, I've been receiving more phone calls than ever. So much so that my phone went completely dead from too much activity. I guess it's been off for about a day or two. I don't know, to be honest, life's a blur right now.

At night, I fight my sleep, for hours on end I lay, eyes wide, afraid to close them in fear of murderous nightmares, starring Alexis. Of course it never completely works, I always drift off, and there she is, each time, killing herself in a new more heinous way. I wish I could say I'm growing numb but that would be untrue. Still, with that being said, once I'm asleep I fear waking up. What's life when you're not living?

In a way, I guess I kinda wish God just finds it in his heart to silently take me out of my misery. The thought of eternal peace soothes me. No heartache, no pain, I can only imagine the feeling.

At times I find myself thinking back to the past, happier times. And you know what's funny? Most of those moments usually stem from my life of crime. Those were the times when I kept a pocket full of cash. And even days when I didn't, I had friends who took my mind off of being broke. Everything's different now.

I don't even know who the fuck I am. Actually, who the fuck am I kidding, it doesn't even matter who I am. My broke ass probably can't even afford to be who I'm truly destined to be. Aint shit in this world free. Most likely being me is far too expensive for my premature pockets. I hate myself.

Thank God for Weed though. Aint no telling where I'd be without it. So far it's been my only comfort. Alexis had just copped an ounce the day before I killed her. I've been getting high as hell, smoking like a chimney. I hate reality, weed had become a mandatory escape.

Sadness lives in my heart right next to the veins, I can feel it pumping.

Whatsup God,

Man I don't even wanna go to this dumb ass funeral. Why me man? Why? As if I aint got enough on my plate. Damn dog, I been asking for some fuckin signs every damn day. You aint telling me shit. Tell me something! At least let this funeral bring me some sorta closure or something. Come on man, I need it. You see me having these nightmares? I know you do. Are you giving them to me? Man fuck. I'm just ready to quit; everything. I admit I didn't know a lot in the past. If I would have become successful I might have messed it all up. But right now I feel as though I know a few things. I'd be able to survive. I know I can. Just give me a shot. Please man, please. I been through it all. Just gimme a shot Lord Please. Just gimme a shot, one shot, that's all I need. I promise, I'm begging you. Man I'm sad as a bitch. I really wish I could find permanent happiness and an opportunity to change my life for the better. I'm lonely as hell man. I need you Lord. I need you. Nobody in this world truly gives a fuck about me. Show me something different Lord, I need you. I'm breaking. I'm broken. I'm dying. Help me. Help me. Please.

Finally after what seemed like forever, I was dressed and as ready as I was going to be for the funeral. No, I didn't match, yes I have on sneakers, and hell no I didn't iron but this was by far the best I had to offer.

Moping to my car, I swung open my driver's side door before falling inside, throwing my feet to the pedals as I struggled to find the ignition before cranking up the car. Dropping my head onto the steering wheel, tears gushed from my eyes.

Whatsup God,

Help me, help me please. This is a new feeling. My heart isn't broken. It stings.

Digging deep, I somehow found the strength I needed. Clutching on to the damp steering wheel I rose my head, took a deep breath and slowly headed to my destination, using God as my GPS.

Whatsup God,

I know I aint came to the viewing or talked to the family but please allow it in their heart to understand. I just want peace. That's all I need. Peace, I swear that's all I need.

I hadn't been in the Church's parking lot for 20 seconds before I heard a knock on my window. I looked over. It was my Cousin Mike.

"Whatsup Cuz," he said as I opened the door, stepping out.

"Whatsup man," I replied, dryly.

"Cuz I'm so sorry for what happened. I've been calling, texting, I even came by," he added, as we embraced.

"Man, I'm sorry dog. I just couldn't talk."

"I hate to say I understand because you and I both know that's not true. But I swear I feel your pain man. I do."

"Yeah man. Can't lie dog, shit is hard. Aint been in my right mind lately," I said, fighting my emotions. "It took everything in me to even get up and show my face today."

"I bet man. You did the right thing. You're a strong dude, always have been."

"Thanks man."

"Yeah you know I had to show my support."

"Appreciate it man," I replied.

"Hey man. You still coming to my Bachelor Party week after next?" Mike asked. "I know its bad timing and all, but shit, you've already paid and it might be just what you need to get your mind off of things."

Truthfully I had completely forgotten about the Bachelor Party. We were going to Costa Rica. I've never been out of the country. Maybe he was right. This could be therapeutic, hopefully that's where my peace dwelled. It damn sure can't hurt.

"Yeah, I'ma still go," I replied.

"Cool. We're going to have a ball man."

We walked up to the church doors to enter.

"Yo I've been waiting for you all day," barked Alexis's cousin, one of the same cousins she'd written about molesting her in the letter. In a flash he shot over to me, tackling me down to the ground as the entire church gasped and everyone rushed over. Flashbacks of my Mom's funeral were impossible to escape.

"Stop it Marc, Stop it," screamed family members.

"Fuck that," he yelled back, holding me down by my neck. "You the motherfucker who killed my cousin."

"I aint kill your cousin," I struggled to say.

"Yes the fuck you did nigga, why else would she do some shit like this, she been around your ass every day. She won't even talking to us anymore. I know you did it. I know you did," he said swinging his fist irately, desperately trying to strike me as I did my best to block him. "I should kill you right now motherfucker."

"Let him go. He aint worth it," says the family as they pull him off.

"You lucky motherfucker," he screamed and pointed as he was dragged away. "Get away from here and never come back. You hear me bitch! Never."

Slowly I rose to my feet, enraged, not knowing how to feel, how to act. To say my thoughts were all over the place would be an understatement.

"You alright Cuz?" said Mike as he trailed behind. "I tried to pull him off you, he came out of nowhere."

I ignored him as I made my way to my vehicle.

"You know you can come stay with me. I got plenty room." he said as he continued to follow.

I shook my head before falling inside my vehicle.

Whatsup God,

Yo what the fuck! Am I even talking to anybody? Is anybody up there? Is this shit some sorta joke to you or something? Because the shit aint amusing to me. Not one fucking bit. I mean damn. I aint even really got nothing to say, I actually don't know what to say, I said it all. . Actually I do got something to say, fuck that. Is this pay back for something I did in the past? Naw fuck that. That was a stupid question. I know damn well I aint did shit in my life to deserve this type of pain. I mean day after day, week after week. When will it end? Do you want me to go out the same way Alexis did? Because I swear that's what's next. It's really no other choice. And I think you know that. But you don't care. You don't give a fuck. You don't give a shit about me. To tell the truth you kinda got me thinking that happiness is just a want, like I don't really need it or something. It only makes sense considering the fact you've always given me what I needed. Guess you don't really give a damn about what I want. If that's the case just let a nigga know. Damn. I need answers. ASAP. You hear me! I said I Need! I know I'm talking all over the place right now, but I'm lost and losing my last bit of patience. Not sure how much more I can take.

I drove off, again in complete silence. Once I got to the crib I packed everything I could. This wasn't home to me anymore. I don't know where I'm going but I'm going, a fresh start was required.

In no time I was finished packing. I'm ashamed, after gathering everything I had in this world I still had plenty of room in my car. What has my life become? I aint got shit in this world. Fuck.

Before leaving, I walked back into the house. I had to ask myself one more time, 'How had things gotten to this point'? This place started off so good, it was my second chance in life, so many great memories. I could still picture Alexis and I laughing, smoking, binge watching something on Netflix, or her in the kitchen cooking in her panties.

It's crazy how memories can bring so much joy but on the other hand bring so much agony. In no time the image of Alexis hanging from the window flashed through my head like lightening. My body shook as chills sprinted down my bones. Who knows if I'll ever get over this? Probably not, it's been years since my Mom and Grandma died and I still can't seem to forget about them. And it aint like I even saw them hanging from a window. This is different, life changing.

I just don't get it. How could this happen when I had done so much to be successful? Fuck is going on? Where are the fucking rules on this thing called life? I need to read them because I'm obviously doing this thing all wrong. And whatsup with this Karma thing? I know for a fact Alexis did a lot of good, where the fuck is her good Karma going to? Where's all that good energy going to go? Shouldn't I get it? I'm serious, shouldn't I? Who else but me? As much as we've been through. As much as I put up with. Shit, I bet aint nobody else losing sleep behind her like me. I deserve something. I aint too sure what but I know for a fact, I deserve something. Fuck that.

I can't believe her stupid ass family. Motherfuckers wanna embarrass me and place blame on me for her actions. Yeah I said it was my fault for what she did but now I'm starting to have second thoughts. It aint my fucking fault, it's theirs. They're the motherfuckers who allowed her to get hurt like that. Fuck them, they was abusing her long before I came along. I should go back up there and shoot that whole family up. Fuck them! Damn right I deserve to get everything good she had coming to her, just for the fact I aint snap in there. Shoulda exposed her Uncle and Cousins. I guess my loyalty to her lasts even after death. She was a private person, I know she'd never want everyone knowing her business like that.

Man, the longer I stood looking around the crib, the more my temple started to pound, harder and harder. I can't win if I tried. I dropped down to my knees, still looking around, searching for hidden answers. What the fuck am I supposed to be learning? It's gotta be a lesson in all of this. I gotta figure this shit out. What am I doing wrong?

I don't get it. Why does everyone who just conforms to society's norms seem to be living so much better than me? Obviously I must have made the wrong decision. Invested everything I had and still came out with nothing.

People say God answers prayers, but when? When does he do it? How much pain do I deserve? How much more do I have to bare? Why does happiness come with such an expensive tab? Yet another thing in this world I can't afford. Why can't everyone just be happy? Why the fuck isn't that shit free? The world would be so much better. I got so many questions. What the fuck is my purpose on earth? What I thought I was here for has to be totally wrong. I'm worthless.

Gathering strength, I stood tall, walked to the door, stormed out, slamming the door behind me before tossing the house key as far as I could. Fuck that crib. I shoulda burned that motherfucker down.

I Can't Give Up

Ring Ring Ring.

I was awoken by the sound of my phone. It was Erika. This was the third time she'd called since Alexis had died, the third time I hadn't answered and the third time she'd left a voice message.

"Hey Von. Hope everything is ok. I've been thinking about you. Remember, you're special. Everything happens for a reason. Love ya," she said.

Whatsup God,

Yo can you wake me up from this nightmare. It's like shits getting worse by the second. Look at me, lonely as hell, still ignoring calls. Losing valuable friendships. Am I stupid or something? Never mind I already know the answer to that. Of course I am. It would be easy to just blame Alexis for all my problems. But we both know it wouldn't be true. I been fucking up long before I met her. Especially when it came down to my friends. A nigga's been distant for years. Putting in so much damn time hustling and tryna figure out ways to get where I wanna be caused me to kinda shut a lot of people out. If I'ma be honest, I gotta say, I suck at being a friend. Can you blame me? Most days I lack the strength to talk. Besides what am I supposed to say to them? My life sucks, I'm drained, and I think I may have forgotten who I am. That's part of the reason I don't wanna talk to people. Being me is the reason I have friends. I don't want to lose them all but maybe it's 'God's will'. Aint like no one understands me anyway. Everyone's perfectly happy living a life that would be miserable to me. But foreal dog, can you just place one person in my life who really understands me? Like come on now. I swear I'm alone. Do you even understand me? Do you even care to understand me? Fuck am I asking that for. Of course you don't. I guess my job is to understand you. Or maybe it's just to do whatever you say. And hey, I'm cool with that. I'm willing to do anything you want me to do to be happy. But sometimes I'm a little too confused on what you even want. It's heartbreaking to realize I have no real control over the way things happen to me. It's like I'm forced to sit depressed, not knowing when the pain will end. And when it ends, if ever, I fear that another storm will come. But anyway, I'll say it again in case you forgot, if this is a nightmare, please, please wake me up.

As I stretched my arms and legs I pinched myself, nope it wasn't a nightmare, this shit is real. How the fuck did I drop so low? Here I am, a grown ass man, waking up in my car, sitting in the back of Wal-Mart's parking lot. I slept here because it was open 24 hours. No one could really bother me about trespassing or whatever. I'd been posting up for about a week now trying to figure out my next move. So far, giving up, getting a regular 9-5 and becoming a regular fucking guy has been my top option. Honestly, I'm not too sure I got it in me to keep going. I know I say that a lot but I've never been more serious.

My only glimpse of hope was getting a call back for the role I'd auditioned for. So far I hadn't heard a peep, nor had Kyle Upshaw been answering his phone. Last time I'd spoken to him he said to be patient but I don't know how long this can last. The world is moving and I gotta somehow find a way to keep up, sitting in the same spot forever will be the death of me.

Lately my minds seemed to slowly transform into a ticking time bomb waiting to explode, so many thoughts, so little space. I'm going crazy, not sure if brains can be broken but if so I can for sure say mine is at least sprained. Man, outta all the times to be outta weed why the fuck does it have to be now. Moments like this have you questioning every decision you've ever made with your money. Have you thinking shit like, damn if I wouldn't have gave that one Bum on the corner a dollar every day I wouldn't be in this situation, now look at me, I'm the bum and he's probably somewhere laying in the shade.

Still, one thing I've realized, no matter who or what I place the blame on, at the end of the day, it still doesn't negate the fact that this is indeed my reality. Guess it's a good thing I'll be headed to Costa Rica next week. Only one problem, yep you guessed it, no cash. Yeah the trip is paid for but as of right now I have zero spending money. I thought about asking some of my family back home to borrow a little something, but I'd been ignoring them all, I can't just pop up outta nowhere with my hand out. Fuck that, looks like I'ma have to figure something out on my own; as usual.

Gotta admit, seems pretty unlikely that I will. Just look at me, only person I gotta worry about in this world is me and I can't even do that right. I'm ashamed of myself. Only thing I got to my name is my Instagram. How fucking sad. On top of that, aint like I can really even post and interact like I used to. Who the fuck wants to scroll down the timeline to see me take raggedy selfies in my car? Exactly, no-fucking-body.

On the bright side, with all this bullshit going on in my head, it's been kinda hard to focus on Alexis's death. Don't get me wrong, to say she doesn't cross my mind on more than one occasion a day would be a lie, a boldface lie, I miss her, every day in every way, everything and everyone reminds me of her. Seeing couples laughing, holding hands and just enjoying one another's company has grown to be unbearable. At times I've found myself closing my eyes, pretending they didn't exist.

The thought that I may never feel love again is something I've found myself coming to terms with. I've never been to good at love, it may be time to be honest with myself, maybe it's me, maybe I don't have what it takes to truly be loved. Or maybe I don't know how to express true love. Who knows, it could be a thousand reasons, I'm not sure. But what I am sure of is the fact that I won't let anyone that close to me again. I have to protect myself, to feel as vulnerable as I do at this moment is something I refuse to ever live through again. Once I'm out of this funk, there will be a new me. I'm forever changed, scarred for life.

As the morning sun beamed down, clashing with my face, I sat watching the Bums congregate by the bus stop a few feet away from me, an activity they indulged in every morning, most not even waiting on the bus, just chilling. I think it's like the local Bum hangout or something. They all just sit around talking about everything going on in their world. Usually I hear shit like.

"You know Lil Donald's selling two for fifteens?"

"If you know anybody who need food stamps I know somebody."

Sometimes I even hear them talking freaky. There's this one old Bum Lady who's thick as hell, uglier than a motherfucker, but that ass, damn, if I aint know for sure that it probably smelled like earring backs, I might shoot my shot. Seriously, this Bum lady won't nothing to play with. All the old Bum niggas always got some slick shit to say to her. She's smart though, far from a dummy, each day, she knows exactly who she's dealing with.

Every morning it's a new Bum nigga. And it never fails, each day, it's the Bum nigga with the most money. I haven't figured out exactly how she scopes out the Big Spenders, all I know is that her radar is on point. Man, her old ass milks them old suckers dry before moving on to the next bum the very next day, leaving the guy from before broke, sober, hating from the sidelines. It's a cold game.

But hey, I aint hear to judge. I may not ever join in on the conversations but since I'm out here I guess I'm sorta part of the Bum crew. You can call me 'Baby Bum'. Only difference between them and I was that they all looked happy. Even with crack stained, decaying, or missing teeth they all seemed to keep a smile on their face.

Fuck them. Joyful faces were starting to piss me off. In a weird way I sorta wished we could switch places. That thought only lasts for a second, I always snap back to my senses. Deep down I know if I keep thinking like that I could end up just like them. Who knows, they were probably once just like me. Life probably beat them to a pulp forcing them to a life they never imagined. Scary. I can't allow that to be my fate. No way. Somethings gotta give. I can only imagine what it does to a person's spirit to sleep in the street with trash for years on end. I guess just to see them smiling is a blessing. Who know the traumas they've witnessed.

"My nigga," said a Bum standing in front of my car to another Bum walking up.

"Sup ol timer. What's going on jack," the guy responded, excitedly. "I aint seen your ass in a month of Sundays."

"I ain doin shit, just maintainin, bouta head on down to the Plasma bank to make my donation. Where in the hell you been at?"

"Man I'm fresh home from the Pen, I need me some money, which Plasma Bank you go to?" he asked.

"Right up there on Bouldercrest," he replied as he sparked his cigarette.

"They pay pretty good?"

"Damn right. First time donors get $75 the first donation and $100 on the second," he replied.

"Oh shit. That aint bad. That aint bad at all," he followed, nodding his head.

"Hell naw it aint. If you comin you betta come on now wit me before it gets all packed."

"U'ma be up there in bout an hour. First I gotta go get some shit outta Wal-Mart. They dont have nobody at the door between 6-7. You can walk out that mo'fucka with any damn thang."

"Oh shit I ain know that."

"It ain for erbody to know, keep it on the low," he replied, looking around. "But you can't come with me. I ain tryna get the block hot. Them section 8 bih's already be in there stealin up every damn thang."

"Mo'fucka I been gave up boostin. Shit, my last bid was for a B&E. I gotta job now."

"Oh shit. You workin?"

"Yup. U'm right up there at the McDonalds on Cascade."

"Damn that's aite there," he replied, nodding his head approvingly.

"Yup they posed to be makin me a manager soon."

"Can you hook an ol mo'fucka like me up with some free food and shit?"

"Man hell yuh, you jus gotta come up there when it aint too many customers."

"Right on, I'll prolly be up there sometime this week. It was nice seeing you man. Glad you hangin in there."

"Yuh man, and I'm glad you home man."

"Me too, I'm gettin to ol for that jail bullshit," he replied. "But hey man, you thank I can get one of them blows up off you?" he asked pointing to the other Bums cigarette.

"You know I usually dont do this but since we go way back, hea," he said as he looked around, assuring no one saw him, before cautiously whipping out his box of Newport's and handing one to the other Bum.

"Thanks bruh, I needed this shit."

"No problem man," he replied as they both rode away on their bikes.

Now outta that whole entire conversation only one thing stuck out to me. The 'Plasma Bank'. I always said I would never donate, where I'm from that's a sign of being at your lowest. But I guess I gotta face the facts, I'm at my lowest, probably a little lower than my lowest. I'm out this bitch breaking my own records. I need that money more than ever. Donating would at least allow me to hit Costa Rica with about $175. May not be much but it's damn sure better than the $7 worth of change I got in my pocket.

With that being said, I started my car and was on my way. But first I had to stop at the Holiday Inn. I ate at a random Hotel every morning. They always have complimentary breakfast for the guest. All I do is walk in casual as hell, eat a quick plate or two and then take one for the road.

100

Today was no different, I ate then headed straight for the Plasma Bank. Once inside, it's like every conversation in the crowded building ended and every eye beamed down on me. No bullshit. It was as if everyone knew I didn't belong. Suddenly I heard whispering coming from each corner of the room. As I walked to the front desk I locked in on the lips of everyone in my view. I swear I heard my name come out of each one of their mouths. I know, I know, I'm probably tripping, maybe I am, I don't know, I'm just saying that's what it looked like to me. Still, I shook it off, finally making it up to the front desk.

"Sup. I wanna give some plasma," I whispered to the secretary, a young chubby black girl.

"Ever donated before?" she asked, never looking up to me, face stuck in her phone.

"No."

"Ok. Fill this out and bring it back up here when it's completed," she said as she tossed a clipboard up to me.

"Appreciate it."

I sat down on a chair behind me before taking a look around. There was a long line of Bums, and yes, I still felt they were talking about me. What the fuck were they saying though? Did they know something I didn't? If so, they need to fill me in. I need answers. What the fuck did they possibly know about me? Did they know that I would someday look like them? Was this the first step to becoming a permanent Bum? Could this be my destiny?

In desperate need for answers I leaned in closer to get a good listen to the conversations around me.

"Yeah man I got so high last night."

"Do roaches eat bed bugs?"

"You know the temp agency giving out good jobs."

Looks like they weren't talking about me after all. Still, the urge to walk out was more prevalent than ever. My hands shook uncontrollably as I filled out the questionnaire. What should have taken three minutes, took me twenty before I was able to return it to the Young Lady at the desk.

Times like this I wished all those rumors about signing your life away to the Illuminati for fortune and fame were real. I'll definitely do it, in a heartbeat. Thank God I found the strength to continue on. After about an hour and a half of more questions and blood work it was finally time to stand in line with the regulars to officially begin the process of donating plasma.

"First time?" asked a woman standing behind me.

"Yeah," I said as I turned around, glancing at her for a quick second.

"Do I know you?" she asked. "You look real familiar. "

"Naw I don't think so."

"What's yo Mama name?"

"I'm from Virginia I don't think you knew her."

"Oh well maybe I don't," she said as she looked down at the paper work I was holding in my hands, displaying my name. "Lavon Jordan," she screamed. "That's where the fuck I know you from. You was in that damn play 'Us vs. Them'. Yep. Sure was. My daughter took me to see it. You did a hell of a job," she said before pausing and screaming. "Ay we got a celebrity in the building. This the little handsome actor I been talking about."

"Oh that's him," said a lady who worked there.

"Boy she been talking about you for a month straight," said another.

"Damn get off his dick," said a male Bum in front of me.

"Yeah, he broke just like the rest of us," said another.

"Yeah what the fuck are you even doing in here?" asked some old guy standing in the front of the line.

I didn't say a word. Still they kept talking amongst themselves.

"See that's xactly why I took my daughter outta that damn actin class. Ain nobody getin no money in entertainment. It's all a fraud. He's proof right here," said the lady who had initiated the conversation.

I took a deep breath, turned on my headphones and attempted to remain as cool as possible.

"Could you turn that down," said some White Lady standing behind the Lady who'd seen the Play. "There's a sign that says keep music to a minimum," she followed as she pointed forward to the sign.

I clinched my fist, everything in me wanted to cuss this bitch out. Man, it don't matter how bad a White Person is doing, they can be broke, dirty and on their last breath, they'll still think they got the right to tell a nigga what to do. Just five damn minutes ago I overheard her yelling on the phone with what I'd bet my last dollar was her pimp. How dare her little trickin ass tell me to turn some shit down? Fucking whore.

Holding in my aggression, I simply turned and looked at her with a grit she'd never forget.

"Don't you worry bout her. She's jus mad cause some trick ain pay her ass last night," said the guy in front of me.

"Fuck off Jerome," said the White Lady.

"Bitch fuck you," he replied. "I got your back Young Blood," he said as he tapped my shoulder proudly.

I nodded.

"You know I used to do a little acting back in my day too," he continued.

"That's cool man," I replied, dryly.

"Yep," he followed. "Ay, where you get them shoes from, I gotta get me some," he added as he pointed down to me kicks.

"I ordered them from eBay," I replied. I don't know why broke people always wanna know where you bought some shit from, aint like they gonna actually go out and buy it.

But yeah, finally after taking my blood pressure and weight it was time for me to hook up to the machine to begin the donation process. I walked over staring straight ahead. There were about 40 or 50 small beds hooked up to some computer monitors and needles. Once I found a vacant spot I laid down as a young nurse located a vein in my arm before strapping a needle into me, sucking the plasma from my body.

Sitting back, I was truly humbled. I said I would never be here and look at me, here. From the corners of my eyes I could see dozens of eyes locked in on me. The big ol actor was sitting right next to them at the rock-bottom. I think it gave them some sorta joy, they were probably thinking maybe their short comings weren't too bad if their decisions had landed them in the same position as me.

Wow, failing in front of the world is something only a few will understand.

Whatsup God,

I know I should never say never. But I'm sorry, after I get back from Costa Rica I can never come back in this motherfucker. Ever. I can't take it. I can't fucking believe I'm in this bitch. Guess I can never know how much I can endure until you actually make me endure it because I swear I never saw myself here. Shit is wild. This is like the closest thing to being accused of something I didn't do. It's like I know I don't deserve this. I feel like I'm in the middle of the ocean, stuck, only a miracle can save me. I'm holding on for dear life. This shit is borderline disrespectful. But what can I even say. Man, just let me make it through these last two visits. I won't need anything after that. Come on man, I'm in pain. And you know I'm used to pain. But shit, it don't make it any easier. I keep telling you it's a different kinda pain knowing you're in pain but also realizing the worse may be yet to come. It's so crazy man. Who would have known that chasing your dream requires you to be disappointed so many times? This shit is wack.. I wanna quit so fucking bad man. Just wanna go live a regular life. Fuck it. But I can't. Deep down I already know it will leave a bitterness inside of me that may never go away. Deep down I know I'll never get this acting bug out of my system. Never, it's stuck with me. But continuing to sacrifice only to fail isn't something I feel I can continue to go through right now. At least I don't think so. I don't know. Fuck. I guess the saddest part is knowing I may never be happy. You hear me man? Are you even listening to me? Do I matter? How many times do I have to ask you that? Am I talking to myself? I don't know dog. Sometimes I feel talking to you is like asking somebody for help and they agree to do it. Yeah, they said they would help but they never said when. That's the messed up part. Only person I can really trust is me. And I'm losing trust in myself because I can't even find a way to make myself happy. And it's crazy because I've always been so good at making other people smile. When is it gonna be my fucking turn? Look at me now, I wanna blow my brains out so bad but I know I'd hurt the few people who love me. My dumb ass, after all this, still worrying about other people's feelings. Man, I'm stupid, I should have broken up with Alexis the minute she started tripping. Why the fuck do we still aim for forever knowing nothing in life truly lasts? I'ma fool. Fuck! I'ma dumbass. It sucks when you can't blame anyone but yourself for the way your life turned out. I needa damn hug.

"Hey Von," said Whitney as she opened the front door of her home.

"Hey Whitney," I followed as I stepped inside.

Whitney was my cousin Mikes Fiancé. After seeming to take forever, the time was officially here, in a matter of hours I'd be over 30,000 feet in the sky on my way to sunny Costa Rica. Hopefully I'd not only be leaving my car behind but my problems too.

Can't lie, this is the happiest I've been in forever. Shit was exciting, I even had a little change in my pocket, not much, but it was something. Not to mention I was bouta go to a foreign country for the first time. And probably the best thing of all, I'd be taking my first flight, I've been wanting to do this shit since I was a kid.

"Whatsup Cuz," said Mike as he trotted down the stairs toting his luggage.

"Nothing man. Chilin. Ready to get this show on the road," I responded as we embraced.

"That's what I'm talking about. We gonna leave as soon as Jay gets here. You remember Jay right?" he followed as he sat his luggage by the front door.

"Yeah the tall Guy who works with you," I replied.

We all sat on the couch, small talking for about five or ten minutes before the door bell rung.

"Whatsup Motherfuckers," yelled Jay as he entered. "Yall motherfuckers ready?"

"Hell yeah," Mike screamed as we all got hype like we were about to play in the championship game or something.

"Whatsup Whitney," he said, lowering his tone as he gave her a hug. "Appreciate ya letting my boy go on this trip. It's about to be lit. Me and my motherfucking dogs."

"Yeah but don't get too lit," followed Whitney, sternly.

"Oh no. We gonna keep it respectful," Jay replied.

"Trust me babe, you don't have anything to worry about," followed Mike.

"Oh no, I'm not worried, trust me you're the one who should be worried," she replied deviously.

"Yeah, she means business," said Jay as we laughed.

"I wouldn't dare play with her ass," I followed.

"Well I'm glad you know," she said with a smile. "Bring yall butts to the car before I change my mind," she said jokingly as we all followed behind, toting our luggage.

We all packed up inside of her Ford Focus and headed to the airport. Considering Whitney was in the car, no one really said too much on the way but once we exited the vehicle it was a totally different story.

"Yo we gonna fuck so many motherfucking bitches. I heard this place is like hoe Heaven or some shit. Land of the thotties," shouted Jay.

"Facts," replied Mike.

"Hoe Heaven? Foreal?" I asked.

"Damn right. My buddy went down there a couple years ago and said he had to leave his cousin."

"What do you mean leave him?" I asked.

"Exactly what I said, leave his ass," answered Jay. "Man they said he met some bad ass Model looking chick and just moved in with her. Last they heard he was living like a king, with a daughter and dog."

"That's crazy," I replied, laughing. "Well you aint gotta worry about me doing anything like that. I aint really the type to Wife hoes," I followed.

"Boy you're tripping. I love me some hoes," blurted Jay.

"What?" I asked.

"Yeah he aint lying," replied Mike. "He really does."

"You remind me of my nigga Rell," I said laughing. "Care to explain?"

"Ok, think about it, Kim Kardashian was a hoe. We all seen her butt ass naked, sucking dick, but my nigga Kanye looked passed all of that. He saw her potential. Look at her now, taking care of her kids, freeing inmates, I even read that she's about to be a lawyer."

"Man that bitch doesn't care about freeing inmates or the law. She just saw Donald Trump become President and knows that she and Kanye might really have a shot now," I replied.

"You really think that?" asked Mike.

"Hell yeah," I replied. "That's the reason Kanye's performing at all of those churches and the reason he wears that dumb ass MAGA hat. They just tryna weasel their way into the White House."

"Crazy thing is, it might work," replied Mike.

"See, I rest my case, aint nothing like a hoe, they got limitless possibilities," added Jay. "Shout out to my nigga Kanye for continuing to be a visionary. Who would've thought?"

"You funny as hell," I said laughing.

"Real shit." he said before looking over to Mike. "But Mike I don't want to give you any ideas, I don't want you missing your wedding due to one of these Hoes."

"Naw fellas I love Whitney. I'm just gonna go out here and let my hair down for a few and enjoy myself, I don't even really need any Hoes around me."

"First of all, you're bald, you aint got no hair to let down. Secondly, motherfucker if you come all the way to Costa Rica and don't fuck no Hoes, you gay."

"Damn why he gotta be all that?" I asked as we continued walking.

"Naw man, its cool Von, he's right. Because I'm definitely fucking me some Hoes," Mike shouted. "Its bouta get crazy fellas," he added as we all got hype once again.

"Hell yeah, everybody bring rubbers?" asked Jay.

"Of course," said Mike.

"Aw shit, I forgot," I followed.

"It's cool, I got you, I bought plenty," replied Jay.

"My nigga," I followed as I nodded my head.

Soon, we arrived at the gate and it was at that moment I realized I'd be forced to pay extra. My dumbass fucked up once again, my damn bag was too big to be considered a carry on. What the fuck. Aint like I had too much of a choice, shit, this was the smallest bag I had. If you ask me this was a rather small bag, too bad no one asked me. Turns out this little ass bag was gonna cost me 25 damn dollars. Yeah, 25 beans might not be anything to others but to me, at this moment, it was a huge chunk of all the money to my name. I know, sad right.

Dog, forking over the cash was torture, I gritted my teeth as I reached into my pocket, part of me wanted to just run out of the airport. If I'm already paying for stuff and we aint even got on the plane, I can only imagine what it's gonna be like in Costa Rica. But fuck it, I took a deep breath, asked myself what other choice do I have and proceeded to get robbed, or at least that what it felt like.

Spending that cash really did something to my spirit, I could hardly even move, it was as if cement had somehow been trapped inside the soles of my shoes, causing me to sluggishly struggle to keep up with Mike and Jay. As I trotted behind it was clear to see that the airport was far different than being at the Greyhound bus stations I'm used to. Here, everyone looked a little classier, a little more confident, even if they were only sporting flip flops and a tee, it was evident that they were somebody, or at least appeared to be.

The longer we walked the more out of place I felt. Especially after looking down and taking a glance at my right arm, it was impossible to ignore the pebble sized scar sitting on my vein. And to think, I'd probably walk around with it for the rest of my life. Got me scared to wear short sleeves because everyone will think I'm some junkie or something. Disgusting.

Stupid ass plasma bank. My hands dripped with nervous sweat as I pulled down my shirt sleeve, hoping to conceal my war wound.

Slowly I scanned the building, looking at the hundreds of smiling faces, wondering if their happiness was sincere. If so, again I must ask, how? How the fuck did they do it? Teach me. How do they all know how to be happy and I don't? Was it a secret that I'd yet to discover or some shit? I need answers, now! I'm bouta start holding these niggas by gun point, fuck that, somebody gonna tell me what the fuck going on, somethings gotta give, aint no way I'm supposed to be feeling this unhappy. Aint no way.

It's crazy, I keep hearing people say happiness is a choice. Ok cool, I get it, but if that's so, why can't I control my emotions. Where the fuck is my happy button because my sad button been on for a minute? Who the fuck even cut it on? I aint approve that shit. Again, like I said, I need answers. Fuck. Life got me feeling like I'm doing a math test and putting 4+4 in and getting 5. Shit just doesn't make any sense, it aint adding up, I just can't figure out how I keep getting the wrong answer, I'm doing all the right shit.

Maybe I should worship money a little more. That gotta be the answer to my problems. Yep, I gotta worship money more. A lot more. I been doing shit all wrong. If I woulda cherished the money more I would never even be in this situation. Shit, Alexis may not have even be dead if I did. Or would she? Man, I don't know. Actually, I don't know shit, I guess that's really the only thing I do know for sure, I don't know shit.

I took a deep breath.

Whatsup God,

Ay can you knock me out of my funk? I'm tripping right now. I'm trying to get my mind off this bullshit.

We sat, awaiting our departure. Thank God Mike's always thinking, he bought a few personal bottles of Hennessey in his carry on. We through back shots as we laughed and joked about life. Kinda took the edge off of the anxiety I was dealing with. Before I knew it, it was time to board the plane. I was a little nervous but I was ready.

I stood to my feet, tipsy, before hopping in line trying my best to act as if I belonged. Not sure if it was working, the liquor was getting the best of me. As we boarded I took a look at my ticket. Luckily I had a window seat, I'd be able to see the world from the sky. I plopped down, strapped on my seatbelt, listened to the Pilot go over all the rules and before I knew it we were taking off.

The higher we flew the more beautiful the world became. I stared from my window in admiration. A tear drop fell from my eye lid as I realized this was the closest I'd been to my Mom, Grandma and Alexis in what seemed like forever.

"I Love yall," I mouthed as I replayed all the good times I'd had with each in my head. I sat in a nostalgic daze and before I knew it we were landing. I didn't realize how short of a trip it was going to be. Of course we hadn't landed in Costa Rica just yet. We were in Charlotte. There we would meet the other guys before boarding.

I hopped off the plane eagerly. I couldn't wait to see my people. I knew most of them all of my life. Mike's my 3rd cousin but we grew up like brothers so everyone going on the trip were basically my people too, well besides Jay. But yeah, I hadn't seen any of them in a while. No question shits about to be epic. They were all some fucking characters.

Didn't take long before we saw them. Or should I say heard them. They were famous for being loud as hell. The first voice to come blasting through my eardrums was Mikes Uncle Red.

I don't even know where to start with Red, he was your typical black ol school Uncle, Loud and thought he knew every damn thing. Most of the time he was wrong but he was so damn funny it didn't even matter. I always loved to be around him.

I mean how couldn't I? He was responsible for me getting my first piece of ass. I'll never forget it, remember it like it was yesterday. I gotta tell you about this shit, it was life changing. See, even though neither of them ever attended the school, every year Uncle Red and Mike's Pops took Mike and I to Norfolk States Homecoming game back home. In our city Homecoming was a certified holiday, everybody put on their best fits, hit the liquor store and paraded around campus all day, reuniting, politicking and just having a good ass time. We'd be out that bitch all day.

Usually afterwards Uncle Mike would drunkenly drive me back home around 9 or 10 and my night would be over. Not this particular time though. Their homeboy Mad Dog was throwing a big ass strip party at his spot, and at the tender age of 14, we were finally allowed to hang with the big boys.

The whole ride over I'm nervous as hell. Excited, but nervous, a young nigga couldn't even sit still. I hadn't even really seen any girls my age naked, I aint know how the fuck I was going to handle seeing grown women, bouncing bare ass all in my face. I guess I wouldn't have been so nervous if I was just going to be around people my age, but grown folk, I aint even know how I was supposed to act.

Still, I faced my fears, stuck my chest out, held my head high and walked in that motherfucker holding my nuts. From the second I entered, I knew this was some shit that wouldn't be hard for me to get used to. It was a movie, an x rated movie, big booties, and titties every damn where.

Mikes Dad gave us both $20 a piece in ones. Wasting no time I found a spot on the couch and attempted to act as mature as possible. No smiling, nothing, I meant business and as I looked over to Mike it was clear we were both on the same page. Dude had this serious ass look on his face the whole time. He actually looked pretty goofy, I aint say shit though, can't lie, it was damn near impossible to fight off my laughter.

Don't get me wrong, I won't paying too much attention to Mike though. It was obvious who really had my eye; them hoes, they was on some other shit, popping pussy, throwing it all in my face, no lie coochie juice was flying everywhere. This was amazing, I cherished every second, a lil nigga was even sniffing the air after they moved away from me. The sweet scent of grown woman vagina was taking my young ass to Heaven.

Before long one of them even turned to me and said, "Smack it," in this sexy ass voice as she twerked in front of me, throwing her ass in a circle slowly. So yeah, you already know what the fuck I did. I smacked that motherfucker, yep smacked the hell out of it. Boy, I remember cocking back damn near leaving my left hand print on her shit. Her ass started jiggling like a damn tsunami as my eyes followed the wave. Of course I aint see my face but I'm pretty sure my damn jaw was on the floor. Safe to say, I was hooked, I must've smacked her ass at least 48 times, at least.

Oh yeah, I guess I was throwing a little money too, but after about the 8th dollar, I started scooping them motherfuckers back up when she won't looking. Fuck that, I had to make that shit last. I had just learned in school about conserving and that's exactly what I was planning on doing, conserving that damn money. Yeah them hoes looked good, but I was 14 and broke, I was gonna need that change later.

Not sure, but I think the stripper caught on considering she walked away with an attitude. But who gives a fuck. Besides, that's when I saw Uncle Red with this phat ass dancer, I'm talking Buffy the Body phat. You gotta remember, this was back in the day, we aint know nothing about ass shots. This bitch was a stallion. I stared amazed as I peeped Uncle Red whispering in her ear, pointing at me before handing her a wad of cash.

Before I knew it, she was strutting over to me, fucking me with her eyes the entire time as I stared.

"Whatsup Von," she said.

"Whatsup," I followed, taking a huge gulp as sweat trickled down my forehead.

I blinked for no more than a second before I discovered her leaning closer to me, reaching down, slowly unbuckling my jeans. I had no clue what the fuck was going on. I looked around slowly, I was the center of attention. I already know what everyone was thinking, 'How was this little nigga gonna act?'

Can't lie, I was asking myself the same damn thing. Intimidated aint the word, I was petrified, but I fought it, blocking out everything around me, I looked the stripper bitch right dead in the eyes as she licked her glossed out lips. In an instance my dick was out of my underwear.

Yeah it may have been a bit weird being exposed in front of a room full of old niggas but I'm telling you, this bitch hypnotized me or something, they were irrelevant, my body was stuck.

Then, outta nowhere she whips out a condom from her boot, ripped that motherfucker open with her mouth before slapping it down on my dick, all while pulling my pants all the way down to my ankles. Man, this girl had to be a part time magician or something, I swear, and for her final trick she made my dick disappear inside of her, reverse cowgirl style.

110

Ying Yang Twins 'Whistle While You Twerk' blasted through the stereo as she rode me slow than fast, fast than slow, ass clapping the entire time. Now, in the beginning, if my memory serves me correct, I was acting a little timid, but I broke out of that shit. Something came over me, a hulk like instinct took over and suddenly I was pumping my little ass off, beating that stuff down.

The crowd was going wild, soon it became hard to even hear the music, everyone was cheering me on.

"Fuck that Bitch!"

"That's what the fuck I'm talking about."

"I got next."

Then it happen, I came. Honestly, the whole ordeal was probably only about 45 seconds long. But to me, it was forever, I cherished each Nano second. In the end, I remember falling back on the couch, drained, paints down, dick still hanging as I stared off dreamy eyed into space.

Till this day I never asked Uncle Red why he decided to pay for the pussy for me, shit I guess I never really cared, all I know is that I owe him one, his old ass changed my life forever.

He aint the only one to change my life though. Uncle Roman, Aka Uncle Rome, better known as Mikes Dad was somebody who I owed everything to. Unc's been putting me up on game since I was a youngin. Just a hell of a nigga. Can't even think of nothing bad you could even say about the guy. If you ask me, he's the main reason Mikes successful now.

Sometimes I wonder if the reason I'm not where I wanna be is because I didn't have a Dad like him. Don't get me wrong, I aint mad at my Ol Man or anything like that. I'm over it honestly. The older I got the more I understood. Aint his fault. I blame the military. Whatever he saw in that War he went to back in the day fucked him up, bad.

I remember playing sports, mad every Saturday because my Dad wasn't ever at any of the games. Just seeing Uncle Rome and all his friends cheering Mike on, wearing his own personal jerseys and shit made me jealous. I never really showed it, I always prided myself on being strong, showing no weaknesses, but deep down inside I dreamed of trading places, even if just for a day. I would have given anything to feel that type of love.

Now it wouldn't be fair of me to talk shit about my Pops and not say anything about Uncle Rome's shortcomings. Naw he wasn't perfect. Like everyone, he had his flaws. He drinks a little too much, can't keep a woman to save his life and to this day, I still can't remember him ever having a real, steady job.

Most would call him a hustler. No, not one of those big time King Pins or nothing, a lot of times he wasn't even selling drugs, when I say hustler, I literally mean hustler, he was the type who you could basically catch doing anything for a buck. Nothing outrageous, just normal hood

Ol Head shit; painting, cutting grass, laying carpet. I guess you could call him a jack of all trades, master of none type nigga.

At the end of the day I don't believe he really cared too much about mastering anything besides being a Father, and he damn sure accomplished that goal. Even when he didn't have much money he still made sure he spent time. Time is important. Every Sunday he took me and Mike to watch the Cowboys game with his homeys. And at least one Friday out of the month he'd take us to the Cinema Cafe.

Now that I think of it, he might be part of the reason I'm an actor. He was big on movies. He knew fun facts about the directors and everything. And it never failed, every time we left the Cinema he'd talk about what we'd saw the entire ride home. I liked that because most of the time he took us to Rated-R movies and at ten years old I more times than not didn't know what the fuck was going on. Him explaining shit was right on time.

He had this special way of making the films seem so realistic. As if it won't just some make believe bullshit or something, he made it special. It was kinda like he took me to a whole new world, a world that I would find more at home than the one I was actually occupying. I remember going to the crib and counting the days till the movies we watched would be coming to video. I'd feign to get a second chance to watch it with my newly acquired knowledge. Eventually I started studying the characters and wondering why they made certain decisions. I didn't know what I was doing back then but I'll never forget it. It came so natural to me. I'ma always have love for Unc for that, he basically introduced me to the reason I feel I'm on this earth.

Walking next to him was another one of his good friends, Uncle Pit. I can't say too much about Pit. I really only saw him on those Sundays when we all watched the Cowboys growing up. But what I do know is that Pit was one of the craziest Ol Heads I've ever came in contact with. Just wild as hell, opinionated like a motherfucker. Most of the time he was wrong as two left feet but to tell the truth I don't really think he gave a damn, his old ass just liked to argue. Fuck it though, he was always the life of the party so nobody really cared that he didn't know what the hell he was talking about.

He and Uncle Red were first cousins who acted more like twins. I guess I'd say he was the evil one though. Not so much in a bad way, he was just raw. Uncle Pit was just the type nigga you needed to have a good ass time. Not an hour went by without him doing something off the wall.

The wildest shit I ever seen him do was that night I lost my virginity. After I bust my nut, the party continued. And I don't know for sure but I'm guessing he aint want no 14 year old out doing him, so he took it upon himself to take it up it up a notch.

Ok, so close your eyes, picture this, light skin stripper, tattoos all over her body, not some of those jailhouse ones either, I'm talking nice ones. Thick as hell in all the right places, butt naked on all fours, spinning, twerking, just doing her thing. Everybody enjoying the show, having a great time, before out of nowhere, Pit is on the floor with her, face in her booty.

Yeah, you read that correctly, I said face in her booty, I swear all I saw on him was neck and shoulders, he was all in her shit. I aint know what the fuck was really going on. Up until that night, I didn't even know eating booty was a thing. Never heard of it. Shit, I was at the age where eating pussy was still disgusting to me, but boy did this motherfucker school my ass.

I don't know if I was in shock or what but a young nigga couldn't take my eyes off of it. Pitt was giving that bitch the hurricane tongue. And you'd think niggas would be pulling him off; nope, hell naw, niggas was cheering him on just like they'd been cheering me on earlier, maybe even harder. From the outside you'd think the nigga was about to win the 100 yard meter in the Olympics or something.

"Go Pit!"

"Eat that shit Nigga!"

"Put your neck into it!"

Whole time me and Mike just looking at each other, puzzled. Was this what being an adult was like? I gotta admit, a lot of the stuff they did I couldn't understand until I was older. But that aint one of them. I'm a grown ass man and I still don't know what the fuck would possess his old ass to eat a strippers booty in front of 20 niggas. Bruh, he aint even know if the bitch wiped good. Crazy. Aint no telling what he bouta do on this trip.

Next to him we got Sydney, but don't call him that, he prefers to go by something more suitable for a cat such as himself. 'Money' is what they call him. Now Money wasn't one of Mikes Dad's friends. He was Mike's older cousin on his Moms side. Yeah I'm on his Moms side too but Money wasn't my cousin. But yeah, he's like ten or fifteen years older than us. To be honest I don't even really know him too well. Realistically no one really does. How could they? Dudes been in and out of jail ever since I can remember.

Back in the day he was a big time hustler. Real big. Not sure if he was a millionaire but that's the word on the street. Wasn't hard to believe either. Growing up, the few times I saw him, he always had some exotic ass car, and designer ass clothes. He was clean as a whistle, jewelry used to be shining, waves used to be spinning, he was one of them niggas who just embodied success, never said legal success, but success indeed.

As a youngster I admired that shit. He was a boss. Sadly those days are long gone, he just came home from doing about 8 years in the feds. He's legit now, got some job using his welding trade he'd learned in prison. I'm glad he's on the straight and narrow. Everybody is, only one problem, he thinks he's still Balling when he's not. Last time I saw him, he kept talking about what he was doing in 2003.

Whole time I wanted to say, 'nigga that was centuries ago, nobody give a fuck about that'. But I didn't, I just listened, and commented things such as:

"Damn you was the man."

"They don't make em like you anymore."

"You said how much that shit cost?"

I got a kick out of egging him on. Truthfully it's kinda sad, it's unbelievable how stuck in the past he is. He even keeps pictures of him balling out in the club in his wallet. I swear he shows them to anyone who makes eye contact with him.

Speaking of pictures, I gotta tell you about Money's older brother, Boo. He was here too. Boo's a self-proclaimed photographer. Never been to school for it or nothing like that, he just does it. And with so many Instagram models popping up, he makes a pretty good living. He's one of those niggas who's only way to get girls is by booking photo shoots with them. Everybody knows every girls imaginary profession is a model, no matter how ugly or outta shape they are.

Still, why any girl would get naked and pay for him to take dumbass pictures of them in the most random of places is beyond me. He always kicks it to them like he's going to make them famous. I don't know why they believe that shit, the nigga's 5'4, bald with a beer gut and damn near 50 years old. He don't even look like he got any connections. Besides, if he could make them famous why the fuck hasn't he made his own self famous yet?

Fuck it though, I can't knock the man's hustle, shit, he's probably making more money than me. Besides, it's his passion. I don't think I've ever seen him in all my 27 years of life without a camera around his neck. Family functions, graduations, weddings, he's there. Actually, he's there even if you've already hired a photographer.

I'll never forget back in the day when Mike and I were younger and played football, Boo got into a fight with the photographer the team had hired to take our team photos all because he decided he was gonna take pictures too. I mean most people who desired to take personal pictures waited till the real photographer was done. But not Boo. He was right beside him, giving us directions like the professional they hired wasn't even there.

Next thing I know, the kind photographer screamed, "Get the fuck outta my way," before jabbing Boo in the jaw. All hell broke out, camera lenses and film everywhere. That day was crazy and so was Boo. Still, in a way I kinda salute it. He's doing what he loves every day and not giving a fuck what anybody says or thinks about it.

But yeah, walking behind them was Lee, he was one of Mike's best friends. Growing up he was a big athlete in the city but he got injured his Freshman year of College, so now he lives back home and works as a Teacher. I aint really hung out with him in years but I know back in the day dude had all the Girls. They all thought he was going to the league, everyone did. All that's over now. He's a married man.

He doesn't even look the same to me anymore. Looks like life's sucked all the juice up outta him. I can still picture him, baby-faced, bright-eyed, looking forward to the future. Now he's chubby, hairlines receding and his bright-eyed are slightly overshadowed by his bifocals.

But hey what can I say, at least he knows how he's gonna eat every day. He aint waiting on no phone call from no dumb ass Film Producer. Not to mention he's got a wife and kids that love him unconditionally. Sometimes that's all you need in this world. Examining his life makes me wonder if I made the right decisions. Maybe I should've took the safe route.

I don't know, but when I look over to KT, who was walking next to Lee, he kinda makes me glad I didn't. He's my age but the nigga's dressed like he's fifty. I guess it's still better than when he was younger. See, KT lost about 200 pounds, used to be a real Fat ass. And yes I do mean fat, with a capital F, dude was obese, big ass titties, neck rolls, about 7 stomachs and he wobbled when he walked. He aint never seem like he cared too much though. He joked about him being overweight more than we did.

One day really sticks out though. We had to be about 13 or 14. We were all in his garage, bored as hell. This was back when we first experimented with weed. We got high as a bitch and his fat ass started playing with this little portable leaf blower, just blowing niggas hats off, putting it in niggas faces, just little childish shit.

Then somebody said, "Leave me alone before I blow your tittie in the air."

That was all we needed to hear.

"Yo I got $5 if you actually blow it," one kid said.

"$5?" KT asked. "Hell yeah I'll blow it."

That motherfucker wont lying. He took his damn shirt off, put that leaf blower under his big ass boy boob and pressed down on the power button. Shit was hilarious, titties flying everywhere, we damn near pissed on our self.

"Hand me my cash," KT, screamed in triumph over our laughter.

This was the day KT became a hood legend. For then on we started calling him King of the Titties and the Nipples. Later that got shortened to King Tips which finally got cut to KT. Man, those was some funny ass times. My nigga KT, cool as hell, food and cars, all his ass used to talk about.

The way he spoke I woulda bet my last dollar that he would own a restaurant or a dealership or something by now. Instead he drives a Kia and works at the Norfolk Naval Shipyard. Back home, it don't get no better as far as jobs for a black man. You work at the ship yard and people think you're rich. Especially if you're a welder or painter or some shit like that. They make real good money.

I mean not as much as I could make as an actor but it's still pretty decent. I worked there once. I was just a firewatcher though. That's the bottom of the barrel. Your job is pretty self-explanatory, you literally carry a fire extinguisher all day and sit with the Welders to make sure nothing catches on fire. The thing is, nothing ever does, so you don't do shit all day. Actually nobody at the shipyard does shit all day. Outta the ten hours you're required to be present, probably about an hour and a half go to actually doing something productive, the rest of the time you were busy trying to hide out from old White Men in white hard hats. They aint do shit either, well besides getting niggas fired for doing the same shit they were doing, chilling.

115

Gotta admit, that life sounds pretty good right about now. Who wouldn't wanna get paid to do nothing? But fuck that, the boredom and lack of purpose is something I can't handle. I couldn't imagine doing it every day for the rest of my life. Fuck the money and benefits. But hey, if you got a family to feed I guess it's pretty cool. Again, I think about if I would have stayed there and worked my way up. I'd probably be making good money by now. But again, I realize I wouldn't be happy. Of course I'm not really happy right now so I guess it doesn't really make a difference. But I know you get what I'm saying.

Anyway, that right there is the gang, all of us. I can honestly say I learned a lot from them all but probably the most important lesson was, 'When arguing with black men, usually the loudest one is right'. Only problem with that, occasionally that causes fist to pop out. Fuck it though, at least it aint guns.

Ten black men on our way to a Bachelor Party in Costa Rica. This is gonna be pretty interesting.

"Motherfucking Uglathang," yelled Uncle Pit to me as we all met up.

"Whatsup Unc," I said back.

"Who the fuck is Uglathang?" asked Jay, confused.

"You don't know who the fuck Uglathang is?" replied Uncle Pit as he looked around to Uncle Rome and the rest of the old heads.

"Oh hell naw, don't tell me yall call him by his real name," replied Uncle Roman.

"Yeah Pops everybody does now," added Mike.

"Man I know you a big Hollywood actor and all but you can't forget your roots," said Uncle Red.

"I aint forget Unc," I replied.

"Hold on, yall gotta fill me in on this," followed KT.

"Man it's just a little inside joke between the Unc's," I replied.

"Hell yeah, just a little family name," said Mike.

"Ok. Ok, but how the hell you get it?" asked Jay. "I gotta hear this shit."

"Go ahead, tell them Unc," I said looking over to Pit. "I know you want to."

"Man," he said, elated. "See Big Rome took us to one of Mikes' football games back in the day. Young boys out there 6 years old with little helmets and shit. They skipped straight passed flag. So one day after the game the kids ran over to us. Mind you, we was all drunk as hell, been drinking Ice House since 8 that morning, we tore the fuck up. But yeah, like I was saying, they had just won a big ass game. So they run over to us, happy as hell," said Uncle Pit.

"Yep, I can still picture it now. Mike took off his helmet smiling and shit, then Ugla-, I mean Lavon took off his helmet and we went into shock," added Uncle Red.

"Hell yeah, I don't know if it was because we was drunk or if it was true but when I looked at Von, the first thing I said was 'Rome, Who the fuck is this little nigga? I swear he gotta be the 'Ugliest Thang in the world'," said Pit.

"Then I said, hell yeah, we bouta call that nigga Uglathang for short, and after that, the rest was history," Followed Red.

"Well as yall can see, their Karma's finally caught up to them, cause all yall old mo'fuckas ugly as shit now," I replied.

"Fuck you," said Uncle Rome laughin.

"Yeah nigga, I won't too ugly when I fucked yo mama," replied Pit.

"Yo chill," said Mike as I shook my head.

"Oh shit, my bad I forgot she passed away," replied Pit.

"You just don't know what the fuck to say out your dumb ass mouth," added, Uncle Roman.

"Fuck you motherfucker, my Mama dead too. Yall can joke about it, death is a part of life."

"Yo chill," butted in Uncle Red.

"Ok, ok, my bad Uglathang, I aint fuck yo mama," said Uncle Pit.

"I know you didn't, it's cool though I aint tripping," I replied.

"Yeah, but I did get some head," Pit followed up.

"Man," everyone yelled throwing their hands up, walking away.

"Fuck yall motherfuckers, we bouta have some motherfucking fun. Aint nobody got time to be sad," replied Pit in amusement.

He was right. I couldn't even do anything but laugh. If anybody else would have said some shit like that to me, I would be mad as hell, ready to fight, but I know these old motherfuckers are crazy. If I'ma let that piss me off I'ma be pissed the whole damn trip.

"Flight 232 boarding," came across the speaker.

"That's us," said Mike.

"Let's get this motherfucking show on the motherfucking road," said Uncle Rome.

"Costa Rica, yall motherfuckers better be ready. Big Dicks are on the way!" yelled Pit.

Not saying a word, me and the rest of the young niggas just looked to each other and smiled, these old ass motherfuckers are about to be a piece of work.

Dirty World

We boarded the flight and just like the other, I got a window seat. And just like the other, I couldn't get my folks off my mind.

Whatsup God,

I just don't get it man. Answer this, is it really a Heaven? I'm looking around, where exactly is it? I don't see no door up here. Where is it man? I'm confused. And let's just say Heaven is real. Is it true that if you kill yourself you don't go? I'm just saying, what if Alexis's pain was unbearable? What else was she supposed to do? I can understand her. I know she was probably talking to you the same way I do. Probably more. And if I know you like I think I do, I know you aint really give her too many answers. You just sit up there quiet, listening, well at least I think you're listening. This death shit is crazy, it's like I'm surrounded by it. It all started with my Mom. I swear so much shit be running through my head. Like, what were her last words? Was she thinking about me? So much changed when she died. Shit, so much changed since my Grandma too, I'm just out here man, alone. Ay, I can say this though, flying over the land, looking down at the world kinda makes me realize that all those times I questioned were you real, were stupid. Damn right you're real, look at this shit. It's beautiful. Only someone as great and powerful as you could be responsible for this. If you can create all this to look so flawless, why can't you make my life feel the same way? On the other hand, I'm sure all of this wasn't just made in a day. Maybe I just need a little more patience. Like always, I don't know, I'm just trying to understand. Shit, if anybody knows, I know you do. Ok, I'm done rambling for now. Just keep me safe out here. Please.

I reclined back in my seat and closed my eyes. Before I knew it, we were arriving and I was being awakened by the loud Ghetto sounds of Uncle Pit.

"Yo how old is your sister?" he asked a guy sitting ahead of him as they both stood to retrieve their carry-on luggage from above.

"This isn't my sister," the guy replied, annoyed.

"Oh," said Pit as everyone laughed. This seemed to turn him up.

"You knew it wasn't my sister," the man said in anger.

"I'm sorry, I'm sorry, well I gotta say that you have a lovely cousin," added Pit.

"She's my wife," the guy rebutted.

"Oh hell naw, I know I'm bouta get me a dime piece out here if your ugly ass got somebody like her," Pitt said as everyone continued to laugh.

Dog, dudes wife was looking so damn uncomfortable. In a way, I felt sorry for the nigga. I could tell his wife was too by the way she tapped him urging him to hurry up and exit the plane.

"You lucky you have a gang with you, I don't play," he said pointing aggressively as his wife tugged him along, making sure to never make eye contact with any of us.

"Play these nuts, you aint gonna do shit," fired back Uncle Pit as we continued to laugh as we exited the plane.

"Ay motherfucker, don't take your ass to jail out here. I aint bonding a motherfucker out for shit," said Uncle Rome.

"Oh trust me I know your broke ass aint bonding nobody out. That's why we got Uglathang up here, I heard he was the rich one," he said as everyone looked over to me.

Why the fuck did he say that shit? Instantly I began to perspire. Yeah I know, it's just a joke and all but I get real jittery and jumpy when people start talking about money. Trying to deflect the attention, I smiled and shook my head. I aint even want the conversation to go any further, fuck that.

I slow strolled looking around at the scenery, wasn't too much different than the airport back home but the air did kinda feel weird now that I was out of the country. Maybe I'm tripping but it felt pure for some reason. I took in a deep breath, soaking it all in as we walked in side. It was finally time for me to get my first passport stamp. Can't lie, a nigga was feeling a little special, like a boss or something. I can now check this off of my bucket list.

It didn't take long for everyone to get their stamps.

"Yo they gotta liquor store in here," said Mike to the crew as he pointed ahead.

"Cool, we can all get a bottle each for the crib," said KT as we entered the small store.

My heart started to pound once again as everyone picked their poison. Scanning the shelf I slowly searched for the lowest price. Bingo! I found a five dollar bottle of gin. I damn sure could afford that, but just as I was about to pick it up, Uncle Red walked up.

"Ay Ug, they got two bottles of Bombay for $30, let's go half."

"Cool," I replied even though it was far from ok. Sometimes I can be such a bitch. Why the fuck didn't I just keep it real? I dragged my way up to the counter before pulling out my cash. "Here," I replied as I handed him $15.

"Thanks," he said as he gave the cashier his Debit Card and Passport.

"Sorry but your card is declined," said the cashier.

"What the fuck. Oh hell naw, you better try that motherfucker again."

They swiped once more to no avail.

"It's probably not gonna work because you're out of the country Unc. You have to call your bank and let them know you're here," Mike said as he stood behind.

"Man why the fuck aint nobody tell me that shit," he replied, annoyed. "Hey Ug, just pay for it I got you back later."

Man hell naw. I damn sure don't trust no black man saying they gonna pay me back. But again I bitched up. Besides, it's still kinda hard telling him no, knowing that he was responsible for getting me my first piece of ass. Yeah it may have been 13 years ago, but still. "Ok," I replied.

After paying I fell back once again. Talking wasn't really something I was in the mood to do at the moment. Spending unnecessary money tends to have a way of pissing a broke nigga like myself off.

"Ay fellas, I just talked to the concierge on the phone," said Mike as we stepped outside to await our ride. "They wanted us to know that they only get paid off of tips. So whatever you can give, give it to them. They're gonna look out for us this whole weekend."

"Man fuck these motherfuckers," said Pit.

"Come on, Unc chill out," said Mike.

"I'm just playing, I got something for these broke motherfuckers," he followed.

"You always calling a motherfucker broke. Nigga I know that damn city job aint paying your sorry ass that damn much," added Uncle Red.

"Motherfucker it's paying more than that dumb ass construction job you got. Got your gullible ass outside in the cold at five in the morning sludge hammering rocks. Fuck that," said Pit.

"Motherfucker I don't sludge hammer shit, I sit in a machine all day, and what the fuck you talking about, your old fat ass has get up early too," shot back Red.

"So motherfucker, I don't do shit all day at work but pimp. You out there working for the White Man."

"Nigga you think the motherfucker who sign your raggedy ass checks aint White?"

"And motherfucker," he yelled. "I don't see the nigga. I heard yall owner walk around the site like a slave master, I'm surprised the cracker aint got a damn whip."

"Motherfucker fuck you, I'll whip you," shot back Uncle Red.

"Just a heads up for the people who don't know, these two old niggas gonna be arguing bout nothing the entire trip," said Uncle Rome.

"Motherfucker I'm getting tired of yall calling me old, yall ugly motherfuckers older than me, and your bitches look older," said Pit.

"Motherfucker don't talk about my wife," barked Uncle Red.

"Nigga fuck you and her, I went to your house the other day and aint smell nothing but Bengay and mothballs," followed Uncle Rome to Uncle Red.

"What the fuck is Bengay?" asked KT.

"Man oh hell naw, we can't even joke around these young motherfuckers, they don't know a damn thing," said Red.

"Young ass pill popping motherfuckers. I heard about yall," followed Uncle Pit. "Which one of you young motherfuckers snuck some of that lean over here?" asked Pit.

"Unc we don't drink no damn lean," added Mike.

"What the fuck?" Pit shouted. "What kinda young motherfucker's aint getting high? Square ass niggas. You hear that fellas," he added as he looked over to Uncle Red and Rome. "We cooler than these young motherfuckers."

"So you trying to tell me we're not cool because we aren't getting high?" asked Jay.

"Motherfucker, damn right. Because you best believe I'ma ask one of these Spanish speaking motherfuckers where the motherfucking Cocaine at," shouted Pit.

"Motherfucker you aint did no Coke in damn near 30 years. Fuck around and die out this motherfucker," said Uncle Rome.

"Well if I die it was my time. Hopefully I have a big booty hoe right beside me rubbing my nuts. Tell my wife I said I love her."

"Nigga you crazy," said Uncle Red.

"I aint crazy. Yall the motherfuckers who crazy. Mad at me because I said I'm getting high. Fuck yall, I'm getting high till I die. I've actually been thinking about starting to smoke crack once I turn about 70, fuck it."

"Motherfucker you sound silly as hell," added Uncle Rome.

"Nigga how? You ever seen a sad crackhead, them niggas be happy as a motherfucker, full of energy. Yall motherfuckers got the world fucked up, when I go out I'm going out just like them. Aint leaving nobody a motherfucking dime, my money's going to the Dopeman."

"So you aint leaving your kids nothing?" asked Lee.

"Did you hear me motherfucker? I said not a dime. I love em but fuck em. My Daddy aint leave me shit, they better get it like I got it. Like I said, I'm getting high till I die. Bury me with a Redskins jersey and a crack pipe."

Everyone laughs.

"See yall laughing at this fool, that's all he wants yall to do," followed Uncle Rome.

"He gotta be the dumbest motherfucker on earth. Who the hell says they want to get hooked on the most addictive drug known to man before they die?" added Uncle Red.

"I wouldn't say it's the most addictive," Jay butted in.

"Young nigga, this is above you, I seen crack since the day it came out. That shit has took down whole family trees," replied Uncle Red.

"I'm not saying it's not powerful. I just wouldn't say it's the most addictive high," replied Jay.

"Yeah, I'd probably say heroin," added KT.

"Naw I wouldn't say that either," followed Jay.

"Then what the fuck is it?" asked Uncle Rome.

"Happiness," answered Jay.

"What?" we all blurted.

"Happiness, think about it. It's the one high that we've all felt. Its addicting and will have you doing anything to get it. A lost motherfucker will follow just about anybody who seems to know the way to it. Shit, we get in relationships with toxic ass people because more than likely they once made us happy. That's when we find our self chasing that very high they once gave us because we fear deep inside that their might not be anyone else who can truly give it to us. If you ask me happiness is a motherfucker."

"Yo Mike where the hell you find this weird ass nigga?" asked Uncle Pit.

"See, yall just don't know how to think outside the box," added Jay, pointing to his dome.

"Naw young nigga, I think Pit's right, you might just might be weird as hell," followed Uncle Red.

"I aint saying you weird bro, I just don't quite see it," said Mike.

"Yall tripping, happiness dictates everything. It's even the reason these little niggas out here gangbanging and selling drugs and shit. Those guys aren't animals, they're just sad and lost, yeah they might hurt people in the process but at the end of the day all their doing is something that they feel could potentially make them happy."

"Man aint nobody tryna hear that shit," said Uncle Red as he waved Jay off.

"Yo here come the van guys," yelled Mike.

"Fuck yall, yall aint gotta listen to me," said Jay, feeling ignored.

"Trust me, we won't," added Uncle Pit.

A big ol grey van pulled up squeaking before two natives hopped out mean mugging. Not too sure if they looked like that to scare off tourists or they were just crazy. I'm gonna go with

123

just crazy, who knows what kinda shit they had to endure growing up around here. I know one thing, I aint testing they ass.

"We don't know if they told you but we only get pa-," said one of the drivers.

"We know, we know," interrupted Uncle Pit. "Yall motherfuckers want some of our dollars."

"Yes," he replied as his partner stood nodding his head.

"Man yall think yall slick, yall dollar aint worth shit. Yall wanna take our little American money and get rich. I should give yall a dollar a piece. But I'm feeling kind today so I'ma give yall a five," added Uncle Red.

"Yeah, me too," followed a few more of the guys.

Not me though. I won't giving them niggas shit. Hell naw, fuck that, I needed a damn tip my own motherfucking self. Good thing I was standing in the back, out of the way, I aint need nobody all up in my business. If I don't wanna tip, then that's that, I aint got to.

"Ay Ug, give me a five all I got is a ten," said Uncle Rome, walking over to me.

"I don't have any either," I said as I dug into my pocket mistakenly pulling out a five.

"Motherfucker, yes you do," he replied.

"Oh my bad," I said as I pulled it out, taking a deep breath as Uncle Rome and I swapped money.

How the fuck did that happen? What the fuck is going on with my luck lately?

"Thanks, I'll pay it back later," he replied.

We all through our luggage onto the van and bunched in. I sat to the back with Money and Boo.

"Yo let me see your phone," Mike screamed back to me.

"For what?" I asked.

"I'm bouta play some music off it. My phones dead."

"Oh alright cool," I said as I tossed it up.

Mike turned on some tunes as everyone passed around cups and liquor. I'm not sure what the fuck them drinks had in them but niggas seemed to feel them ASAP. Before long it was damn near impossible to hear the music over the loud ass talking. Motherfuckers was wasted.

Except for me. I wasn't really in the drinking mood. I sipped a little but was chilling for the most part. I was still soaking it all in. I couldn't believe what I was seeing. Mountains of beautiful grass and trees as tall as the sky next to big ol clear lakes, I sat, mesmerized.

That was only until we made it to the neighborhoods, no lie there were dozens of miniature dollhouse sized shacks scattered alongside the road. Just when I was feeling sorry for myself, thinking I had it bad, I was humbled. I couldn't even imagine living like them. Kinda made my car look like a mansion.

As a member of the human race, it was impossible not to slightly feel their pain. Trapped in a third world country with no way to really ever escape. They stared and pointed to the van as they paused, stuck in a daze as if we were being transported in a spaceship. I stared back, locking eyes with a young boy before quickly turning away, ashamed. How could I ever complain? To them I was rich, still something in me knew that inside I was probably more broken then they would ever be.

As we drove further along, my mind wandered. What really was the difference between them and me? Didn't take long for it to hit me; hope. I had hope that things would change. Not only that but I had the luxury and blessing of tasting a piece of success. That right there is enough sometimes. The fact that I knew that success existed gave me hope that I could somehow acquire it once again.

Hope, I never knew how powerful it was until now. It can force you to find a way to get back to the glory days or worst case scenario, sink you into suicide. But shit, I'll take having once had success and losing it to never having none at all. At the end of the day the memories will never fade and sometimes that's all you need. This instantly boosted my spirts. Shit, I may not know where I'm going, but at least I have clear knowledge on where I've been.

On the other hand I still felt afraid. If God can make them suffer for the majority of their life, who's to say my suffering won't be forever. Scary. Fuck it though. I shook off the thought and snapped out of my zone right when 'Futures' 'Mask off', came blaring through the speaker.

All of us young niggas went crazy rapping along to the music only to be interrupted.

"What the fuck is this bullshit, turn this dumb ass shit off," demanded Uncle Red.

"Hell yeah," added Pit. "Turn some motherfucking R. Kelly on or something."

"Hell naw we aint listening to that damn child molester," followed Lee. "Fuck that."

"Yeah Unc, you got daughters, how could you listen to that shit?" added Mike.

"Motherfucker I still wear cotton after my ancestors picked it for years," replied Uncle Pit.

"Unc that aint got shit to do with nothing," added KT.

"Yeah that's not really the same thing Unc," followed Mike.

"Ok motherfucker maybe it aint, I'm drunk, but all I'm saying is since when motherfuckers start caring about the law like that?"

"It's not really the law, its just-," attempted Lee.

"Motherfucker what is it? Because to me it sound like yall a bunch of damn hypocrites. We just listened to yall get all hype to motherfuckers screaming 'fuck the Police', but now yall motherfucker's care about the law."

"Unc it's not the same," said Mike once again.

"How? I don't see no motherfucking difference."

"You tripping Unc," added Lee.

"Naw, even though he just talked all that shit about me, I actually kinda see his point," butted in Jay.

"So you would let an old ass nigga fuck your daughter?" asked Lee.

"Hell no. But I get why he's saying we're hypocrites," answered Jay.

"How?" followed Lee.

"Yeah I gotta hear this," said KT.

"Tell em young blood. I knew I liked you," said Uncle Pit. "I was just joking when we called you weird."

"See, to me his problem isn't sexual," stated Jay.

"What?" exclaimed KT.

"Chill, let me explain. To me his issue is control and manipulation. It's fucked up that he's doing it to young impressionable girls. But people in everyday life do this to helpless people all the time. On all levels. How can so many people with so many skeletons in their closet judge him? What really makes him so different than all of us? If he's so bad, why the fuck we aint mad at everybody who abuses their powers? Because to me, it seems as if it's only a crime when us Blacks do it. When in actuality this whole country's four fathers have been guilty of far worse and they got statues and Holiday's."

"Preach," shouted Uncle Red, finally chiming in.

"See that's exactly what I was gonna to say," added Uncle Pit.

"Naw man, I guess I can sorta kinda see your point but fuck that, dude was pissing on kids, niggas a disgrace. He was dead wrong, simple as that," followed KT.

"Not saying he isn't, but at the end of the day if everyone who used Control and Manipulation to get what they want is bad than lets lock everyone away. I guess what I'm saying is we need some balance. It's hard to really gage what's right and wrong in this country because skin color and money alter a lot of situations."

"Yeah, I hear what you're saying but like KT said, it aint no way I can get over him fucking young ass girls, that shit is disgusting," added Lee.

"Nigga and so was your Granddaddy," added Uncle Red. "Everybody back in the day was Marrying and fucking on Teenagers."

"Yeah, you think they should have took their asses to jail back in the day?" added Uncle Roman? "Not saying its right. But—."

"But nothing. I thought you was better than that Mr. Rome. I can't really speak on how they was living back then," interrupted, KT. "We're talking about today, and in today's time that shit is wrong."

"Well to me, if the shit's been going on for centuries, I think we need to find a solution to the problem. Because obviously it's a serious issue if niggas can't break the trend," added Jay.

"Man fuck all that. Yall talking too much. I'm about to turn on some Jay-Z. I know we all can agree to that," said Mike.

"Hell yeah," added Lee.

"Cool, we can do that," agreed Uncle Pit.

"That's my motherfucking nigga, him and my nigga Diddy," said KT as Mike turned on Jay-z's 'Feelin It'. "They showed me that I can do any motherfucking thing."

"I want to live just like them. Big ol bosses," said Lee as he and KT dapped up.

"Fuck that, yall niggas tripping, I want to live like Snoop," said Jay.

"Snoop?" asked Lee.

"Yeah, who the fuck wants to be like Snoop. He's cool and all but why Snoop?" added KT.

"Why Snoop? Nigga, Snoop is the fucking man. Dude gets to do whatever he wants, cooking shows, movies, game shows, gospel albums, reggae, gangster. The guy seems so stress free. That's how I wanna go out, no worries, Diddy and Jay always got too much business and shit to handle, fuck that," said Jay.

"I aint never thought about that," said Mike.

"Man I don't wanna be like none of them motherfuckers, besides maybe 50 cent," added Uncle Red.

"Unc yo old ass is older than all of them, how the fuck can you possibly look up to 50?" asked Mike.

"Motherfucker I can dream, matter of a fact, cut that Jay-z off and crank up some 50 cent, turn on 'In da Club'.

"OK," said Mike.

We all sung along as the music blasted.

"See, young blood I can get with this kinda rap," said Uncle Red as he looked back to me, I hadn't said a word. Neither had Money and Boo. We were all basically just enjoying the show.

Next Sam Cooke's 'A Change Gon Come' came blasting, we all sung that too.

"Now this some real music," said Uncle Roman.

"See Unc, you peep how we know all this old ass music," I finally said, breaking my silence. "We respect it. We just want yall to respect our music."

"Man but these was real hits, had the whole world singing em," replied Uncle Red.

"The same goes for the rappers we were just listening to. Future's a platinum artist, everybody knows his shit," added KT.

"He's platinum?" asked Uncle Red.

"Hell yeah." All the young guys said, including Money who thought he was young too.

"Alright then, maybe I'm just outta touch. Maybe I need to shut my old ass up," said Red.

"Yeah yall got it young blood," followed Uncle Pit, as he bobbed his head.

We played some more old school shit before, 'Ceo Moc and Beo Smook's' song 'Ima Dog' came blasting through the stereo.

"Say you a dog, well bitch I'ma dog and we got that dog food," all of us young guys rapped in unison.

"Oh hell naw," shouted Uncle Red. "Now this is some real bullshit. What the fuck is this?" he asked, face screwed up.

I could only laugh this time. I forgot who the fuck I was talking to. Those niggas aint give a fuck about the music. They just liked a good ol fashioned argument. I aint have time to go back and forth with these niggas. Word to Lil Duval.

That's What They Like

Before long we arrived at what I guess is their version of some sorta outside food court or something. I had no idea what most of the restaurants were, mainly due to the fact that the names were written in Spanish. I did happen to see a Subway. Can't lie, a nigga was hungry as a bitch. Still, there was no way in hell I was wasting my little money on some bullshit ass food, fuck that. Not to mention going to Subway would remind me too much of Alexis.

Niggas said earlier that we were going to stop at a grocery store later and rack up, I'll just wait to chip in on that. Aint like nothing was looking so tasty that I couldn't resist. In fact everything was looking pretty sketchy. Looks as if they'd just through this little area and these stores right in the middle of the ghetto. They knew tourist like us would have no choice but to spend money over here. Smart idea, but yeah I'll pass. Motherfuckers probably didn't have food licenses or nothing around this bitch. They probably don't even know what a food inspector is.

"What the hell we stopping here for?" asked Uncle Pit, looking around. "I better not have paid all of this money to be living in the damn hood."

"Naw Unc this is where we have to stop to pay for the ATV's," replied Mike.

"Hell is a damn ATV?" asked Uncle Red.

"Unc I told yall all about it in the group chat," answered Mike.

"Nigga I aint know how to read that damn group chat," Uncle Red blurted. "I aint know what the fuck yall was talking about half the time, after a while I stopped reading the motherfucker."

"Unc, it's just like texting one person," said Jay.

"Man we come from the days where you just call a motherfucker," said Uncle Roman as he gave Pit and Red a high five.

"Well I ant bouta argue, the ATV is like a four wheel dirt bike," said Mike. "We gonna ride them tomorrow up a mountain."

"Why the fuck you aint just call it a damn four wheeler?" asked Pit.

"Young folk always tryna talk fancy. Just say what the fuck it is, a damn four wheeler," added Uncle Red.

"Yo are we gonna argue about every little thing?" asked Mike, annoyed.

"Maybe. Sometimes us Old Heads gotta keep yall young motherfuckers on your toes," replied Pit.

We laughed.

"Well like I said, we all gotta give $100 apiece. Yall can get a bite to eat while you're over here," said Mike.

We all rushed off the van as Mike stood outside, directing everyone to the shop where they would put down their money.

I got the fuck outta site. I aint know how I was gonna break it to Mike but I was going to have to let that nigga know that 'Uglathang' won't participating. Fuck that, yeah it sounded like fun, I'd love to do it but forking over $100 would be damn near everything I had. Sorry. They was gonna have to just fill me in later when they got back or something. Better tell Boo to take some good ass pictures, to tell the truth I don't give a fuck what they do, I just know my black ass aint gonna be involved. Sorry Cuz.

I crept over to the restroom. My stomachs been bubbling, plus it was a perfect opportunity to hide out in the stalls until it was time to get back in the van. Once inside I wrapped the toilet with tissue and sat my ass down before my silence was broken by Money and Uncle Pit's loud asses.

"I can't believe we just paid $100 to ride up a damn mountain," barked Uncle Pit as they both walked over to the stalls.

"Shit, that aint nothing, I remember blowing 20 g's in Puerto Rico one year."

"Hold on Motherfucker, I aint come here to hear you talking about 1996 again. You did that shit last time we was together. I've been enjoying myself since you and your motherfucking brother been quiet. Don't ruin it for me."

"Motherfucker fuck you. What you mad because I use to be a rich nigga?"

"Keyword, used to be."

"Nigga I still got money."

"What? Monopoly money."

"Fuck you."

"Nigga Fuck you, I'm just telling you what everybody else wants to. If you gonna keep talking about the past, than just keep your mouth shut like you been doing. Nobody cares about what you had. What in the hell do your ass got now?" asked Pit as they both flushed the toilets and walked over to wash their hands?

"Yo fuck you and anybody who got something to say to me. Niggas out here counting my motherfucking pockets. Fuck yall. All yall, yall don't know what the fuck I got. I'm straight, I got some of the most exclusive fabrics in America," he said as he flashed his Gucci belt.

"Nigga that old ass designer bullshit you still got from before you went to the Pen don't count. What do you have that means anything?"

"Nigga don't worry about me. What the hell you got?"

"A home. And I'm about to get me a Lexus. And I'ma clear out my whole garage. Aint shit gon touch it. I don't even want nothing within ten feet of the motherfucker."

"A Lexus? I had one of them."

"Here we go again," said Pit as they walked out.

I sat, impatiently waiting their departure until finally the sound of the door slamming came ringing through my ears. I stepped out of the stall, annoyed. Fuck everything they were talking about. How in the hell are both of them motherfuckers doing better than me? Jealous once again, I slid out of the bathroom head down, I know I can't keep letting little bullshit like that get to me, but I can't lie, shits hard. How the fuck is everybody blessed but me?

Once I got back outside, everyone was making their way back onto the van. I walked past everyone, ignoring the new conversations. I'm not sure what they were talking about but it had to be about Cash or something because Money was fully engaged. Boo still wasn't talking but I can tell he was prepared to defend his brother at any moment. From what I can remember that's how their relationship had always been.

We drove a little further before hitting the local Grocery Store "Mas X Menos'. It was just like the stores back home except they had Spanish names for everything. Instead of Doritos they had 'Bravos' and instead of Sprite they had 'Fresca' and so on and so on.

I'd heard the money went further but apparently not when they saw Americans, just like true hustlers the prices were boosted up for tourist. With me being a former criminal I'd already figured they was gonna try and finesse us. They knew we aint know nothing about their dollar. I guess everybody wasn't as prepared as I was.

"Yo this aint my right change," screamed Jay to the cashier.

"Huh?" replied the cashier as if he couldn't understand.

"You heard me motherfucker. I just looked up the money exchange, you owe me more."

"Sorry," the cashier said as he reached into his drawer and gave Jay what I'm assuming is his correct change.

"Nigga aint no sorry. You knew what the fuck you was doing. If not you would have argued or something. I should whip you ass," Jay said as he jumped at the cashier.

"Ay young blood, I told yall earlier I aint got no bond money for none of yall," said Uncle Rome. "You go to jail and you're on your own."

"You're right Unc," said Jay. "I aint tryna be stuck over here."

"Hell naw you aint, end up some sex slave or something," said Uncle Pit as he handed the cashier his items.

After everyone copped, we all hopped back into the Van in route for our crib for the next three days. Soon we arrived. Dog, I couldn't believe what I was seeing. Crib was big as shit. And not just big, gorgeous, luxurious, man basically any fly word you can think of. The darkness of the night sky made for the perfect back drop. I could hardly believe what I was looking at. This shit was too dope. Never in a million years would I think I'd be staying in some shit like this. I guess I gotta up my expectations. Thank God Mike's always thinking big.

It was like a Villa or something. There were two big ass cribs facing each other being separated by a 12 ft. pool with small bright lights circling around with a heated Jacuzzi at the head of it. Scattered around were little palm trees with big healthy leaves that sorta floated in the night air as a cool breeze slightly hit.

"Yo is all this ours Mike?" asked KT in amazement.

"Yeah, both of these houses?" asked Boo as he snapped shots with his camera.

"Yep fellas. For the next three days, we're gonna live like kings."

"You the man Son. I gotta go check out the rooms," said Uncle Roman. "You the motherfucking man."

"Hold on Dad, we gotta listen to the concierge first."

I looked to my left and there appeared a woman. A beautiful woman. She fit in with the scenery perfectly. If someone would have told me that the Architects who designed the resort were inspired by her I'd have no choice but to believe them. I didn't have much, but she had the type of beauty that would make a nigga give his last. She had a glow, one that comforted you upon site. It was like her soul was visible and I knew I could trust her with my life. I know that sounds like a lot for a first impression, but I'm telling you, it's true.

As I looked around it was clear everyone else felt the same, every eye widened, studying what may be the most exotic creation in the entire country. The more I looked at her the more intrigued I became. Damn. Her butter smooth complexion, sparkled like the stars in the night as her thick, jet black hair flowed like the ocean. And her smile, wow, don't even get me started, it didn't take long before I found myself lost in her presence. Mind you this was all before she even spoke a word.

"Hello fellas," she said in a signature Costa Rican accent.

"Whatsup," said everyone.

"My name is Stephanie and I will be your evening concierge. I will handle all of your needs."

"Oh really," said Uncle Pit.

"What if I got some special needs?" added Uncle Red.

"Then I will handle them," she said with a smile.

"Oh snap, I see Stephanie bouta get all my damn money. Fine ass," said Uncle Roman.

"Look so good I'll fight your Baby Daddy over your heart right now," shouted Uncle Pit.

"No, no, no," she said still smiling. "I'm not that type, but I will provide you the services you desire. But first let me run down a few of the house rules."

"Run em down baby, run em down," said Boo as he stood back snapping pictures.

"Ok, we will be at your service between 10 a.m. and 3 a.m. If you need to run to the store, go into the city, or if you would like us to bring over one of Costa Rica's many beautiful Women, feel free to ask. I work the night shift and in the morning, my friend Maria will come, this is our driver Antonio," she said as she pointed back to a Man who was standing by the van. "Also any damages will be taken out of Mike's deposit, so please be careful."

"You hear that young niggas, yall know yall the only ones she's talking to," said Pit.

"Shit, yall the damn alcoholics, yall better not trip and fall and break something," added KT.

"Youngblood we been drinking before your mama drunk your daddy cum," Pit shot back.

"Yo that was too far. Whatsup with you and these damn mama jokes," replied KT.

"Nigga everybody mama sucked dick, stop being sensitive," barked Pit.

"Yo can yall let her talk?" interrupted Mike.

"My bad Stephanie, continue," said KT.

"Ok like I said, those are basically the house rules," she continued before appearing to think. "Another thing, I don't advise any of you to go into the city alone. It's pretty dangerous. The locals have been known to kidnap easy targets. Also beware of pick pocketer's, the locals are very poor here and will steal anything they can get their hands on."

"What about you, you need some money? I don't even care if you pick my pocket," asked Uncle Pit.

"You can pick anything you want on me baby," followed Uncle Rome.

"Hell yeah," followed Jay.

"You guys are funny," she said smiling. "I hope you enjoy your stay. You are free to check out your rooms now."

We all dipped out to the estate. I walked slowly, marveling at my surroundings, trying not to miss a thing. Bright lights shined throughout. I've never been but this must be how the homes in the Hollywood Hills or Las Vegas look. I didn't even get a chance to make it up to the room before I heard everyone yelling.

"Yo I aint never going home."

"This is the shit."

"I'ma fuck the shit outta somebody on this big ass bed."

For some reason something told me to look up, I wasn't sure but from my view it looked as though there was a bed on the roof. Had to see if my eyes were deceiving me. This shit was too lit. I jetted up the steps, if I was right I had to have it. Quickly I arrived and to my luck it was. Who would have thought to put a whole bedroom on the roof top? In all my years on earth I've yet to see anything like it. There was a king sized bed, nightstand and even a shower. It was even a see through Canopy sitting over the top of the bed so that you could see the stars before you fell asleep at night. This was crazy.

Besides having some little dingy ass Chihuahua dog that wandered around, this place was perfect. Actually I was so damn lonely I picked the motherfucking dog up, he'd followed me up the steps. I needed a friend right about now.

"Whatsup little nigga. What's your name?" I asked as he stared at me innocently. "Well since you don't know, I'ma call you-," I said as I thought for a second. "I'ma call you Lucky. Hopefully you'll bring me some while I'm out here or something."

Lucky didn't object to the name and soon we both fell back and looked up to the night sky as my mind drifted off.

Whatsup God,

Ay I'm glad you allowed me to come out here. I talk a lot about what you haven't done and what I'm angry about but maybe this is just what I need. I already feel weight lifted off of my shoulder that I haven't felt in a while. For the next three days I'll be stress free. I'd kinda forgotten how this felt. Feels amazing. I just gotta stop thinking about what's awaiting me back home. It's hard though. Man please let me really get this role when I get back to the states. I need this opportunity. I don't know what I'll do if I don't get it. I don't wanna go back to my old criminal ways. And I can't go back to Virginia. Everyone thinks I'm someone I'm not. I know I'd be able to get a job. But I just don't want to have done all of this for nothing. You of all people know what I've been through. Shit, I thought you had been the one giving me the signs to keep going. I still remember back when I lived in New York, my rent was due and I didn't have a job or way to pay it. You got me a painting job that paid $500 that day. Or what about the time when I first moved there and you gave me a place to stay even though I only had $300 in my pocket. Shit like that told me that I was doing the right thing, it assured me that I was on the right track. That's basically why I've been waiting on you. You really never made me wait this long though. That's what's got me worried. I've been walking on faith this long though. Guess I gotta just keep on walking. It hurts though. But I'm gonna just enjoy this trip. Again, hopefully you place it in the Producers heart to give me a call by the time I leave. Please Lord I need you.

"Yo this motherfucker done found the best seat in the house," said Mike as he walked up.

"Yeah man. I think I need this," I said as I sat up, releasing Lucky, allowing him to run off. "Kinda feel free, nigga been caged in for a minute now," I followed as I joined Mike. We both leaned back against the rail.

"I know Cuzzo. That's why I'm glad you came."

"Yeah man me to."

"I don't tell you this enough but I'm proud of you man. You're living your dream. You know how many people would kill to do that?"

"Yeah man but sometimes I wish I was more like you," I replied.

"Trust me you don't, this whole corporate America shit aint really what it's cracked up to be."

"Gotta be better than chasing some fairytale ass dream."

"Fairytale? Cuz, you're more successful than any actors I know."

"We gotta be real though Mike, you don't know any other actors."

"That's true," he said, snickering. "But man you're going on auditions, working on Plays, most Actors probably don't even make it that far."

"Yeah I guess I can see what you're saying. It's just that this shit gets overwhelming sometimes. It's like I'm chasing something a million miles away with no map. I feel like I know exactly where I want to go but I have no clue on exactly how to get there."

"Yeah but to me that's so fucking raw, that's cool as hell. Think about it, you made it this far without even knowing how you're getting where you're going, obviously you're headed in the right direction. You got this man, you're smart as hell."

"Thanks Cuz, but naw you're the smart one, you went and did something that you knew could last a life time. There was a clear path on how to get where you wanted to go, go to high school, graduate, get your bachelors, and go get a masters and bam you were bound to get a job. While me on the other hand, I can do everything that I saw Denzel or any other successful actor do and still not get famous. I swear man, broken dreams lead to broken hearts. You made the right choice dog."

"Man fuck that, you're gonna make it. No doubt."

"I hope man. It's just sometimes I think I chose the wrong path, maybe I was wrong about my life, maybe acting isn't my thing. I don't even think I'm the kinda guy those White Execs are even looking for."

"First of all, one thing I learned about white folk, whenever you're wondering what they're thinking, trust me their only thinking about one thing; money. They don't care about how you look, where you're from, their only question is can you make them some Cash, be an asset."

"Yeah, I guess you're right."

"I am. And trust me I don't know if I made the right decision either. I wake up every day and have to listen to White folk tell me what to do. Seems like all they do is use you up and take all the credit for it. They act like I'm just doing my job when I make the company money. But then they overwork me and don't give me the proper employees and damn near act like their ready to fire me when I don't do something right," Mike said, shaking his head. "But you, you get to wake up every day and go do what you love."

"You love doing what you do to don't you?" I asked.

"Bruh, do you even know what I do?"

"Shit, hell naw," I replied. "I just know you're getting money and you gotta wear a suit every day," I replied, jokingly.

"Crazy thing is, that's all everyone knows. In a strange way, that's sorta all I know too. I always thought going to college and getting a corporate job was all I needed to be happy, but man, waking up to do something I hate every day is taking a toll on me. Kinda feel like I'm missing something. I don't feel like I'm helping the world in anyway. Like I'm not fulfilling my purpose."

"Damn. So what do you wanna do Cuzzo?"

"I'm still tryna figure that out. That's why I admire you man. You may not have as much materialistic bullshit as I do at the moment. But you know who you are and what you're here for. You're ahead of the game man. It's only a matter of time before you're a millionaire."

"Man, I hope so. Thanks Cuz."

"Naw thank you, watching you chase your dream motivates me every day to find my true passion. I admire you Cuz. You're strong. You're on the right path My Boy, you're gonna make it so them white folks have to come to you, trust me."

"Man I admire you too dog. Always have."

"Well I guess we can both learn a thing or two from each other," said Mike.

"Yeah I guess you're right. I really needa learn how to pick women like you though," I followed.

"Man-."

"It's cool,' I said, cutting him off. "I know you don't know what to say. To be honest, I don't either."

"Did Alexis ever give you any signs that she would do something like that?" Mike asked.

"Well I guess she did, I don't know. Maybe I was too caught up in myself to notice."

"You don't blame yourself do you?"

"No- I mean ye-, man I don't know. Shit, I don't really know anything nowadays. My mind is all over the place."

"I bet man, you know I'm always here if you needa talk, a place to crash or just anything."

"I know man. I'm good though," I replied.

"I'm just saying man, I love you Cuz."

"I love you too my nigga," I replied.

"Oh yeah. And you might want to holla at Erika," he said with a smirk. "She's been talking about you a lot."

"Man she's just worried about me because she heard what happened to Alexis."

"Naw man. I think it may be more."

"You think so? You think a girl like that would actually like me?"

"Bruh, I really wish you could see yourself the way the world does."

"Yall niggas gay as hell," interrupted Jay as KT and Lee followed behind him up the stairs.

"It's a room full of hoes down stairs and yall out here having emotional, heart to heart talks and shit," said KT.

"A room full of hoes?" Mike and I asked.

"Yep. And they shaking ass everywhere," answered Lee.

"Hell yeah, they call us Cho-co-latte`s" said Jay in a Spanish accent.

"Say word," I said.

"Word," replied Jay as Mike and I jetted over to the steps.

"Damn slow down, yall niggas looking thirsty as hell," said KT as they trailed behind us.

Once downstairs we casually walked into the little lounge area where everyone was kickin it. Safe to say, it was true, three Spanish chicks were half naked, dancing, passing around shots.

"Cho-co-latte`s," they screamed as we walked over.

"Hi, I'm Noa, you're cute," said a Spanish Brunette.

"Whatsup," I said back.

Yo these bitches was some real live prostitutes. I could smell dicks on their breaths from a mile away. Little cheap ass dresses, 6 inch cheap ass stripper boots and last and certainly least, cheap ass make up. To be honest they would have been better off saving their money and just coming naked, I can almost guarantee they would have looked better. Safe to say, these hoes aint

137

have shit on Stephanie. But hey, they were still females, so I can't really complain, won't like they were ugly, like I said, they were just cheap.

"Ay fuck all this booty shaking. We came here to fuck," said Mike as he looked at the old heads. They were all having a ball.

"Man these old motherfuckers, in love," Lee said as we looked around.

The Old Heads might not like rap music but they damn sure looked like they was in one of their videos. Them old ass niggas was tossing money in the air, sipping out the bottle ,smacking ass, just straight having the time of their life. It was obvious they aint felt no young skin in years. Kinda reminded me of that strip party from when I was a kid.

"Yo how did they even get over here?" I asked Lee, pointing over to one of the girls.

"They just popped up. I think that's how it's gonna be all weekend," he answered.

"Yeah once they hear Americans are in town they flock over. This whole town is full of Prostitutes, I heard girls from all over the world come here to trick on the weekends since it's legal in this town," added KT.

"So I'm assuming all these hoes cost money," I said.

"Nigga hell yeah, you think they'd be twerking on their old asses if they wasn't getting paid," followed Jay.

"So there's not any regular girls in this whole town?" I followed.

"Who knows," answered KT.

"I'm bouta go ask that girl Stephanie where we can go to find some more Females," I said. "These hoes aint even worth no money. These old niggas just like anything that looks young."

"Nigga you aint never lied," said Mike as I walked off.

Didn't take long before I found Stephanie. She was sitting with the driver in a small booth in the front of the house, listening to music through her headphones. I knocked.

She opened the door, allowing her sweet fragrance to meet my nose.

"Hey," she said.

"Whatsup, My name is Von."

"Hi Von."

"Hey," I smiled. "So exactly what's popping tonight? We need some plans."

"You not happy with the girls?" she asked as she looked down to where all of the commotion was coming from.

"Their cool, but not really my type. I know we're going to the club tomorrow but is there like any little place we can go tonight, not too much, just a good little crowd?"

"Yep, you're in luck, I think I know the perfect place."

"Cool. Cool," I replied.

"What time do you want to go?"

"Soon," I answered.

"Ok."

"You coming with us?" I asked.

"No. not tonight. I'll be riding over with you though," she replied.

"Bet."

I went back inside and told the fellas. The Old Heads were still entertaining the other women. We showered, made a couple sandwiches, got dressed and met at the van.

"Yo where are we going Stephanie?" asked Lil Jay as we all crammed inside.

"We call it the Candy Store," she replied.

"The Candy Store?" asked Mike.

"That sounds lit," followed KT.

"It is, you'll love it," she said as she smiled.

We rode, drunk as hell, blasting trap music, obnoxiously rapping along to every word before hopping out. Boy I tell you, something about that type of music forces you to feel untouchable. I aint hardly have a dime in my pocket but at that moment you'd never in a million years be able to tell. My confidence and swag were unmatched. On the way over I'd just robbed a couple plugs, sold a few bricks and fucked a couple niggas Babymamas, all before tucking my daughter away in bed and paying my Mama's rent. Won't no way you could tell me I won't the shit. Fuck what those Old Heads was talking about earlier. Aint nothing like some good ol Trap Music.

As we all strolled into the club the bright lights from above beamed down upon us. It was lit, literally. Dice games and slot machines all around and I know I might have been drinking but on God I swear it was nothing but bad bitches all over the place. No men. Well, maybe it was some men. But I aint lying, they must have been hiding or something because I damn sure aint peep em. Maybe because the bitches were overshadowing them. They were everywhere, hundreds of them, some in bunches, some by themselves, some dancing, some smoking, but most of them were busy staring at us, mouths watering, like we were tender pieces of meat.

"Yo I see why they call this shit the Candy Store," I said as everyone stood at the entrance looking around.

"Hell yeah, we got all different types of flavors in this motherfucker," said KT.

"I don't even know where to start," followed Mike.

"I do," added Lee as he walked over to a short, thick chick and her friends.

Everyone split up and started to shoot their shots.

I slowly walked through the club. This is how bad bitches must feel, girls were tugging on my shirt, undressing me with their eyes, and a couple even grabbed my dick, no lie. Now I know I have a reputation for exaggerating things, but dog, I'm telling you, this aint one of them times. I'm dead ass serious. It was kinda fly, but uncomfortable at the same time. It aint every day bitches drool over me.

No bullshit, I had to pause for a second to think of my next move, with all the liquor I'd been drinking on the way over, I couldn't think straight. Slowly, after a minute or two I finally got my thoughts together, it was time to try and bag me a female for the night. I looked around, my goal was to find the one who was the least pressed. There was no question, the hoes staring at me wanted money. That's a no deal, I'm broke. I needed me a free girl, somebody who just wanted me for me. Of course that's like finding a needle in a haystack around here. But to be fair, aint like I'm looking for the prettiest thing, shit, I'll take a nice 7, maybe even a 6, hell if she's thick I might take a 5. Truthfully I don't give a fuck. I just aint wanna be the only loser without a girl at the end of the night.

I swear this ol, 'Hiding my problems' thing is getting old, fast. Letting everyone in on the fact that I was broke as hell would take a huge weight off of my shoulders. But on the other hand I just can't keep talking to people about my problems. At the end of the day I chose this life. I can't complain. I mean I guess I could, but what the fuck would that solve. It's a fucked up feeling to need everyone around you and no one needs you. But it's even more fucked up when they know you need them. I won't give them that power over me. Fuck that I got too much pride.

"Hey whatsup," I said, as I gently grabbed a hold of some dark skinned Spanish chicks hand.

"Whatsup," said the girl as she grabbed my dick.

I knew right then and there this bitch was a Prostitute but I still had to shoot my shot.

"How you doing? You're beautiful," I said.

"You beautiful too, how bout you buy me a drink and then buy me," she said as she licked her lips, inching closer to me.

"Huh? Excuse me?"

"Buy me. I make you feel good," she replied.

"Why I gotta buy you though? How bout we get to know each other?"

"No, no, no, you pay, you pay. Look at you, I know you got money. You too sexy to be broke."

"Shit, you're too sexy to be broke," I said as I walked off.

I looked around, KT, Lee, Mike and Jay were all cuffed up with bitches all around them. They had the advantage; cash. I know if I wanna take something home I gotta work fast. I've always had a way with the ladies, it's time to work my magic. I was growing more determined than ever to get one. With every second it seemed to be getting harder and harder.

"Cho-co-late`," said two Brown skin bitches as they walked over to me.

"Whatsup," I followed.

"Why you by yourself? You need a real woman in your life," said one of them

"You're right," I agreed. "Are yall the women I need?"

"Yep. And we're running a special, two for one," said the other as she grabbed my hand and placed it on her breast.

"Man I'ma keep it real. I don't even have any money."

"You must think we're ugly. Trust me. We'll make you feel good," the first one said as they slid closer to me.

"I'm sorry I already feel good."

I darted off, ready to just give up but before I could even get 10 feet away I was grabbed by the hand. First reaction was to pull back. Fuck did I even need to talk for. I knew I wasn't gonna pay for a damn thing. But once I turned around it was obvious that wouldn't be so wise. Man that bitch was too bad. Dark skin with curly long black hair, big pretty white teeth, big ol titties, with a big ol ass to match. This may be TMI but my dick jumped just from the touch of her hand.

"Hello handsome. Why you all alone?"

"I was looking for you," I replied.

"Well here I am."

"Look," I said after taking a deep breath. "I'ma tell you the truth. I aint got no money."

"Who said anything about money," she replied.

"I'm just saying, look around," I followed as I pointed to the crowd of thirsty women. "I know what you want."

"So give it to me," she said as she got closer, rubbing her fingers down my chest as she pressed her body to mine.

"Only thing I can give you is this dick for free, which I'm sure you don't want. I'm smart enough to know aint shit free around here."

"I never said for free. But I like your ear rings."

"You want me to fuck you for my earrings?"

"Yes. I can tell they are real."

"Man," I said thinking. Looking at her, it was hard as hell to say no. Damn near impossible. Truth be told I couldn't even get the words out initially. But the fact that Alexis had bought them for me was all I had to remember. Not to mention that's all I really have of value besides my car and clothes. "Naw," I replied as I walked away.

Next I decided it would be best to just hide out. Find me a little corner and chill. Try again tomorrow night or something. All that disappointment had taken me out of the mood to even try to fuck anybody. I'm mentally exhausted. Shit, at least back home if I knew I probably wouldn't get the girl I could at least enjoy the thrill of the chase. Aint no chase around here though. It's either you got cash or you don't. And I don't. So fuck this. I aint never been a fan of wasting my time.

I chilled dolo for about 30 minutes or so next to the craps tables. I could tell I was annoyed on another level because that shit was kinda pissing me off too. Just sitting there watching motherfuckers have fun was torture. Back in my day I was what some would call a gambling addict. Never really had too much luck but those days when I did were magical. Cee-lo or craps were my games of choice. Man, the adrenaline rush of winning money is incomparable. The good ol days. I sat reminiscing before finally the guys barged over, drunkenly making their way over to me, each with a Bad Bitch on their arm.

"Ay motherfucker, hell you doing over there without a bitch?" asked Mike.

"Look at this motherfucker, same ol Von, always tryna shoot some damn dice," added Lee.

"You can take a nigga out the hood but you still can't take the hood out a nigga," followed KT.

"Fuck that. Nigga you better go in there and get you one of these Hoes," added Jay.

"Yeah, we bouta get outta here cuzzo, we'll wait for you" said Mike.

"Naw I'm good," I replied.

"Nigga what do you mean you're good? All you gotta do is grab one and say come on. It'll be the easiest piece of ass you ever got," said KT.

"Yeah come on, the van aint even here yet. You got time," said Lee.

"I'm good I'ma sit tonight out."

"Aw man you're trippin. Suit yourself though. I'm bouta get freak nasty with this bitch. You see her ass! It's fake," said Jay as he smacked her on the backside. "I always wanted to fuck a fake booty. And she said they use numbing cream on their pussy so I can beat it up," Jay exclaimed.

"Nigga how do you live in Atlanta and aint never fucked a fake booty?" asked KT.

"Yeah you're buggin," followed Lee.

"First of all don't neither one of yall motherfuckers live in Atlanta, so how the fuck yall know how easy it is to fuck a bitch with a fake booty?" asked Jay.

"Man we just know," followed Lee. "You fucked a fake booty right Mike?"

"Yeah maybe once or twice before I met Whitney."

"Well fuck yall, I'ma fuck me one tonight," said Jay. "Aint that right baby?".

"Everything you say is right Papi," his Girl replied.

"Oh my God. I think I'm in love!" Jay Screamed.

"Oh shit there go the van," said Mike as he pointed outside.

We all hurried over before piling in. Everyone sat cozied up with their girls while I instead sat up front with Stephanie.

"No girl?" she asked.

"Naw. Not really in the mood."

"Wow. I've never seen someone like you. Usually men come down here just to be dogs."

"Yeah. Not me."

"You a faithful man?"

"I don't have a girl."

"Really. Why, you're so handsome?"

"Yeah, thanks," I replied, dryly. "It's a long story. What about you?"

"No I don't have a girl either."

"Ha-ha very funny, you know what I mean."

"I know," she said, smiling. "But yes I have someone."

"What does he do?"

"A little bit of this, a little bit of that. Basically anything he can to make money. There's not many opportunity out here."

"Damn so why don't you guys leave?"

"And go where?"

"To America. It's so many opportunities out there. You can get rich."

"Are you rich?"

"Shit, I wish."

"So if you're not rich, how would I?"

"Well what I should have said is that I'm not rich, yet. It's coming."

"What are you going to do to get rich?" she asked.

"I'm an actor."

"A movie star?"

"Not quite but that's the goal. It's just so hard finding opportunities. Sometimes it seems impossible."

"Well, you want any advice?

"Sure," I replied.

"Maybe you should create your own opportunities. No one has more power over your life than you."

"Yeah that sounds good. I wanna believe it so bad."

"You have to, you've got to think positive, believe."

"It's just so hard, one of the worse parts of the journey is not knowing where you will end up next."

"Like I said, think positive. Believe."

"No offense but its easy saying 'think positive'. To me that's the words of an unexperienced person. A person like me has gone through this countless times and sometimes God takes you out of one uncomfortable situation and places you in another and there aint nothing you can do about it but accept it."

"Sounds like you need to work on your faith."

"Huh?"

"You're being tested and from the looks of it, you're failing. You gotta believe. Only the strong survive."

"Yeah I guess you're right."

"I am," she replied, confidently. "Suffering for long periods of time alone can do one or two things, make or break you. God didn't put your talent in you for you to not do everything in your power to showcase it to the world. It's sorta a sin to take it to the grave."

"I never thought about it like that," I said as I smiled, sitting back. "I like the way you think."

"Thanks," she said with a smile.

We pulled up to the spot. Everyone clumsily stepped out and headed up to their rooms. I sat by the pool with Lucky, thinking, looking up to the sky.

"You mind if I sit with you guys?" asked Stephanie after about 20 minutes alone.

"Nope," I replied as Lucky hopped from my arms, darting away.

"Cool," she said as she took a seat next to me. "What you thinking about?"

"I-."

"Make a wish, it's a shooting star," she said excitedly interrupting me as she pointed up to the sky.

"Oh shit, it really is," I replied, looking up.

"Let's close our eyes," she followed.

I closed mine.

Whatsup God,

I usually ask for happiness and stuff like that but I think I have to switch it up. I need money. Lots of it. I need to be rich. I need money.

We reopened our eyes.

"Did you make a wish?" she asked.

"Yep. Did you?"

"Yes I did," she answered. "Now you know what the key to it coming true is, right?"

"What?" I asked.

"What we were just talking about on the bus. You have to believe, have faith."

"I wish it was that simple, just believing."

"There you go again, I never said it was going to happen just because you believed in your wish. It's going to happen because you're on the path that God designed for you and you spoke it to existence. That's all it takes. He never said when it will happen but trust me it will, like I said, believe."

"You believe in what you asked for?"

"Of course. I have no choice."

"I guess you're right. I agree with everything you're saying, I just don't know. It's complicated. "

"Why Complicated?"

"I guess because they say God answers prayers. But on the other hand they say before you're born he already has a plan for your life. What if everything you ask for goes against what he has planned?"

"Yeah I understand. Calling and screaming to God really doesn't seem to matter sometimes. I'm not 100 percent sure but I think he just moves when he wants. Better yet, moves when you're ready."

"Yeah and that got me confused as to what the fuck prayer is really for. I have firsthand experience that God doesn't give us what we ask for. At least not in the first 8 years of asking. I haven't really had any experience after that."

"You gotta listen to me, maybe you just aren't ready."

"I hear you but how is that possible? I feel ready. I've been grinding my ass off for years. I deserve it. I'm tired of waiting. But hey, what other option do I have besides to kill myself."

"Don't say that."

"Not saying I will. I'm just saying."

"Can I ask you a question?"

"Ask away?" I replied.

"Can you honestly say that you've done everything you possibly could do?"

"Ye-"

"Take a second to think about it, don't answer it now, just think about it. There may be something crucial you've yet to grasp. From my understanding the entertainment business is a Devilish place, he may be getting you fully prepared for what you may face."

"Damn, I'd be a liar if I said you wasn't on to something. Maybe there are a few things I need to switch up."

"We all can stand some improvement. It's nice for someone to actually listen to me," she said looking over to me, smiling once again. "I wish I could get my Boyfriend to."

"He'll come around. Sometimes it takes us men a minute before we get our act right."

"Yeah, I hope so," she replied.

"So, what does he think about you working overnight with horny Americans?"

"He knows we need the money," she said with a slight giggle. "Besides he trusts me. I'm a very loyal person."

"Well he better hold on tight, that's pretty rare in these days and times," I replied.

"Tell me about it," she said. "Are you loyal?"

"Shit," I said as I thought for a second. "I think I am. I try to be a good person. I haven't always been. But to tell the truth, sometimes I think I was happier when I was doing the wrong things. It's like the right thing to do is always so damn hard."

"But in the long run it will pay off."

"There you go. Ms. Positivity."

"I'm sorry," she laughed. "It's not like you really have any other choice. Either keep pushing and die trying to make it or give up and regret it for the rest of your life."

"You talk like you've been here before. How old are you?"

"23."

"Only 23? Damn. You're pretty wise Stephanie. How'd you get that way. You got some regrets in your life or something?"

"I do actually."

"Like what?"

"I guess the biggest one is that I had a chance to move away. But I chose to stay and help my family. They don't really appreciate me. But now I feel as though I'm stuck. But I made my bed. I said I would do something, so I'm here."

"Just change your mind, fuck that. Your happiness comes first."

"Yeah. But remember I told you I'm a very loyal person. Sometimes it's to a fault."

"Damn. So you just plan on staying here for the rest of your life? You don't have anything you'd want to be?"

"Yeah I do actually," she said reluctantly.

"What?'

"You're gonna laugh."

"No I won't. Come on, I'm over here spilling out my feelings, it's your turn," I replied.

"Ok. Ok. A comedian."

"A comedian?" I asked with a giggle.

"See I told you."

"No I wasn't laughing at you, it just caught me off guard. I would have never expected you to say that."

"Yeah I understand, it's just to me, they are the most talented people in the world. Just think about them. The greats always are equipped with so much. Think about Eddie murphy or Jamie Foxx, they can both sing, dance and act. Its beautiful gift to be able to take some of life's pain and draw laughter from it. And trust me I have a lot of pain."

"Well I hope that was what your wish was for."

"Too bad I can't tell you," she said with a slight grin.

"Yo yo," said the fellas as they all stormed out of their rooms with their girls.

"Man that pussy was amazing," said Jay as he smacked the ass of his lady friend.

"Some of the best ever," followed KT as he did the same.

"Look at the time," said Stephanie as she checked her phone. "It looks like I'm off."

"Aw man," I replied. "It was nice talking to you," I said as we stood to our feet.

"Nice talking to you too," she replied, with her signature smile. "Good night guys."

"Goodnight Stephanie," everyone replied as she walked off.

"Yo is it me, or were yall flirting?" asked Mike.

"Naw man it's just you. She says she has a man at home," I replied.

"I'm sorry but I aint trusting no bitch around here, fuck her man," said Lee.

"Hell yeah Von, you need to hit that," added Jay.

Ignoring them, I watched as Stephanie glided away. A certain sadness came over me. Life seemed so simple when she was around. A feeling that had grew unfamiliar. Felt good. I could definitely get used to that again. Maybe there was hope for my life after all.

The Rain

"Alright everybody get your motherfucking asses up. Breakfast is served," screamed Uncle Pit. I hopped out of bed and looked downstairs. All the Old Heads were sitting around the pool drinking brews. I'd heard them for the last couple of hours but had been trying my best to ignore them. I'd forgotten how early these motherfuckers like to get up.

I stretched and yawned as I took a good look at my surroundings. The sun was already beaming down as the clouds drifted through the sky. This is they type of shit I could wake up to for the rest of my life.

Whatsup God,

Wow Lord another beautiful morning. Please let everything work out for me and allow me to have a good day.

After awaking Lucky, I slid on my slippers, through on a wife beater and headed down with the fellas.

"So yall mean to tell me the Candy Store was jumping like that?" asked Uncle Roman.

"Hell yeah Unc," said KT.

"What time does it open? I'm tryna go check it out," added Money.

"I don't know. Probably later tonight. We can go there after we leave the club. We got a V.I.P. section at the hottest spot around here," said Mike as he bit into his eggs.

"Damn that's whatsup, we bouta do it big," said Lee.

"And I definitely could use a little Candy in my life," added Uncle Roman.

"Damn right. I need to find me a new bitch. Because I fucked the shit outta my bitch last night. She aint gonna be able to take no dick for a few weeks. Bitch started screaming as soon as I stuck it in," bragged Uncle Pit.

"Hell naw," said Lee jokingly.

"Motherfucker I aint gotta lie. I'm serious, I told the bitch, you aint ready for this American Big Dick. This a foot long. Had that bitch climbing up the wall."

"Yeah your bitch was cool but them hoes aint compare to the ones at the Candy Store Unc," said Lee as he and KT hi fived.

"Man fuck that. My bitch was bad," followed Uncle Roman.

"Man fuck you and your bitch. Woke me up out my damn sleep," said Uncle Pit.

"Motherfucker how?" asked Uncle Roman.

"Your snoring ass," butted in Uncle Red.

"Yeah, I walked over to your room to tell you to shut the fuck up but once I opened the door I discovered both of yall stankin asses butt naked, spooning, cuddled up looking bout dumb as hell" added Pit.

"You slept with the bitch?" blurted out Money.

"Ya damn skippy I did motherfucker, yall got a problem with it?"

"You tripping Unc. Aint no pussy good enough to have me sleeping cuddled up with a Prostitute," added Jay.

"Fuck yall worried bout me for?" barked back Uncle Roman. "I fell asleep in her. Pussy was so damn good I cried in that motherfucker."

"Motherfucker that aint got nothing to do with how good the Pussy was. Your old ass just simple as a motherfucker. You probably ate the bitch pussy too, nasty motherfucker," said Pit.

"Motherfucker you better believe it," he yelled. "I came over here to have a good time and that's what the fuck I'm gonna do."

"That is pretty nasty Dad. But hey, I'm just glad you enjoyed yourself. That's the reason we're here," said Mike.

"Who you fuck Ug?" Pit asked me out of the blue.

"I aint fuck nothing," I replied softly.

"What?" Uncle Roman exclaimed.

"You the pretty boy actor, and you aint get you no pound?" followed Pit.

"Naw," I replied.

"You aint gay or nothing is you? I know how that acting can world be," added Pit.

"Man hell naw," I replied.

"Leave the young blood alone. I aint get no ass either," added Uncle Red.

"That aint no damn surprise, you been gay for years," blurted Uncle Pit.

"Motherfucker, aint shit gay bout me. Yeah, it might've been 30 years ago, but don't forget the fact that I fucked Shina, the bitch you wanted so bad back in high school."

"Nigga fuck you. You gay," Pit shot back.

"Motherfucker I got a Wife that I love."

"So motherfucker, what you tryna say? I love my Wife too," shot back Uncle Pit.

"Nigga all I'm saying is that this is my second Wife. I cheated on my first Wife the night before the wedding and the next night after the wedding I was right back cheating again. I fucked up a good thing by not being faithful. I aint tryna go that route again. I made my vowels and I'm gonna stick to em."

"I made my vowels and I'm gonna stick to em," Pit mocked. "Motherfucker shut the fuck up. Talking bout some damn vowels," barked Pit, disgusted. "Nigga fuck them vowels. Don't no damn vowels count when you on vacation in a foreign country. We in Costa Rica, stupid motherfucker."

"Yeah you trippin. You better get some of this out of the country ass, aint nothing like it," said Uncle Roman.

"Yeah, we know you know. You around here raw doggin Prostitutes," added Pit.

"Ay young niggas, don't be like these fools when yall get older. Two of the most simplest motherfuckers I know," said Uncle Roman.

"Fuck you," followed Uncle Red.

"Naw motherfucker don't fuck me. Fuck one of these Hoes. Old motherfucker," said Uncle Roman as he and Uncle Pit laughed uncontrollably as the morning concierge, Maria walked up. I was happy. Not just to be seeing another beautiful Woman but because I didn't want to keep going back and forth about who had sex and who didn't. I didn't feel like hearing it anymore honestly. I'd much rather listen to Maria.

"Hey guys I'm Maria, I'm the day time concierge."

She was just as breathtaking as Stephanie but I'd be a lie if I said they were equal, if that makes any sense.

"Hey Maria," everyone says.

"Trust me, we know who you are, we've been waiting for you all night," followed Pit.

"Ok," she said with a smile. "I counted ten of you but it seems you guys only paid enough for 9 guys to ride the ATV's."

"Oh no, we all paid yesterday," interrupted Mike.

Of course it was me who hadn't paid. This instantly bought an extreme nervousness over my body. Luckily no one looked over to me, I'm sure my dishonesty was written all over my face. It was becoming damn near impossible to hide the fact that I was broke as hell. With no other options coming to mind I decided it was time. Time to stand up and admit what I'd done.

"Man fuck it, I aint going anyway," said Uncle Red before I could speak.

"Why not Unc?" asked Mike.

"I just aint in the mood anymore. Fuck that shit," he said.

"You always acting soft," said Pit. "You just mad cause we're joking your ol goofy ass."

"Aint nobody paying your bald headed ass no mind. I just don't wanna go motherfucker."

"So what the fuck you gonna be doing while we're out?" asked Uncle Rome.

"Doing what the fuck I want. Hell, I might just walk in all yall rooms and fart. I aint made up my mind yet."

"Nigga you fart in my room and I'm beating your ass," shot back Pit.

"Fuck you. I might just take a long ass shit in your toilet without flushing."

"Alright, try me if you want," Added Uncle Pit.

"Yo can yall please stop fussing like an old ass married couple?" asked Money.

"Oh naw I aint the married one. I'm single in Costa Rica, that's his simple ass," spat Uncle Pit as he pointed over to Uncle Red.

"Fuck you and fuck you too," said Uncle Red to Boo and Pit.

"Fuck Me? What did I do?" asked Boo.

"I'm getting tired of you taking all these damn pictures."

"Yo leave my Brother alone," defended Money.

"Naw tell your Brother to put the damn camera up," fired back Uncle Red.

"Yo, yo, yall calm down. Yall old motherfuckers gotta stop drinking so damn early in the morning," interrupted Mike.

Tensions eventually calmed as Maria finished giving us the run down, everything was working out perfectly. I was gonna be able to keep my money in my pocket all while still joining the guys. Excited, I through on some old gym shorts and a wife beater before we all awaited the van to pull up so we could pile in.

Once it arrived everyone hopped inside. Instead of music this time we simply laughed and joked. So far, so good.

That joy didn't last long, it only took about five minutes to get down to 'Adventure Tours', the place with the four wheelers. That's when it hit me, I'd never rode one. Just the site of them intimidated me. So big, so powerful, how did I know if I could handle it? I aint never been one of them adventurous ass niggas. Shit, I was the last one on the block to ride my bike with no training wheels back in the day. I aint no bitch. I just like to be safe. I just don't really see the purpose in experimenting with unnecessary things. Feel me? But fuck it, I've never been one to back down from a challenge.

Besides, we were going to have 3 tour guides, Manny, Ramiro, and Victor. From the looks of them they appeared to have done this millions of times. They were little jungle men, long hair and athletic frames. Not sure what that has to do with driving a four wheeler but for some reason I trusted them. Together we stood in a circle gathered around as they explained to us how to work the bikes and what not.

"Ok. Is anyone afraid of heights?" asked Manny as everyone stood silent. "Good, because we will be traveling thirty miles up a mountain. I will warn you that there will be sharp cliffs that are extremely dangerous if we don't take our time."

That's what got me. Sharp cliffs? I aint sign up for all this. Shit, actually I hadn't signed up for anything. My heart sank to my stomach as I snuck a look around to everyone else, they aint give a damn, looked like they aint have a care in the world, they all stood, chilling, twiddling their thumbs, anxiously awaiting our new adventure.

"If no one has any questions, we can get started," said Ramiro.

I know I should have asked a couple. Instead I followed everyone outside where we all hopped on our bikes, preparing to drive over to the start line. It was at that moment when my ass hit the seat that I realized something extremely critical. I had hardly understood a thing he had explained to us on how to ride. Two seconds of my time could have went to asking. But of course I'm retarded. My dumbass wanted to blend in with everyone else. Now look at me, I'm about to teach my own damn self.

I sat calmly, tryna be cool, scoping out the scene, tryna see what everyone else were doing. As usual I grew impatient, and I had to try for myself. I hit the gas, thinking, 'Oh this aint so hard'.

Shit was all good up until the moment I saw a large puddle of water sitting inside what I guess was some sorta small pothole. My first instinct said press down on the break, but the break wasn't where my foot was at, instead they were on the handle bars. I panicked and before I knew it I'd ran into a big ass gang of bushes.

I looked back and everyone was pointing and laughing.

"Yo how the hell you crash before we even start?" asked Pit.

"Aw man," said Mike Laughing as he and Boo both took pictures of me.

"Are you ok?" asked Ramiro as he rushed over to my aid.

"Yeah, I'm ok," I replied.

"Good. Give me your keys," he demanded with his hand out.

"Why?"

"I've already told you how dangerous this journey is. I don't think we can let you take that risk."

"I got it. I promise," I said as I looked around to the other guys. Wont no way in hell I could let them go on without me. They were already calling me Gay because I aint fuck nobody,

I'll never be able to live this shit down. Not saying I wouldn't love to sit this one out, but this some 'Man' shit. I gotta do it. "Please," I said as I looked him in the eyes.

"Ok," he replied, hesitantly. "But you must be careful," he insisted.

"Thanks, I will," I said as I carefully backed up, alongside the other guys.

"You get in front," Manny instructed me.

I followed his orders before following behind.

Everything was going smooth. Some of the guys could ride faster than me but I didn't try to put on a show. I kept my own pace. After slamming into the bushes I knew I had to be cautious. So far so good. After a while I sorta kinda got the hang of things, shit actually became somewhat relaxing.

It was cool watching the little kids laugh and joke with one another as we rode passed farms and old rundown homes. It didn't even look as if they had electricity but they were still so happy. I smiled and nodded to them.

Soon we began to elevate higher and higher up the mountain. My ears started to pop as I stared straight ahead. Looking to my left could be detrimental. There were 100ft cliffs 5ft away from me. To say it was a struggle to stay sane is an understatement. Growing up, I've always kinda been afraid of heights. For some reason I thought I'd grown out of it. Especially considering I'd just rode on a plane. But naw, I guess the Pilot being in control put me at ease. Knowing that my clumsy, bad luck having ass is in charge right now has me worried, extremely worried.

For the remainder of our journey my goal was to stay as far from the edge as humanly possible. The road seemed to become narrower the further I rode. So much so that it got to the point where I had to completely stop because incoming cars were driving down the opposite side making it impossible for us both us to drive at the same time.

I focused every ounce of my attention onto the road. The further we drove, the more I wanted to quit. If someone would have asked me did I want to stop, without a doubt I'd tell them yes, hell yes. Fuck my pride and what everyone had to say.

Too bad I aint really have a choice. We'd come too far for me to turn around. It seemed to be taking centuries to reach our destination. After finally arriving at a small Lake I was completely exhausted. Wasting no time I hopped off the ATV next to some Natives who were selling lemonade and homemade arts and crafts. Everyone checked out their merchandise, not me though, what for, I'm broke. Ignoring them, I walked my ass right over to our instructors who were posted by the lake.

"Ok fellas, this right here is Lake Precioso," said Ramiro as everyone finally gathered around. "Anybody interested in jumping in?" he asked as he pointed over to a small cliff above the lake, it was probably about a 30 ft. drop.

"Fuck no," said Lee.

"Hell no," followed Pit.

"I will," added Mike.

"Fuck it, I will too if my son's going," said Uncle Roman.

"Shit, me too. We came here to have a good ass time and that's what the fuck I'm about to do," I followed. I couldn't let my boy go up without me.

"Cool," said Manny.

"Before you go. I do have to let you know that you need to drop straight down. Do not grab onto any of the branches from above and attempt to swing. It may look fun but its very dangerous." said Manny.

"Ok," we all said.

I stripped down to my underwear and followed behind as everyone climbed to the top. The higher we got the more I started to realize I was trippin. Who the fuck do I think I am? Tarzan or some shit? This aint me. I'm fucking afraid of heights what the fuck am I even doing up here. I cursed myself out as I stood behind Mike and Uncle Roman, awaiting my turn. I gots to be the dumbest.

"You ready?" asked Manny as Mike successfully made the jump.

"Yep," I said confidently. Mike and Uncle Rome had somehow boosted my confidence. They made it look so easy. I was ready now. "This can't be too bad."

"Remember-."

"Yo I'm good. I got this," I said interrupting. "They aint the only ones who know how to turn up," I said before taking a leap.

I moved to fast though. Damn near slipped off the rock as I leaped. Told you I was clumsy. Unable to think quickly enough, I reached up for what I thought was a tree branch. It wasn't. It was a fucking snake with a grill the size of a shark, with razor sharp teeth. From my view it looked as if he was about to swallow my entire face. Shocked and petrified, I screamed, letting go of the snake, plummeting down to the water as my legs and arms swung aimlessly in the air.

Next thing I remember I'm lying flat on the ground staring up at the sky as everyone circled around, looking down to me.

"You ok?" asked Victor.

I looked around trying to figure out what exactly had happened to me.

"Yo nigga your ass just passed out in the damn lake," said Mike.

"That's why I tried to tell you not to grab any branches," added Manny.

"Yeah nigga they say its snakes up there," said Money.

"I know now," I said as I stood to my feet shielding my face from Boo who was steady snapping pictures. "Why the fuck yall aint say that shit first."

"We tried to warn you before we started," said Ramiro.

"Yeah your ass just panicked," followed Uncle Pit.

"Fuck it at least I'm still alive. Let's get the fuck away from here," I said as Lee tossed me over my clothes.

Shit was wild. I couldn't wait to get off this damn bike, I was wet as fuck. Man, I swear, no matter how big my faith in God is, I still gotta wonder if I'm cursed sometimes.

I rode extra careful, clutching the breaks with a pliers grip, I don't know what kind of bullshit would be thrown my way next but I'm gonna be prepared.

The ride was totally different going down the mountain. Niggas was still riding fast but I won't with that shit. Hell naw, fuck that, I could already picture myself flying off the cliff, no sir, I refused to let that go down.

After what seemed like forever we were finally halfway down the mountain. We took a break at an outdoor restaurant, 'Los Amigos Jaco`'. From our view we overlooked the entire city. I stared out mesmerized at the mountains of grass and sturdy century old trees surrounding the town. I wondered what kinda animals lied beneath.

Before long we received our orders. It was crazy because Manny, Ramiro and Victor were our waiters. People always talking about Jamaicans having numerous jobs but no one ever talks about these niggas. They was working like slaves for probably pennies. Hey, at least they're working though.

And I'm not sure if they were in the kitchen cooking the food but that shit was off the chain. Real Costa Rican shit. I had a big ass plate of nachos. Shits was a scud, tomatoes, extra cheese, big ass chunks of grilled chicken, guacamole, the works. We crushed as the Old Heads got drunk.

"I remember I came here bout 20 years ago. We had all the bitches. Had a ball. Had about $50,000 on me. I was blessing these motherfuckers out here," said Money as he bit into his taco as Boo took pictures of him and everyone else eating.

"What the fuck you doing now though?" barked Pit. "All you ever talk about is what the hell you used to do. Any fool can get rich. It takes a real man to maintain it."

"Nigga you just mad because you aint never did or had shit. Get off my dick."

"Nigga I know one thing I aint never did was go to prison," replied Pit. "You think it's cool to ball all those years and then have to do prison time? That's stupid as hell. And the fact that your dumb ass always bragging about it lets me know that you aint learned shit and you'd do it again. Stupid Motherfucker."

"Nigga you don't know me. Shut your drunk ass up. You aint got but one more time to speak on my life before I straighten your fat ass out."

"Nigga you aint gon do shit. I don't give a fuck how many muscles you gained in the Pen."

"Oh ok. Show me then," said Money as they both stood to their feet before squaring off. We all rushed over to break up the fight. It was obvious Pit was drunk as hell, he'd been throwing back shots all morning. Money's big diesel ass would have demolished him, no question.

Suddenly the mood had been shifted. I couldn't wait to get back on the road, I think we all couldn't. No one said a word for at least 15 minutes, we ate in silence.

"Ay motherfucker you're too drunk to be riding down that mountain," said Uncle Roman to Pit as we finally exited.

"Nigga fuck you. I aint drunk."

"Nigga you stumbling and leaning over right now," Uncle Roman shot back.

"Yo Victor. He can't drive back," intervened Mike.

"Hold on, aint neither one of you motherfuckers my damn Daddy," Pit, replied, slurring.

"Nigga I'm bouta save your life," said Uncle Roman.

"Motherfucker fuck you," countered Uncle Pit.

"Ok. He can ride with me," said Victor as he tugged Uncle Pit along.

We hopped back on our bikes and headed down. I was more afraid than ever, the cliffs seemed to be inching closer. My heart raced as I slid down the rocky mountain. The further we rode the more the thought of never making it back crossed my mind.

For miles I drove at a turtles speed, prepared to bare down on the breaks at all times. I could hear everyone complaining how I was riding too slow but I ignore then and just let them go around me. Everything was copasetic when out of nowhere I felt what seemed to be a huge gust of wind collide with my backside.

Instinctively I turned my head to check and see what was going on, big mistake, I nearly lost balance as I swerved on the narrow road nearly crashing into Uncle Roman, thank God I stopped on my breaks just in time. "Oh shit," I screamed.

With my heart in the pit of my stomach, I turned around once more praying no one was about to run into the back of me. Good news; they had all stopped. Bad news: someone appeared to slip off the cliff. Hopping off of my bike I rushed over alongside everyone else as they peered down the edge of the mountain.

Everyone yelled, "Pit!!!" as I finally arrived.

"Thank God," screamed Uncle Roman as I saw Pit's scarred body climbing up to us. There was a small piece of land only a few feet down from the cliff. Apparently he was able to hop off the back of the bike right in the nick of time.

"NOOO," Manny and Ramiro screamed in agony. They'd hopped down to where Pit had climbed up from. Victor hadn't made it, he'd fallen hundreds of feet down to the ground along with the bike. The pain in their voice touched me. I knew how it felt to watch a loved one lose their life.

"Yo why the fuck you take us on this dangerous ass bullshit," screamed Pit to Mike.

"Motherfucker I was just tryna show yall niggas a good time. I know yall never did anything like this," he barked back.

"And motherfucker I never will again," yelled Uncle Pit.

"Hold on motherfucker you aint bouta jump down on my motherfucking son," screamed Uncle Pit. "I'll throw your motherfuckin ass off this damn cliff where you shoulda been."

"Fuck you," barked Pit before charging over to Uncle Roman.

Again everyone intervened.

"What the fuck are yall arguing about? A man just lost his fucking life in front of us and yall wanna fuss," screamed KT as he pointed over to Manny and Ramiro who both continued to scream.

"Yeah," shouted Mike. "Those niggas lost their motherfucking friend and yall arguing. We blessed to even still be here."

"Nigga fuck that shit," Pit shot back. "We shouldn't have been on that motherfucking shit anyway. This some ol White boy stupid ass shit. I'm Black. Fuck yall I'm out. I'm walking back to the house, calling that little Costa Rican bitch, going back to my room and paying for me some fuckin pussy. I aint bouta sit out here and worry about some motherfucker I don't know."

"I'm sorry but I'm with him. That's the smartest thing he said all night. I can't let this nigga dying stop me from have a good ass time. I'm out," said Money.

"Wait for me bro," said Boo, before snapping one last picture.

"Yo I can't believe yall niggas man. It's a human fucking life down there," screamed Mike with tears in his eyes. "A human fucking life!"

I stayed over at the scene. There was no way I could leave Mike. He was visibly sick, I hated seeing him like that. This aint what he wanted, this aint what he deserves. All he was trying to do was show us all a good time.

Together, the remaining crew attempted to comfort Manny and Ramiro, they weren't feeling us though. I couldn't blame them. They demanded we leave and we obliged. Once back at the compound all of us young guys sat around the pool, no one saying a word.

158

Whatsup God,

Why? Just why?

"Damn why they send these hoes? Man I don't think my mind is even ready to talk to any bitches after what just happened," said Lee.

None of us were really in the mood to be fucking with any females. We'd all just had a near death experience and it wasn't even 3 pm. For the first time in most of our lives, females were the last thing on our mind.

"Yeah me either. Dude really just lost his life right before our eyes." said KT as more girls walked up. Bad ones too, not like the ones who came over last night. These hoes actually looked more like the ones we'd met in the Candy Store. Of course they immediately started flirting and sitting on laps and shit. I had no business talking to them.

"Yeah man, I definitely understand," I agreed. "Yo I'll be back I gotta hit the bathroom," I said before walking off.

I didn't feel like running all the way up to the balcony to use my restroom so I shot over to Mikes since it was the closest. Those nachos from earlier were starting to get to me. I was only on the toilet for 2 minutes before I heard Mike burst into the room with a female. Not wanting to ruin the mood, I decided to simply sit there and wait. I could hear everything that was said.

"Oooh Daddy, you so sexy."

"Thanks, thanks," said Mike.

"Where do you wanna do it at? I wanna fuck you all over this room," she said, seductively.

"Whoa, whoa. I gotta tell you something," Mike followed. "Look, its cool if we don't do anything. I'm still gonna pay you."

"Huh? You don't want none of this," she asked.

"Naw," said Mike. "I'm the groom. I'm getting married when I get home. I don't wanna cheat on my wife. I wanna go in a clean man."

"Or is it that just don't find me attractive?" She whined.

"Please. Look at you. You're beautiful. But not more beautiful than my Fiancé. It's nothing personal, I did the same thing to the chick last night."

"Wow. I've never heard of anything like this. Married men have sex with me all the time. They are actually better customers than single men. Single men have the luxury to fuck girls whenever he pleases. A married man has less time."

"Yeah. I just believe in God and I know he's watching."

"Wow. You're definitely going to Heaven," she replied.

I sat, shaking my head. My nigga Mike, he's always been a good nigga. This right here doesn't surprise me one bit. But damn. He could have gave me that money instead of that Hoe. I wonder if I should let him know that I'd overheard what happened. Naw, never mind, what am I thinking. He's good. I can't tell him how to handle the situation. Shit sure is funny though.

After about ten more minutes they exited. I peeked out the window before slowly opening the door and sneaking up to my room, I had to ensure that Mike had no idea I knew his little secret. Once upstairs, Lucky and I watched from above as he told the guys all his fake ass juicy details. I couldn't help but laugh. Only if they knew.

After a while, Lucky and I both fell asleep only to be awaken about an hour later.

"Man I can't believe as Black Men yall would believe in some shit like that," barked Jay as I hopped up and looked down over the balcony. Mike, Lee, KT and Jay were all sitting around the pool drinking. "That must be some Virginia shit," added Jay.

"Nigga how is it Virginia shit? Everybody believes in the bible," said Lee as I walked down.

"Yeah, you tripping," added KT.

"Yeah bro I don't even wanna be involved in this convo. God might strike us all down," added Mike.

"Nigga for what!" Jay screamed. "Yo Von," he said as he looked over to me. "Yo you know all that Bible shit is some bullshit, right."

"Yo Von, you aint gotta agree with this clown," added Mike.

"Yeah Von, he just wants a nigga to go to hell with him," added KT.

"Damn bro," said Jay. "How you gonna say some shit like that?"

"Nigga what do it matter? You don't believe in the Bible so you obviously don't believe in Heaven or Hell," KT replied.

"You got a point," said Jay.

"Aw hell naw," followed Mike. "You're confused. You don't know what the hell you believe in."

"I know damn well I don't believe in no Heaven. That shit don't even make sense."

"Nigga How?" asked Lee.

"How can you truly believe in Heaven and Hell?" asked Jay. "KT, you're a Dad right?"

"Yeah, but what that got to do with anything."

"Just hear me out. Ok, so if your son, God forbid, killed someone, you're telling me you wouldn't still support and love him?"

"Man of course I would."

"So if God is our Father. How in the hell would he look making his children burn in hell for eternity for committing sins. Shit don't make sense."

"It aint gotta make sense," added Lee.

"Nigga you a slave," Jay added. "How the fuck can a sane Black Man believe in a damn book written and passed around by white people. The same white people who enslaved us for 400 years."

"There you go," said KT. "Always gotta bring the White Man in it."

"Hell yeah I do," replied Jay. "They made it this way."

"Made it what way?" asked Mike.

"Man why you even feeding into this nigga Mike?" asked Lee.

"Fuck yall," said Jay. "Back to my question," he said looking over to me. "Von, how do you feel about the Bible?"

"Well-," I started to say before Jay interrupted me.

"Before you answer, I just wanna say-" added Jay.

"Yo. How you gonna ask a question and then don't let the guy talk?" asked Mike.

"My bad, my bad, but I just gotta say," Jay said looking over to me. "Don't forget to factor in the fact that slave-owners shoved that shit down our throat. Why would they hurt us in every way possible but try to make sure we go to heaven? Make me understand."

"Yeah you got a point," I said as I thought about the conversation Alexis and I had at the Lake. "Yo too be honest, I don't really know what to believe. I really don't think any of us do."

"See, that's the smartest shit you could have ever said. Luckily I do know though. That Bible shit don't make one lick of sense. Those crackers brainwashed us and damn near 500 years later we still got dumb ass niggas like yall reading it."

"Fuck you," said Lee.

"Yeah nigga fuck you," barked KT.

"Naw, I really wouldn't say they were dumb," I followed. "Just because I'm not sure if everything in the Bible is facts doesn't mean I don't respect the stories being told."

"And there's nothing wrong with that," replied Jay. "Those motherfuckers who wrote the Bible was some good ass storytellers. But to me they're no different than any other good author. Their artist, they take life, exaggerate it and teach lessons with it."

"Yeah I see what you're saying," I said.

"Well I don't," followed Lee.

"Yeah, me either, if the Bible says that's what happened. Then nigga that's what the fuck happened, simple as that," added KT, confidently.

"Man you must don't know how dumb you sound," replied Jay. "Ok, I got another scenario."

"Here we go," complained Lee.

"I'm serious, last one, then I'll leave yall alone."

"I know you're lying but carry on," said Lee.

"Ok. So say some kid over here in this country is born poor, his whole family is poor and that's all he'll ever know. He hardly has food and lives off water. What if he came and robbed us and accidently killed one us. You think your God should send him to Hell after he's already been living in hell his entire life?"

"Man that aint my job to judge," answered KT.

"Nigga you sound dumb," exclaimed Jay.

"So what do you believe is gonna happen to him?" I asked.

"Man I've been giving it a lot of thought lately," replied Jay. "And quite frankly I think this reincarnation shit gotta be real. It just doesn't seem fair that God can make people suffer for a life time and then that's it. Naw, I think their coming back in another form or something. They just have to."

"Man I aint tryna hear that shit," said Lee.

"Bro the more you talk the more I really believe you're dumb. I was kidding at first, but naw nigga, you dumb," followed Jay.

"Yo you got one more time to call me stupid or dumb," said Lee.

"Or what? What you gonna do? You can't kill me. That would go against your little fake ass commandments."

"Man-," said Lee.

"Man nothing. That Bible was written by a bunch of lying, white, manipulating, control freaks, shit, I wouldn't be surprised if 'Thou shalt not kill' was written by a murderer," blurted Jay.

"Yo," screamed Mike. "You're tripping."

163

"Makes perfect sense if you think about it," Jay continued. "Whoever wrote it knew that if he told everyone killing was the ultimate sin he'd have the advantage to kill whoever he saw fit with little consequenses. And yall dumb asses believe it."

"Yo, Jay, I understand you got a difference of opinion but that doesn't mean you gotta disrespect what we believe in," said Mike.

"Yeah man. I'm done with this convo," followed Lee. "You're going too far."

"Ok. You're right. My bad, we can agree to disagree. But can I at least ask one last question?" asked Jay.

"Bro, I don't even feel like answering no more damn questions," said KT.

"Yeah bro, you said the last question was your last," added Mike.

"Just hear me out, yall don't even have to answer it, I just want you to think about it," said Jay.

"Man," said Mike as he looked around to everyone. "Go ahead man, but I swear after that, this conversation is dead."

"Ok Cool," said Jay as he looked around. "Ok. So in the Bible the world begins with Adam and Eve, and they document everything that happens after right?"

"Right," said Mike annoyed.

"Ok. So explain this to me," followed Jay, looking around to all of us slowly. "Where the fucking Dinosaurs at?"

"Huh?" asked Lee.

"Nigga you heard me. Where the motherfucking dinosaurs? You mean to tell me it aint one damn story about the dinosaurs in that bitch. Not one of them old motherfucker's aint never bumped into one? Aint like we aint got proof they existed. But where the fuck they at in the Bible? Shit aint adding up."

"That is pretty interesting," I said.

"Exactly. Yall talk all that shit but never mentioned no dinosaurs. That's because the motherfucker who wrote that damn bible never knew they existed, shit, scientist just now learning about them motherfuckers for real. So if they aint know that, you want me to believe that they know how the world started and who created it?"

"Man-," Interrupted Lee.

"Not to mention they found dinosaur bones from over 50 million years ago," continued Jay, cutting across Lee. "According to the bible we've only been here for thousands of years. Whatsup with that?" he asked as he looked around to us all. "I rest my case."

We all sat speechless. No one really had a comeback, can't lie, that Dinosaur shit was simple but interesting. Like why the fuck weren't they in the bible?

Whatsup God,

Yo, I don't know what to even think anymore. Should I question everything? Am I even talking to you? Ok, ok, I know I am. But who are you? Is it more than one of you? Yo if the Bible aint real does that mean Heaven aint? Can't lie, I didn't do a lot of bad stuff in the past because of the fact that I wanted to go to Heaven. But if it aint a Heaven why am I even trying to be a good person? Aint like being a bad person isn't fun. And hey, I guess even if the bible aint true it's still a pretty good guideline on how to live life. I could only imagine a world where no one thought there were any real consequences to our actions. Man, I'm even more confused than ever. Oh shit, does this mean my Mom, Grandma and Alexis aren't really in Heaven? Where are they if not? Are they spirits? What the fuck? I don't know what to think.

"Damn bruh," I said looking over to Jay, breaking the silence. "Yo you made some crazy points."

"Fuck all that," Pit interrupted as he walked out to us shirtless, gut hanging. "You need to point your dick in the direction of some pussy."

"Damn Unc. Why you keep riding my dick like that?" I asked annoyed.

"Motherfucker, I aint on your dick, I just want you to get a bitch to ride on it."

"I'm good man. I'm straight."

"Straight? I hope so. Maybe you need some of this to get you in the mood," he said as he tossed a large bag of cocaine onto the table in front of us.

"Yo what the fuck? How'd you get that?" asked Lee.

"One of these bitches gave it to me after I wore that pussy out. She said she owed it to me."

"Yeah right," added Jay, laughing.

"But no, seriously I really bought it out here to give it to Nephew," he said looking over to Mike who hadn't even looked his way.

"I'm good," replied Mike, "I don't fuck with that shit."

"That's cool, but still, I want to apologize. I was tripping for coming at you like that. That accident wasn't your fault. I was just shook up. Man my life flashed before my eyes. I was in shock. That's the real reason I'm bouta sniff this shit. I gotta make up for what happened. Get my mind off of it."

"Shit, to tell the truth we all should," said Jay. "What we just witnessed wasn't cool at all."

"Yeah you're right. Plus, we are in Costa Rica," said KT.

"Yall down?" asked Pit, looking around to everyone.

"Fuck it," said Mike as he threw his hands in the air. "Why the fuck not."

I couldn't believe I was about to try coke. Yeah I always said I'd do a line after I won an Emmy or something. But I aint win no damn Emmy. I aint win a motherfucking thing. Hell am I celebrating? Ain't shit good going on in my life. But I'm a team player. So I agreed. Fuck it.

"Well everybody go get dressed and in about an hour or so we gonna meet back down here and the party's gonna begin," said Pit.

I headed up to my Rooftop to shower and got dressed. Glad I still had some fresh shit in the stash. I always took pride in my appearance. Yeah my pockets might be on empty but I made sure you'd never know. Fashion is sorta my thing. Too bad I'm probably gonna have to end up selling everything I own. I could get some decent money off of eBay for a lot of my shit, I got Bape, Gucci, Off-white, plenty shit. Most of it I got from Rell. He knew people who used stolen credit cards to buy designer shit and then sale them for the low. But yeah, guess things are really coming full circle, I'm the one selling this shit now. At least I got some good Instagram pics off most of it.

It was fun while it lasted. This weekend will be my last hurrah. Its straight white tee's and sweats till I get back on my feet.

I strutted downstairs and was the first one ready. After looking over to the pool I spotted Stephanie, sitting, relaxing, and looking up at the night sky.

"Oh wow. You look nice," she said as I approached her.

"Thanks," I replied as I looked at my reflection in the water. "You look nice too."

"Yeah right. I just threw this on for work. I can't wear my sexy clothes around here. I know how you men are. Can't control yourselves."

"Yeah, I could definitely see why a man wouldn't be able to control himself around you."

We both smiled.

"So where is everybody?" she asked.

"They should be coming down any second," I replied.

"I heard about what happened earlier, I wasn't sure if you guys were even going to be in the mood to go out."

"Fuck that," I said. "It's sad but we paid a lot of money. It wasn't any of our fault that it happened. I learned you can't really stress things you can't control. What's the point?"

"Yeah that's a good way to put it. Besides, death is a part of life, there is no reason for you guys to stop living."

"I couldn't agree more. How did you find out about it?"

"Trust me this is a small place. Nothing is a secret around here," she replied.

Suddenly all the guys start to walk down the steps.

"Big Dick in the house, big dick in the house," sung Pit as he strutted over. "Yall motherfuckers ready to get high?"

"Motherfucker who said we was getting high?" asked Uncle Rome. "And what the fuck do you have on? You look like a Mississippi Pimp with no hoes."

"Fuck you, crusty motherfucker. But like I was saying, while yall old motherfuckers was sleep, me and the Youngblood's decided to do a little cocaine before we start our night."

"Cocaine?" Uncle Rome exclaimed. "Man hell naw. My son aint doing no damn cocaine."

"Motherfucker your son is grown. Don't act like we aint use to play with our nose a little bit back in the 80's."

"Motherfucker why are you telling all my damn business in front of my son?" Uncle Rome barked.

"Nigga your son is grown he don't give a damn."

"So man," butted in Uncle Red. "Sometimes niggas just don't want everybody knowing everything. You needa learn to shut the fuck up."

"Nigga shut your pussy whipped ass up. Round here holding out, talking bout some damn vowels. I know your stupid ass don't wanna hit the coke."

"Actually motherfucker I do. Drop it on the table," demanded Uncle Red.

"That's what the fuck I like to hear," followed Pit. "Whatsup old motherfucker," he said to Uncle Rome. "You down?"

"Man-," Uncle Rome replied hesitantly. "Fuck it."

We all celebrated.

Next Pit slammed the coke down onto the table. Together, we all stared. I'd seen niggas hit the Paint plenty of times, going to 'Church' is what we used to call it. But now it was my turn. I'm ready. Just the thought of doing something I had never done was exciting.

"Ay Ug. How bout you take the first bump," said Pit.

"Yeah. Show these motherfuckers how it's done," added Uncle Red.

I don't know why everyone always thought I knew about shit like this. But fuck it I wasn't even about to let them know I was an amateur. Like I said, I'd seen it done plenty of times. Can't be too hard.

"Hit it, hit it, hit it," everybody chanted as I crouched down to the table. I took one last good look at the coke before diving in. I hit that motherfucker as hard as I could before what seemed like a small tear drop dripped down my throat. I knew right then and there that I had done it right. I'd always heard about the drip and now I know what it's all about. Not too bad I must admit.

As I waited for my high to kick in, the Old Heads and I coached everyone though. Niggas had me feeling like I was some sorta pro or something. Before I knew it, my high was on full blast and from the looks of everyone else, theirs was too. It was cool. I can't lie. Nothing I want every day. See, I use to be a pill popper. Growing up ecstasy was our drug of choice. We used to pop them bitches like tic tacs. Niggas used to be high for days. Coke gave me a similar feeling. I felt alive and up.

"Let's go get some motherfucking bitches," screamed Lee.

"I can't believe yall got me sniffing powder. I use to sell this shit," followed Money.

"So motherfucker. Fuck what you used to do. Shit, I use to sell newspapers. Now I read em. And I saw your ugly ass mugshot in one," replied Pit, laughing.

"Shut up, you fat head, ol O.J. Simpson looking motherfucker. Big faced bitch," shot back Money.

"I know your stuttering ass aint talking, muscle head motherfucker. You the only nigga I ever seen with a six pack in the back of their bald head," continued Pit as we all laughed.

"What the hell you laughing for Old motherfucker," Money said before looking over to Uncle Roman. "I peeked in your room last night and your old ass was fucking the bitch with an oxygen mask on your face. Ol short of breath ass nigga, one lung having bitch."

For some reason that shit made everyone laugh their ass off.

We wild out for a minute before the van arrived to take us on our mission. Seems like we got there in seconds. Before I knew it we were all stumbling into the club. White Boy Wasted before we could even order our first shot.

They escorted us to our V.I.P. section. The scenery was just right. This would be the perfect set for one of the Migo's or Gucci Manes videos. Or better yet one of them expensive ass Hype Williams videos from the 90's.

Once in our section, niggas got extra loose. I played the cut though, drunk my drink and watched my surroundings. It's a habit, I gotta scope things out. Too many strangers in one place makes a nigga nervous.

First thing I noticed, bitches was flocking to us. And the crazy thing is, they were some of the same girls I'd been seeing at the crib and at the Candy Store. These bitches were everywhere. And it never fails, each time they saw us they treated us like stars. "CHOC-O-LATE"" they screamed.

Soon I had to quit my nonchalant routine. Niggas was having too much fun without me. I don't know where all this coke was coming from but everywhere I looked niggas was doing bump after bump, not to mention shot after shot. Then it happened, the moment I was waiting for, we finally got our hands on some weed. The night couldn't get any better.

"Ay Ug, roll that up for me," said Uncle Pit as he tossed the smoke over to me.

I smiled joyfully. Now this was what the fuck I was talking about. Weed was my thing. I damn near wanted to kiss it. I hadn't been able to indulge in what seemed like forever. I thought I was gonna go crazy. After leaving Alexis's crib I couldn't afford it. I know they say it aint addictive but fuck that. I smoked every day since I was about 14, it was more of a mind thing. Probably wasn't addicted but I did notice without weed you're forced to really sit down with your problems. That shit sucks. I'd rather smoke the pain away any day. This was well needed. I'ma enjoy each and every puff. I never know when I'll get another.

"I need some papers or a blunt or something," I replied, looking around.

"I got one Papi," said a bitch sitting across from me before tossing some raw papers over.

I hit the coke once more before rolling up. After finishing, I examined my product, perfect as usual. I hit the weed as the smoke invaded my lungs. Reunited and feels so damn good.

I felt reborn. So much so that, I even got my black ass on the dance floor. Mind you, I never dance, don't even know how, but tonight I just don't give a fuck. Neither did anyone else in attendance. It was so crazy to me that we were out in the middle of nowhere yet these people knew more of the latest dances and songs than I did. If I aint know any better I'd swear I was back in Atlanta. The power of Black people, amazing. Never really understood the greatness we possess. Our energy travels across the world, influencing millions. Man, maybe this is the type of shit every black kid needs to see. Just to let them know their special.

Looking around, I felt proud. Everything about these people screamed out 'I wanna be Black'. Their hair, the way they walked, talked, danced. This gave me more confidence than ever. I know I'm going to make it. How can't I? I was born into greatness. My people are the shit.

"Ay we headed to the motherfucking Candy Store," yelled Mike as he tapped me on my shoulder.

"Cool," I said as I nodded my head. I bumped my way through the crowd before stepping out into the night light. "Stephanie," I drunkenly shouted as I discovered her standing outside the club. There were hundreds of people walking the crowded block but still, she managed to catch my attention.

"You look like you're certainly enjoying yourself," she said.

"Yep. But how can you tell?" I replied.

"You still have a little something on your nose," she whispered.

I quickly wiped my nostril before saying, "Oh naw that's probably just some-…"

"Trust me," she interrupted. "I know what it probably is. It's cool. You're on vacation, you're supposed to have fun."

"Well if that's the case, you should have fun with me. Hit the weed," I said as I shoved a joint toward her lips.

"No, I'm at work," she replied.

"So, we won't tell. Will we guys," I said as I looked back and saw the fellas.

"Hit that shit, hit that shit," they chanted.

"You guys wanna get me fired?" she replied, smiling.

"Hit that shit, hit that shit," they continued to chant.

"Ok. Ok. Just one time," she said before taking the sexiest pull I'd ever seen anyone take.

"Yo Stephanie you the shit," I said as she handed me back the joint.

"No you are," she replied, blushing.

"Let's take a group pic," said Boo. We all agreed.

"You lucky I'm high motherfucker, you know I hate pictures," said Pit as we all gathered in the middle of the street.

"1,2,3-," said Boo as he focused his camera to us.

"Hold on, Stephanie, you gotta get in the pic," I said as I waved over for her to join in.

"Yeah, come on, Stephanie," said Mike.

"You sure?" she asked.

"Hell yeah," said Pit. "You can help offset some of these ugly ass niggas."

"Fuck you," everyone yelled as Stephanie hopped in.

You should already know who she stood by, yep ME. She smelled so good. I don't know if the coke had opened up some new breathing passage in my nose or something, but damn.

"Now let's go to the motherfucking Candy Store," yelled Lee.

"Do we need the van?" asked Uncle Roman.

"Nope," replied Stephanie. "You guys can walk. I'll drive down later when you're ready to go home. It's only a few blocks up the street," Stephanie replied, pointing.

"Cool," said Uncle Roman as everyone began making their way.

"You're not coming Steph?" I asked.

"No I have to stay with the van."

"Aw man. You sure you don't wanna party with us?"

"I've already smoked the marijuana. I can't just be out here doing what I want," she replied.

"Ok. Ok. I understand, but if you change your mind, I'd love to have a little company."

"I'll keep that in mind," she said with a smile.

I followed the guys down the street. The drugs had me in a fog, but a good fog, like a misty Michael Jackson video type of fog. There were so many people out but I still felt alone, but again, not in a bad way. I mean it in a free way. Yeah, that's what I felt, I felt free. Not a care in the world. The ultimate feeling, peace.

"Ay Ug," said Uncle Pit as I looked up with a smile.

"Whatsup Unc," I replied.

"Nigga stop hogging all the weed," he answered as he strolled with two bitches on his arm. "Pass that shit."

"My bad Unc," I said as I jetted over holding the blunt to the sky before something told me to look over to my left. My high was nearly blown as I discovered two Police Officers sitting at the light staring dead in my face. Immediately I tossed the joint, only it was too late. They hopped out on a nigga ASAP, leaving their vehicle in the middle of the street. First thought was to run, but for some strange reason my feet didn't move, I panicked or maybe it was the drugs. I don't know, but it's probably a good thing I didn't, aint like I know where the fuck I'm at.

For a second I sobered up.

"What's going on," I said as they rushed over, wasting no time, guns drawn.

"Put your hands up," one of them said as they began to pat me down.

"I don't even have anything," I pleaded as I raised my arms in the air.

And I wasn't lying, like I said, I threw the weed. But what I hadn't noticed was the other Cop walking over to retrieve it. As the first officer searched me I watched from the corners of my eyes hoping it would somehow blow away.

It didn't, out of all the damn trash on the ground how in the hell did he find that shit? It was only about an inch long. "Take him down," said the Officer.

"What?" I shouted as the rest of the guys went into a frenzy, pleading with the cops to release me.

Whatsup God,

Help me out Lord. I know I aint come all the way to Costa Rica to go to jail. This can't be right. Help me lord, help me.

"No, no, no," said Stephanie, as she darted over from down the street, stepping in between us. Everyone stood silent as she and the officers talked in Spanish for a second before they reluctantly released me.

"Yo thank you," I said as I turned to her.

"You have to be more careful. You're lucky I have some juice around here."

"Oh shit, you're an Angel. I gotta pay you back."

"Cool. I'm sure I can find something for you to do," she said with a smile.

"Yo motherfucker I thought your young ass was a goner," said Uncle Red.

"Me too," I replied.

"See, I knew yall young motherfuckers was gonna get us in trouble," said Pit.

"Unc," said Lee. "You're the one who called him over to you for the weed. I saw you."

"Shut up. Yall young motherfuckers talk too damn much," he said as he walked away.

We all just looked and laughed as we continued on our high journey, stumbling down the street, before finally arriving at the Candy Store. Again, everyone mingled around. The mood was back, niggas was once again lit. Especially the Old Heads. They couldn't believe what they were seeing, they were like kids in a candy store, no pun intended.

I was glad to not be in Police custody but honestly nothing too special was happening in the club. Same shit from last night. Actually scratch that, I'm being ungrateful. I guess things were better, I'm high this time and like the great philosopher Wiz Khalifa once said, 'Everything's better when you're high'.

Soon, I even found myself dancing with bitches. I kinda started getting a kick out of turning them down. They just knew they had caught a big fish, and every time they shot their shot, I Mutumbo blocked it. Shit was kinda cool, aint every day when you can get a chance to turn down certified dimes.

Before long it was time to hop back on the Van. Again everyone had girls except me. It was cool, well up until the moment Pit and the girl he met had the nerve to take the seat next to Stephanie. Outta all the damn spots why the fuck would him and his plastic body ass bitch have to plop down there. Got me all lonely in the back.

Don't judge me but man I was so high all I could do was stare at Stephanie. She had some little ass shorts on. Not booty shorts or anything but they were small enough. Her thighs and legs looked so soft, I had to wipe my mouth, drool was starting to form. Only the Lord knows what the fuck I'd do to her ass. I closed my eyes, in a high daze, I fantasized about her and me the entire ride home.

Once we arrived back at the spot everyone headed up with their girls as Stephanie and the driver left, it was a little later than last night when we got back so it was time for her to clock out. Lonely, I decided to take a walk. Yeah these streets may be dangerous but fuck it, I'm high. I grabbed Lucky and we made our way down the street.

As the critters whistled and flew through the exotic bushes I couldn't help but to think of Alexis. We always said we'd take trips out of the country together as soon as our paper was right. Man, why the fuck can't I get her off of my mind. Just the thought alone that she'd never take a trip with me sent chills through my body.

Motherfuckers making all these damn cures and shit, when they gonna find a cure for a broken heart? I heard once that the only known remedy was Time. But how is that true? No matter how much time goes by I can never seem to stop thinking about my Mom or Grandma.

On the other hand, maybe my heart has healed when it comes to them, aint like when I think of them I get as sad as I used to. Lately, only the good times come to mind. Hopefully things will be like that one day when I think of Alexis. I don't know though, she's a little different, I didn't see my Mom or Grandma die, I witnessed Alexis take her life, how can I ever forget the image of her hanging from that rope. No, she wasn't my first death seeing, I talked earlier about my best friend Charles getting killed right beside me. It's just that I kinda understand why he died. We were in the streets, that's the kinda shit that comes with it. But Alexis, I just can't seem to get a grip around it. Kinda baffling me. I hope that changes soon.

"I'ma kill you," I heard from behind as I walked. My first instinct was to run. But instead I looked back. It was Boo. He was chasing down some woman with heels in her hand as he irately swung a knife. Bitch was hauling ass, he was too slow. He probably would have ran forever if I hadn't grabbed him.

"What the fuck you doing Boo?" I asked. "What's going on?"

"Get the fuck off me," he screamed. "I pulled that bitches paints down and she had a fucking dick."

No lie, my first instinct was to laugh. But if you could have seen the look on this Man's face you'd understand why I didn't. Dude was out of it, eyes damn near popping out the socket.

"Chill, chill. It's cool. Aint like you fucked her," I replied. "Killing her aint gonna make shit any better."

He stood quiet before taking a deep breath and hollering down to her. "Bitch you lucky."

We walked back to the villa silently. He looked down to the ground as we stepped. Once back to the crib, he headed straight up to his room while I headed over to the pool with Lee, KT, Mike and Jay, as usual they were done with their girls while all the Old Heads stayed cuffed up with theirs.

We all sat around, chilling getting higher till about six in the morning.

"Motherfucker, you're gonna pay for this," said a girl as she stormed down the steps, clutching a large purse.

"Fuck you bitch," said Money as he walked behind.

"Somebody is going to take me home. And that's final," she demanded.

"Bitch didn't I just say fuck you," Money replied.

"Is this how you think you can treat us?" she said as she turned around pointing to him. "Bring me all the way here, don't pay and leave me with no way to get home? One of you is going to pay," she said looking over to us.

"Bitch fuck you aint nobody paying for shit," screamed Money as we all looked away. Won't like any of us could have helped anyway. How the fuck were we going to take her anywhere. On our backs?

"Sorry we don't have any cars," said Mike.

"You're gonna pay for this. All of you, you're gonna pay," she screamed as she stormed off into the night.

"Yo what the fuck did you do to her?" asked Mike.

"Man I bought two bitches here and I guess she thought they were both getting paid or something."

"Why did you bring two?" I asked.

"Man I was drunk and couldn't figure out which one I wanted to fuck."

"So you just bought them both?" asked Lee.

"Yep and the dumb bitch gonna just sit there and watch as I'm piping down her partner. Bitch that's your fault."

"So what happened? Why didn't she get a ride with one of the other girls?" asked KT.

"Who fucking knows? Her dumb ass let them leave without her. The bitch really thought if she stayed in my room long enough she'd get some money outta me. I thought she was getting the hint. She even left out the room for damn near an hour. I thought she was gone then all of a sudden she burst in my room snapping, talking some shit I don't understand. Fuck that bitch."

"You a cold dude," said KT.

"Nigga, I'm Money, I should've been charging her to be with me in the first place. She must don't know who the fuck I am," he replied, boastfully.

"Nigga what the fuck is this?" I heard Pit scream, awaking everyone.

"Oh hell naw," followed Uncle Red, equally as loud.

Annoyed, I turned my head, attempting to go back to sleep. I aint pay them old niggas no mind. Figured they was just tripping like always. That was only until I noticed I had a notification on my phone from the group chat.

Opened it up and was in shock.

"What the fuck," I said to myself.

Someone was blackmailing us. As I scrolled through the pictures I saw so much, niggas fucking, getting head, it was basically a time line of what the fuck we'd been doing all weekend.

"I got you guy's camera and one of your phones. Everything you did will be sent to Instagram. I have thousands of followers and I can make your lives a living hell. Hope you don't love your wife's too much. I told you that you will be sorry. I need 25,000 American Dollars," I read.

It was the girl Money had cussed out.

"Motherfucker I'ma kill you," I heard as I looked over the balcony. Pit was rushing over to Boo as everyone piled up by the pool, phones in hand.

"Nigga you aint gon touch my brother," said Money as he stepped in between.

"Motherfuck you and your brother," replied Pit.

"I got a Wife at home. I told your stupid ass about taking these damn pictures," screamed Red as Boo sat quietly, visibly embarrassed.

"Fucking creep. Why the fuck you got photos of me in hot tubs and shit with bitches?" asked Uncle Pit.

"You better fix this shit," added Red. "If I lose my wife over some bitches I didn't even fuck I'm gonna kill you dead. I swear, I'ma kill you."

"Kill me? Fuck you, I aint got no damn money. You better fix it your damn self," Boo finally said.

"Oh yes you do. I heard you tell that bitch you was Uglathang's manager, you better manage to get some fucking money," spat Uncle Roman.

"My manager?" I shouted as I approached everyone, finally coming down the steps.

"Yeah that motherfucker been telling all the bitches that you're an actor and he's your manager. That's probably why the bitch stole the camera. She thinks your ol stupid ass got some money," Uncle Roman added, pointing to Boo.

"Yeah yall better fix this shit," barked Uncle Red.

"Nigga I aint fixing shit," said Money.

"Nigga you're the one who bought the bitch here," added KT.

"Yeah Cuz," said Mike. "If you would have just paid her none of this would have ever happened."

"How the fuck did she get the camera anyway?" asked Jay.

"It had to be when that dumb motherfucker was chasing that 'man girl' down the street," said Lee, pointing to Boo.

"Fuck you," screamed Boo.

"Fuck you motherfucker," yelled Pit. "One of you motherfuckers is gonna get that damn camera back and pay that bitch."

"I don't give a fuck. I aint fixing shit," said Money.

"Me either I aint do nothing," I replied.

"Motherfucker you aint bought no pussy since you got here," screamed Pit directing his anger to me. "You should have more money than all of us."

"What?" I exclaimed. "I aint paying for shit, you're tripping. I aint got nothing to do with this."

"Motherfucker yes you do, if you wouldn't have let Boo say he was your manager none of this would have happened," replied Pit.

"Huh? I aint even know he was saying that shit. You sound stupid."

"Stupid?" Pit screamed. "Your little gay acting ass is gonna fix this shit," he added, pointing his finger aggressively towards me.

"Gay?" I barked. "Nigga I'll beat your old ass."

"Fuck you young nigga," he barked back.

"Yeah the least you could have did was pay for the bitch to get home since you aint fuck nothing," said Uncle Red. "I would have paid but I was sleep."

"What?" I replied. I couldn't believe this was happening. How the fuck did I become the blame. Was this a joke? Was I being Punk'd or something? "Fuck both of yall," I shouted. "I aint gotta do a motherfucking thing. And aint shit gay about me. Yall got me fucked up if yall think I'm paying. I'm broke," I yelled. "Yall think I'm getting rich off acting? I'm not. I aint got shit.

I came here for my Brother," I added, pointing to Mike. "I'm fucking homeless, yall don't know me."

"I aint tryna hear none of that shit. Motherfucker your gay ass is paying. I don't care what you say," ordered Pit.

"Fuck you," I yelled before taking a swing at him. I missed by a hair as Mike and the guys quickly separated us. The situation was temporarily diffused but still, no one had any words for one another as we all marched off to our rooms.

I laid in bed angry, not so much about the pictures, I aint married, why should I really give a damn about that shit. I was more so mad that these niggas keep tryna play me. Why would they think I was gay? Just because I aint fuck nothing? Were they talking about me behind my back? Fuck them. I sat heated before another text came through.

It was a picture of the Old Heads throwing money on a girl with a caption that read: "This is only the beginning. I need my money pronto. Or it will only get worse. I told you not to fuck with me."

I didn't move out of bed, but I could hear everyone complaining.

"Yo we gotta find this bitch. I got a wife at home," I heard Pit say.

"Oh don't worry about your vowels now motherfucker," added Uncle Red.

"Nigga fuck you," spat Uncle Pit.

Everyone continued laying around by themselves mad all day. No one had a clue on what to do. When Stephanie finally arrived I shot over to her. Hopefully she could help.

"Ay Steph read this," I said as I showed her all of the text that were sent out to us.

"Wow," she said before looking up to me. "I know this girl," she replied.

"You know where she lives?"

"Yeah she's staying in Midtown in my cousin's old house."

"Come on. We gotta go over there," I replied.

"Go over there? Are you crazy?"

"Maybe I am. I don't know, but I have to, Mike is like my Brother, I can't stand to see him lose his marriage over some bullshit like this. Between you and me, he didn't even have sex with anyone while we were here. I gotta save him. He's saved my life too many times. I have to."

"Ok. Wow. I understand," she replied after taking in a deep breath. "Do you at least have a plan?"

"Yeah, I plan to get our shit back. I just need your help. Please."

""Ok," she said hesitantly.

"Come on," I continued.

"Aren't you going to tell your people?"

"Naw," I replied. "I really just wanna do this shit on my own."

"Ok. But are you sure you are aware of how dangerous this is?"

"Stephanie, remember the other night when you talked to me about having belief."

"Yeah."

"Well, I believe this is the right thing to do. I can't really explain why I do, but I do. You just gotta trust me."

"OK, I trust you," she replied looking deep into my eyes.

"Bet. Let's go."

Together, we hopped into the van and headed over. I sat focused, not saying a word, I had no idea what I was about to do or even what I'd say but one thing was for sure, I was coming back with a camera or not coming back at all.

Whatsup God,

Look, I aint even got much to say. I'm just letting you know, I'm gonna go in there and whatever happens, happens. I'm willing to do anything to get that camera back. So if you don't want me to die. I suggest you put it in these girls heart to give me my shit back. No, no, I'm not threatening you. Never that. I'm just telling you what it is. To me, right now, it's a win win situation. With death surrounding me so much I gotta admit I'm kinda curious as to what happens on the other side. I miss my people anyway, maybe I'll see them, or maybe Jay was right, maybe I'll be reincarnated. I don't know. I just feel like if my existence on this planet means anything, if I truly have a purpose, than you'll see that I make it outta here. If not, I guess I'll finally get to meet you.

I sat eyes closed as we drove. Before long we arrived on an eerie dead end street. Only one small house. "You sure someone lives here?" I asked Stephanie.

"Afraid so," she replied.

"Wow," I followed. To think, the guys were clowning me because I didn't get a girl. I bet they'd think twice about fucking them if they saw this shit. There was no way possible there was running water inside, no way. Looking at the house I could see straight through in some spots. There were huge holes everyway. I never seen anything like it. No wonder she was so mad she didn't get paid. This bitch was poor. She truly needed it. "I'll be right back," I said as I clutched onto the door handle.

"What are you doing, are you crazy? I can't let you go inside by yourself. I can help, I promise. They'll listen to me."

"That's sounds good Stephanie," I replied, as we stared at one another. "But I just gotta do this on my own."

"No. You don't know what these women will do to you. I've seen tourist get killed over and over. These people are crazy. This is not America."

"I understand what you're saying. But I just need you to understand. I gotta do this myself. I can't even act as if I know this is the right thing to do. I don't. But I know that my heart is telling me to do this."

"But Von-."

"I'm sorry Stephanie but this shit is personal. I'll be back," I said as I walked off.

Whatsup God,

It's game time.

I knocked on the door.

Whatsup God,

You heard me right?

The girl who stole the camera answered. "Cho-co-late'", she said with a devilish smile.

I looked behind her, there were about five more girls scattered across the living room, laying on dirty mattresses, phone in each of their hand. "Whatsup," I replied to the thief.

"Girls look who's here," she said looking back.

"Ola," they all said, looking up to me.

"Come on in," said the thief.

I took one last look at Stephanie and the driver before stepping inside.

A loud foul order attacked me. These bitches stink. For real. Oh my God, to think niggas pay for this shit. They're walking around here with thousands of social media followers smelling like death, living like hobos. Probably got little girls on Instagram looking up to them thinking their living the life because they got fake asses and long hair. Shit's crazy, felt like I was meeting the Wizards of Oz or something. A house full of frauds.

"Yo we gotta talk," I said.

"Does talking include money?" she asked with the same evil grin.

"I don't have any mon-," I attempted to say.

"Get em," she interrupted as the five Prostitutes hopped up. In what seemed like seconds I was surrounded, as five guns pointed my way.

"What the fuck," I yelled.

"Don't scream now. You got my text. You know what I want. Where is my fucking money?" she demanded.

"Look, that's what I came here to talk about," I said, thinking of ways to defuse the situation.

"Talk about money?" she asked.

"N-,"

"Handcuff him," she said as she snapped her fingers, alerting her Prostitute Posse.

"Hold on," I pleaded to no avail, tossing my hands to the air only for them to be yanked down and cuffed. Together they pushed me down to their mouse infested floor as they continued to point their guns. This was real. Flashbacks of the time Harris shot my car up sprung through my head. This was bad.

"Ladies, let's take a picture. We can send it to his little friends," the thief said as the girls gathered around continuing to point their weapons at me. "Perfect," she said smiling as she snapped a picture with Boo's camera as well as his cell phone.

I smiled, in my head if this was the last picture people would see of me, they'd know I went out happy, or at least appeared to be.

Whatsup God,

Yo you spared me when Harris shot my car up back in the day. It's time to work your magic again. I'm putting my life completely in your hands. How you gonna act?

"Get his fucking phone," the thief demanded as one her flunky's reached inside my pocket.

"We don't have any money. I'm serious. You're gonna ruin a lot of good people's lives if you put those photos out," I pleaded. "I swear, I'm not famous and Boo aint my manager, he lied. Now I know what Money did to you was wrong but don't punish us all."

"Shut up," she screamed. "Motherfucker just because we live here doesn't mean I'm stupid. You think I didn't see your Instagram with all of your fans? You're famous. And your friend bragged to me about how much drugs he sold. We need to get paid. We want your jewelry, everything."

"Man we aren't rich," I whined before she smacked me.

"Stop lying. Where is the fucking money?" she screamed. "I'm going to give you one chance to call your friends. If they want you alive they will bring the money."

180

"Fuck it do what you gotta do to me. Just don't put those pics out. Please. I'm telling you, you're gonna fuck up some good people's lives."

"Do I look like I give a fuck?" she asked.

"Fuck it then," I said as The Thief and I locked eyes. "Kill me. I don't give a fuck either."

"Ok," she said with a smile. "Ladies-."

Suddenly the bright light from the sun beamed down on my face as the door burst open and Stephanie along with two Police Officers barged in. I had completely forgotten Stephanie was here.

"Put those fucking guns down," yelled the Police. It was the same two guys who'd tried to arrest me last night.

"But Papi," the thief whined.

"Shut up," one of the officers interrupted. "I'm tired of you guys blackmailing the tourist."

"But-," she pleaded.

"There's no excuse," he replied before looking over to me. "Stand up."

"Come on we weren't going to hurt him, there aren't even any bullets in the chamber, see," she said as she nodded for one of the Prostitutes to shoot her pistol. Wasting no time, she pointed across the room and shot, as a bullet flew out, drilling a whole in the already tarnished wall. "Oops," The Thief replied, shocked.

"See that's what I'm talking about," said the other officer.

They argued in Spanish as one of the Prostitutes released me from the cuffs.

After snatching the camera and Boo's phone back we headed to the van.

"Yo Steph, how did you do that?" I asked as my heart pumped 1000 miles a minute. "I thought you said the Cops didn't care about tourists."

"You're right, I did say that. But I never said they didn't care about me. I text them on the way over," she replied with a wink. "They've both been having a crush on me since we were kids. How do you think I stopped them from arresting you last night?"

"Damn. You're a life safer."

"Yeah, I've heard that a time or two," she replied as we gazed at one another yet again.

Once I got back to the crib it was a celebration. Uglathang had saved the day. Everyone gathered around as we ate BBQ and drunk liquor.

"Damn, I'm sorry youngin. It looks like you're the real MVP," said Pit as he wrapped his arm around my shoulder.

"Thanks Unc."

"I gotta special treat for you nephew," said Uncle Red. "We gonna take it back to when you were just a kid, I'm buying you some more ass tonight," he shouted. "It's only right."

"I don't think you'll need to buy him anything," said Stephanie, interrupting from behind. "You mind keeping me company while they go party?" Stephanie asked me.

"Hell naw I don't mind," I replied, shocked.

"Ohhhh shit," everyone said as I attempted to hide my excitement.

After a while they all left for the club. Boy, it seemed like they was taking forever. I was dying to see what Steph had in store for a nigga. I sat by the pool, showered, shirtless, smelling good, waiting patiently before she walked over still in uniform. Like always she flashed her flawless smile before kicking her shoes off, sitting down next to me as both of our feet dangled in the water.

"You know what you did was really sexy right?" she asked.

"No, I didn't." I replied. "I just did what I had to do. Aint like I had too much to lose."

"See, that's the only problem I have about what you did. I thought I told you about having faith, you have to believe. There's no reason you should ever think you don't have anything to lose. "

"Yeah you're right, I'm still working on it," I replied as we locked eyes. "But Thanks again for being there."

"You're welcome," she said as she leaned in for a kiss.

"Wow," I followed, surprised. "I thought you had a man?"

"Keyword, had. A lot has changed in 24 hours."

"Really? Like what?"

"I'm not sure you'll understand."

"Try me."

"Ok," she said. "You ever heard of a Spiritual Enlightenment?"

"Yeah I heard of it. Can't say I really know what it is though."

"Well, simply put, I feel as though I have a clear understanding of the world and my purpose in it."

"Oh shit, well lay it on me because I've been tryna figure this shit out forever."

"I don't really know where to start."

"Well take your time. I'm all ears," I replied.

"Ok," she smiled. "Have you ever questioned the world?"

"Fuck yeah. All the time."

"Yeah, but I mean like seriously question it."

"I'm serious, yes."

"Well, me too," she replied. "But lately it seems as if God has been answering all of my questions, sending me sign after sign."

"Like what?" I asked curiously.

"I don't know, I just feel like we're taking this life thing more serious than it actually is. Most of the rules and traditions put in place were made by people who would benefit from them."

"What do you mean?"

"Ok, for instance Marriage. I use to be like every other little girl, I couldn't wait to meet my Prince Charming and ride off into the sunset. But lately it all seems kinda fake to me."

"How?"

"Ok. Are you by chance a fan of Nipsey Hussle?"

"What? Am I? Hell yeah," I replied.

"Me too. I learned about him after his death. He's actually the one who kinda sparked my interest in the Universe. His passing really changed me. I kept finding myself questioning God. But it all changed once he died. I knew that if a person as pure as him could walk this earth, there had to be a Higher Power."

"Hell yeah."

"I just feel like God showed Nipsey the true purpose of life so that he could show and teach us. I never even knew what having a Purpose really was until I began studying and listening to him."

"Yeah he was a great man, I just wish he would have left the hood. He'd probably still be alive."

"No, that's what he was supposed to do. He did exactly what God wanted him to, he lived pure, allowing God to order his steps. And once he fulfilled his journey, there was nothing left for him to do. He'd completed his mission."

"That's deep."

"Right," she agreed. "But, back to what I was saying about Marriage, I was watching his funeral on YouTube and during the Eulogy his girlfriend Lauren London said that one thing he always told her was that 'We couldn't possess people, we could only experience them'."

"Yeah that was deep too. I felt that."

"It got me to thinking, ok, so right now, I have complete control of myself, I have free will and can make my own decisions, right?" she asked.

"Right."

"But when you get married, they say you're now one."

"Right."

"But how is that possible if I can't possess you? We aren't suddenly sharing the same brain or heart. Therefore I could never be one with someone. I can only be responsible for me. People change daily, I believe it's inevitable for two people to grow apart over time."

"So is that why you and your boyfriend broke up?"

"Yeah I guess, it just doesn't make sense to me. I guess Marriage and deep relationships are for some people. But I don't think it's for everyone, most people don't feel whole themselves so they feel the need to fill the empty void inside of them with another person. But I believe that void is reserved for yourself. That void is reserved for true self love."

"Damn. I've never thought about things that way."

"Yeah, most people haven't. I don't believe as humans we question enough things. We like what we're told and believe it because it's easy. Searching for the truth can sometimes be excruciatingly painful, but it's necessary," she added.

"Damn, you're right because if we truly look at marriage we'll see that the Divorce rate is through the fucking roof. Yet we still believe it's the right thing to do because it's what we've been told," I replied, shaking my head.

"Yep," she followed. "Don't get me wrong though, I believe two fully whole individuals who are truly aligned and know exactly who they are can come together to make something remarkable. Only thing is, I'm not sure enough of us are fully whole individuals."

"Damn, so basically most of us are just out here wasting our time."

"I guess in a way you could say that. But then again we have to also realize that there is no one way to live life. Even though I believe we all have a purpose I also believe that we all should be free to live how we choose."

"That would be easier if we weren't so afraid of being judged," I followed. "Ay Stephanie."

"Yes," she replied.

"So you're really prepared to live out the rest of your life alone? You don't think that we need partners to truly enjoy life?"

"Ya know, a couple weeks ago I would have had a direct answer for you. But today, I don't. All I know is that I just really want to be free to experience everything this world has to offer. Sometimes relationships hinder you. Not saying I don't want another one, I'm just not so caught up in spending the rest of my life with one particular person. I'm more so into enjoying the moment, taking things day by day. Besides, I've given my all to people that I love. I think I want to experience the feeling of giving all of my love to myself."

"I feel you, I feel you. So basically what you're saying is that when the fires dies out in the relationship, you're out."

"Yep, moving on, I believe you control your feelings. If you have stress in your life than 9 times out of 10 you've caused it. Most of the time your life whether good or bad is a direct reflection of your actions."

"I can dig it. I never heard a girl talk like you."

"I guess I understand you Men now," she replied as she laughed. "But seriously I kinda feel like I have too much love inside of me to be stuck giving it to just one person. To me that would be selfish."

"Selfish?" I said with a laugh. "Yo this spiritual enlightenment shit is really transforming you into a Guy. Who are you?" I asked sarcastically.

"Just a girl who's dedicating her life to being happy. No, I don't plan on sleeping with the whole world," she said before taking a brief pause. "But if I do, I believe it's my business as long as I know why I'm doing it and can live life with an authentic smile."

"So that's what Spiritual Enlightenment is? Just learning to be happy?"

"Sort of but that's not it, it's so much more."

"Like what?"

"Look around," she replied as she gazed up to the sky. "What do you see?"

"Trees, stars, grass, water," I replied, scanning my surroundings.

"What I see is me," she replied admiring the atmosphere.

"Huh?"

"I am one with the earth, I am one with the universe. We all are."

"Ok. So what exactly do you mean by that?"

"It's the circle of life, we're all connected, everyone and everything, the grass, the sun and the trees, along with every other one of God's beautiful creations. Together everything serves a unique purpose. No one thing is more important than the other."

"Yeah I've heard that before."

"We all have, we just dismiss it because we believe as humans we are superior. When in all actuality we are the only living beings who don't walk with purpose. Yeah some of us do but for the most part we all live aimlessly."

"So you're saying that me and a bird are basically the same?" I replied looking to the sky.

"Exactly the same. I don't understand how we look down on animals. They truly know what joy is. Do you know how great it feels to wake up and do exactly what you love, exactly what you're here for day in and day out?"

"I could only imagine right now."

"Well, animals and trees don't have to imagine. Just look at that bird," she says, pointing up. "Just flying around making nest, not a care in the world, completely at peace. I think that's what we all strive for. Only thing is, they live like that from birth. As humans, somewhere along the line, probably when money was created, we forgot why we were here. I believe in the beginning, on the day of creation, we all worked together, in unified harmony."

"What do you mean?"

"How can I explain it," she replied, pondering. "Ok, I got it. You like sports?"

"Of course."

"Ok, on a team everyone has a purpose, every position is different from the water boy, to the coach, to the star player. Right?"

"Right," I replied.

"Ok, now imagine that everyone on this team was a star."

"Ok."

"Now, if everyone on that team is a star what do you think will happen if everyone plays their role equally and effectively?"

"They usually win."

"Yes, they'd succeed, that's how I view the world. I believe we all started out just like that. Animals, trees, water, humans, we all lived together in unison, in peace, advancing together."

"That seems beautiful as hell."

"It was, only problem, God gave us free will. Now imagine that same team, only now the Coach is off somewhere, high, doing God knows what, chasing a dollar bill, only utilizing his team for his own selfish needs instead of playing his role, directing his people to prosperity."

"The team would be in total chaos, just like the world is today."

"Bingo."

"Ok, ok I feel what you're saying but I still don't see the purpose of it all. Like, why are we here in the first place?"

"I believe it's just simply to enjoy life and advance society, nothing more, nothing less. We overthink a lot of things, and make life more difficult than it should be. If we just realized that we are all the same, I feel we'd learn to understand each other more. To me, there's no difference between you and I."

"Besides the fact that I'm a Man and you're a beautiful Woman."

"Yeah, but I believe it's a little deeper than that."

"How?"

"I believe that we are all just energy, a soul, whatever you want to call it. I think our bodies are just what we are dwelling in for the moment, like a character."

"A character?"

"Yeah. For example the character that your soul dwells in, loves to act, he's handsome, a great kisser," she said as she smiled.

"You funny," I replied, with a smirk.

"I'm serious though, the only difference between the two of us are our experiences. You experienced your life as a Black Man, so that effects the way you see the world and your actions. As well as myself, along with every other human in the world. Our experiences along with our character traits alter the way we see things. That's why it appears as if we are different. But if you stripped our experiences away we'd all be more alike than most of us have ever imagined."

"Damn. Yo I wasn't even prepared for all this shit. You blowing a niggas mind."

"I'm sorry, I'm sorry."

"No. No it's cool. I like all of this shit. I'm all ears."

She smiled. "I believe God is a mastermind, a perfect genius and with his genius he decided to bless each one of us with one of his super powers. Our only job is to figure out what that is and find a way to incorporate our Purpose within it. Purpose is everything."

"I always thought my Purpose was acting, but lately I haven't been too sure."

"No, no, acting is your Passion. It's more so your talent, your super power. That's why it comes so natural to you. Your purpose is what God wants you to get across to people through your acting. It's usually something that will benefit the Universe."

"Benefit the universe? I don't know how acting could benefit the Universe."

"Sure it can, you just have to broaden your mind. Actors are essential, everyone needs to be able to see themselves in others. It's one of the many ways we know we aren't alone sometimes. We all desire to be understood. Not to mention the joy you bring as people watch you on the screen or stage. For an hour and a half you help people take their mind off the stresses of the world."

"So are you saying that's my purpose as an Actor?"

"No. I don't know what your purpose is. That's between you and God. I just know that with anything in life you have to move with intent. When you take that acting job you have to know why. We're all here in service to others. You have to know who exactly you're aiming to help."

"For the longest time I thought I was helping myself."

"Maybe that's where you've been going wrong."

"Damn," I replied. "Well since you know so much what's your Super Power?"

"Well I know I said I'd be a comedian the other day but that's not really my talent, I just admire it. To be honest I have a few talents. Sadly I've never put them to work like you did acting. So I guess as of right now, I'm in the process of figuring out a lot of things."

"So I guess we both got some work to do."

"Yep, luckily I do know my purpose," she followed.

"What is it?' I asked.

"I am a Healer."

"A Healer? Hell is that?"

"In these days and times I guess they'd call me a witch," she replied.

"A witch? Oh man don't cast no spell on me," I said, as I playfully scooted over.

"I never said I was a witch," she said laughing. "I said that's what they'd call me nowadays."

"Ok, ok, I'm listening."

"See, a witch is man-made. But a Healer is sent from above."

"Ok but what exactly is a Healer. What do you do?"

"Lots of things, throughout the history of the world a healer has always been a Dr., a counselor, and even a teacher. Back in the days they would live on the outskirts of town and people would come from all over to receive help. They could feel people's pain, and were able to diagnose them and help rather it be mentally or physically."

"That doesn't sound like a witch to me."

"It wasn't a witch until someone decided it was a better idea if people got paid for the services Healers provided. That's around the time when Dr.'s were created. I believe they were the ones who first called what we do 'witch craft'," she said as she used air quotations. "Healers like myself would be out casted and murdered for doing what we are here to do. I told you, the world changed once money entered the picture."

"Damn. The love of money really is the root of all evil."

"Afraid so."

"Yo you're really making me start to hate people."

"No, no, that's not what I'm trying to do. Just take it as a lesson. Never take it personal when people do harmful things in this world. It's not that their doing something against you. Their usually doing something to benefit themselves. Hurting you is just a reaction to their decision. Once you start to think that way you'll have a better understanding of people along with more empathy."

"Empathy? Fuck that, aint nobody got no damn empathy for me."

"That's because their hurting too. The majority of people on this earth are damaged. People aren't loving themselves. How can they? They don't even understand themselves. It's almost impossible to love someone you don't know. And with so many schedules, past due bills and distractions we have to deal with, we really can't be mad at one another for not loving ourselves. We don't even have time to really search for who we truly are."

"So why the fuck do they teach all that bullshit in school when it's obvious the most important thing in life is finding out who you truly are and what your purpose is?"

"I believe because the more people who know their purpose, the less people will spend money on worthless things that serve no purpose in our lives."

"Ok I get it. Then the rich people, who truly know their purpose won't get all the money that our dumbasses spend on their products, trying to be happy."

"Exactly. We're so confused. I see everyone say 'Self-love' and all this other crap. But I don't think they really know what it means. Self-love isn't loving your curvy hips or lips, its loving what's inside, loving the one thing that will always remain the same, your soul."

"You got it all figured out huh? I hear everything you're saying but I still don't even know if I can even think clear enough to get on your level."

"You can do it. Everyone can."

"I know, it's just hard to focus and stay sane enough to even get the kinda clarity you got. It's so hard doing a profession that requires you to be so creative and free when inside you feel numb and trapped. It's killing me."

"You can't let it get you down, everything happens for a reason. Every negative emotion should be transferred into a lesson for others to learn from you. You're an artist, adversity is required. Besides, some of God's greatest gifts have been created in the dark."

"I never thought of it like that."

"You have to. There are no coincidences. Even the fact that we met. God bought you here for a reason. This is a part of your journey. You stayed strong and God is using me as a vessel to teach you understanding. I told you, I'm a healer, it's my job. I know things."

"You don't know how bad I want to believe you."

"Trust me. I think you going through all of this at this point in your life is for the best, you have to figure out who Von is. It will become impossible to navigate the devilish entertainment business when you don't distinguish who you are within yourself. That's why you see so many Hollywood Stars bottoming out."

"Man Stephanie, I swear I hear what you saying. I'm just wondering do I even have the strength to find a purpose anymore. I'm beat up."

"Stop being negative. When you're on the right path that God designed for you he'll give you anything you desire. When you're on the wrong path of course he's not gonna give it to you. Maybe you're not all the way aligned, you may need to tweak a few things."

"Maybe you're right. But like I said, I understand what you're saying I'm just not sure I have the strength. I'm not being negative. Just real. This journey I'm taking is extremely lonely at times. And I never really feel I have anyone to talk to. Yeah I got you right now, but soon I'll be alone again."

"I understand, failure to connect is one of the leading reasons for suicide. It's hard understanding the world while no one understands you."

"Man, you just made me think of something. I never told you but my last girlfriend recently killed herself right in front of me," I said as I looked up to the sky.

"Wow, I could tell something was deeply hurting you but I never knew exactly what. Don't worry. She's still here," she replied, hand on my shoulder. "Try not to look at death as the end, to me, it's more of a restart, a fresh chance at a brand new life. Energy never dies, that's all we are, one big ball of energy bottled up inside of a body. She's free now. Who knows, her soul may reside inside of a butterfly flying amongst us, or a leaf dangling on the trees, enjoying the summer breeze."

"Yo," I said looking up. "I don't know why but when you just said that I felt a huge weight being lifted off of my shoulders. I've been around death all of my life. My Mom, Grandma, friends. It's draining wondering if your people are ok. But to think that their truly here with me may be exactly what I need."

"I hope it is," she said with a smile.

"It all just makes perfect sense now," I replied as I looked around into the world, wondering if all of my loved ones had been living joyfully around me the entire time. "Yo it's so crazy, Jay was just talking about reincar-," I started to say.

"Oh my God, another shooting star, come on close your eyes," she said as she grabbed me by the hand, looking me in my eyes. "But before you close them, remember, be specific, how can God give you exactly what you want, if you don't know exactly what you want."

"Ok," I replied, closing my eyes.

Whatsup God,

You should already know what I need. I need to find my purpose. Please Lord.

"I did it," I replied opening my eyes. "I may have asked for the wrong thing the last time we did this."

"That's ok. There are always doors opening up. You just have to have your eyes and ears open. God doesn't talk loud. He whispers. You have to block out the world and focus on his directions to truly get where you need to be. I told you about speaking things to existence. It's not really the fact that you're speaking them, it's the fact that when you keep saying specific things you start to focus better. You tend to overlook blessings and miss out on opportunities when you don't know exactly what you're aiming for."

"Man I think you might have just changed my whole outlook on life. I know I told you the other day that I had done everything possible to make it. But now I'm pretty sure that isn't true. I can't say I fully understand everything but I needed this. "

"Of course you did, God places the right people at the right time in all of our lives. I just opened your third eye, you'll start seeing a lot more people like me. Just stay the course. In no way am I saying I have all the answers. I've just found a way to make this thing called life make sense to me. Sometimes you have to create your own reality. I've learned that's really all we need."

"That aint all you need," I followed.

"What else do I need?" she asked.

"Come here," I said as I placed my right index finger under her chin before planting a kiss on her lips.

"I've got an idea," she said as our lips parted ways.

"I'm listening."

"Well, seeing as it's your last night and by the time I see you again you'll be somewhere famous on T.V. I gotta do something to make you remember me."

"I'm sure that won't be a problem," I said as we kissed once again.

"Stay right here," she said as she pulled back, hopping up.

"Where you going?" I asked.

"To grab a couple things out of my office, you mind if I freshen up upstairs in your shower?"

"Of course I don't."

"Good. I'll be right back," she replied as she ran off.

The front gate was locked and we had the entire place to ourselves. I couldn't believe what was about to go down. Boy I wish time could speed up, it seemed like forever before I saw her again. I didn't know what to do with myself.

"Hello Von," she finally said from the rooftop, looking down on me as she posed in lingerie, an open robe and high heels.

"Hey baby," I replied, as I stood to my feet.

"I'll be right down," she said as she walked over to the steps.

I stood speechless watching as she slowly made her way down one step at a time. We locked eyes before she did the unthinkable. In the blink of an eye, she missed a step, causing her to tumble down to the ground, smacking the pavement.

"Oh shit," I yelled as I rushed over. "Stephanie, Stephanie, you ok?" I asked.

Without saying a word, she slowly looked up to me, face covered by the widest smile ever.

"Oh my God," she screamed, laughing hysterically as I joined her.

"Yo I don't mean to laugh. I'm just glad you're ok," I said.

"It's ok," she replied," continuing to snicker. "How did I do that?"

"I have no idea," I replied as I scooped her up into my arms. "But honestly I don't know why you were even coming down here. I think we'd have a lot more fun in my bed."

"Oh really?" she asked.

"Really," I replied as I picked her up, carrying her up the stairs in my arms.

I laid her down across the bed before peeling off her lingerie. Stepping back I admired her bare beauty. Slowly I removed my shirt, next my underwear and shorts. I stood naked. I licked my lips as my chest pumped in and out as I crept over to her before towering over her silky smooth, baby soft body. We kissed as I held her close to me.

"What the fuck," I suddenly screamed as Stephanie and I both looked back. It was fucking Lucky. After not seeing his ass the entire night, this freaky ass dog had the nerve to lick my ass. The motherfucker bamboozled me. I thought he was just my new little friend. Naw, the motherfucking dog had a damn crush on me the whole time. Furious, I forced him downstairs before Stephanie and I could finally continue what we were destined to do.

I woke up the next morning alone. But there was a note.

"See ya later Von. You are special in so many ways. My wish came true last night. I was able to spend the night with the man of my dreams. Your wish is on the way. Trust me. Remember, you're on the right path, pace yourself, walk, don't run. Never forget. Even when you become rich and famous(which I know you will), still remember, walk, don't run. LEARN TO CHERISH THE JOURNEY."

I smiled before tucking the letter away into my pocket. Safe to say I was truly gonna miss her. Just last week I was almost sure I'd never fall in love again. And while I may not be able to be with Stephanie, she gives me hope that there are some good women out here. It's hard coming across someone who understands you when you don't even really understand yourself. But at least I know Love is possible.

We packed and prepared to leave. Before stepping onto the van I took one last look at the place. I don't regret a second. I'd survived. Another part of my journey had been completed. Not to mention I still had a few dollars left in my pocket. Nothing much, but hey, at least I got something.

We hopped on the van. I sat back soaking it all in. I was about to get back to the real world. A world that had become so hard for me. But it was cool. I was gonna make the best of it. I just gotta accept the position I'm in and do whatever I gotta do to get the fuck out of it. I don't know where I want to start or even if I want to start over. Who knows? I just gotta find a way to appreciate all the love I get that a lot of people never get a chance to experience. Yes, I may be down but this isn't my first rodeo. I'll be back on my feet.

"Fellas. I just gotta tell yall I had me a good ass time. I'll never forget you crazy ass motherfuckers. I damn sure don't wanna see yall ugly asses anytime soon but I promise I'll never forget this shit. Thanks for inviting me Mike," Uncle Pit said as he raised his head, looking around to us all as he spoke.

"No problem man. I'd like to thank you guys too," followed Mike. "Man to have this many Black men of all ages come together for a Bachelor Party out of the country is amazing."

"Yeah guy's," added Boo," I know you're all mad at me but this was a really great experience."

"Fuck that shit, trip wouldn't have been the same without you," followed Jay.

"Yeah, that's the past. We're actually gonna need you to take one more pic of us before we leave," said Mike.

"Yeah man I gotta post these shits on The Gram," added Kt.

"See that's the problem with you young motherfuckers," said Uncle Red.

"Aw man here we go," added Lee.

"Naw man I'm serious, that social media shit is ruining the world," followed Uncle Red.

"How?" asked Lee.

"I love social media," added KT.

"Like I said, fuck Social media, look at it," Uncle Red shouted as he pointed to my phone. "Got you young boys acting like pussies. Since when did grown men start liking to take pictures? 'Ay bro take this picture of me, I look cute'," he said in a mocking tone.

"Ay, I can't even lie Unc, you got a good ass point," agreed Mike.

"Damn right I do. Fuck social media."

"And don't let me get started on what it's doing to these motherfucking women," added Uncle Pit.

"What is it Unc?" asked Jay.

"You wanna know what its doing?" Uncle Pit said excitedly to Jay. "It's turning these bitches to whores. See, back in my day women had to really be natural born cheaters to cheat. It was so much work, people had house phones and shit. It was hard to get away with stuff, aint nobody have time for all that. Nowadays a bitch can cheat just by being vulnerable."

"Preach!" Uncle Rome shouted, playfully.

"Her and her Ol man can argue, then five minutes later some muscle head ass Facebook personal trainer inboxes her and you know what the fuck she gonna do?" continued Uncle Pit.

"Tell em," added Uncle Red as we all listened attentively.

"What she gonna do Unc?" asked Lee.

"Exactly what a low down dirty bloodsucking bitch is supposed to do," he said before looking around, face balled up. "The bitch gonna bite," He yelled.

"You better bet she is," added Uncle Rome.

"And you know what happens next, it becomes easier and easier to do some sneak nasty shit. Before long the bitch is a full blown whore, now she's sneaking niggas in the crib when her Ol Man goes to the gas station. I'm telling you, that social media is the devil."

"Fuck that Unc. Yeah it might be bad for some people. But niggas meet their wife's on social media," said KT.

"Wife's?" exclaimed Uncle Pit. "You'll be a dumb motherfucker to get a wife. I aint talking about you Mike, you're already too far in."

"But Unc, you're married," I said.

"You think I wanna be? Bitches can't decide what the fuck they want for diner, you think I believe them when they say they're ready for marriage. Don't be like me young bloods. Go fuck some of them social media whores."

"I'm with you Unc," added Jay. "I don't trust any of these Females."

"Man they aint all the same," added Uncle Red. "I love my wife."

"Motherfucker you just pussy whipped," barked Pit. "Youngin listen to me," he added as he locked eyes with Jay. "Fuck as many of these broads as you can."

"I gotta admit, I kinda agree with Unc on this one," said Lee. "Me and my girl been together for years but I can't do the marriage thing, that's just too big of a step."

"So yall gonna let one or two girls fuck it up for everybody?" asked Mike.

"Hell yeah. That's how the world work," answered Jay. "Just like racism. It's only a few of them white motherfuckers who captured our people and bought us over here to be slaves. But because of their actions I don't trust not one of them motherfuckers. Besides, trusting a chick takes too much energy, I'm lazy."

"Yep, only thing you can trust a motherfucker to do is be themselves, sadly 90% of them Females is all hoes," added Money.

All of a sudden the vans started to put.

"What the hell going on?" asked KT as the van pulled over to the side of the road.

"I don't know what the problem is," said the driver as he hopped out to look under the hood.

"Yo we aint got time to be stranded, we're almost late," said Uncle Red. "I gotta make my flight back. I got shit to do."

"Me too," followed Jay.

"Man we gotta find a ride," followed Mike.

"Does anybody phone work," asked KT, looking around.

"Hell naw, no service," answered Money.

Everyone panicked before I saw a vehicle approaching. It was a van.

Whatsup God,

Yo did you send this?

As the Van drove closer we realized it was one of those Police Paddy wagons. We could all surely fit in there. Together, we flagged it down until they stopped next to us.

"Yo can you give us a ride to the airport, it's important," I said noticing that it was the same police who'd saved my life.

"You again," one of the Officers replied.

"Oh shit. Yall only got one set of police out here or something?" asked Uncle Red.

"What's the problem?" asked the other Officer, ignoring Uncle Red.

"Bruh, we need to pile up in your van. We gotta make our flight back to the states. It's an emergency," said Mike.

"No. It's against the law," said the first Officer.

"Come on man, fuck the law," said Uncle Pit.

"Hold on guys. How bout for this," I said as I whipped out some cash.

"Hop in," they both said, wasting no time, snatching the money from my palms.

It felt good as hell doing something for the fellas. So what if I had to spend a little cash. I know I'll get it back. If not, I'll just go back to the Plasma center. Fuck it. That shit aint gonna make or break me. I gotta do what the fuck I gotta do. Who cares what anybody thinks of me.

We all crammed in.

"Yo one of yall motherfuckers stinks," yelled Uncle Pit.

We arrived at the airport just in time. As the cops released us I knew it was only right to get a pic of us hopping out of a paddy wagon.

"Ay Boo. Take our picture," I said.

After flicking it up, I checked my phone, the picture that the 'Prostitute Posse' had sent to our group chat of me handcuffed was hilarious. No need to be ashamed, pretty sure someone can get a nice laugh out of it. I posted it to my Instagram along with my other pictures.

Caption: 'Weekend in Costa Rica.'

Hopped back on the plane, got comfy and prepared to admire the earth from my birds eye view. Aint no telling when the next time I'll be back on one of these motherfuckers again.

As we took off into the open sky I brainstormed ideas and jotted down a few notes on goals I needed to accomplish. At the end of the day, I gotta remember, I'm still further along than I was when I first started 8 years ago. I've met so many people who may be able to help. But what's even better is all of the knowledge I've obtained. Even if I have to start over from where I began at least this time I'll know what steps not to take.

Time flew and before I knew it I was hopping off of the plane into the overly crowded Atlanta airport. I didn't make it 20 feet before some kid waved me down to take a picture. I was surprised but it wasn't my first time being recognized by a fan.

"When did you see the play?" I asked as he held up his camera for a selfie.

"What play? You're the guy from the meme that Chris Brown posted," he responded.

"Huh?"

"This one," he said as he showed me his phone. It was a picture of me handcuffed with the Prostitutes smiling with the caption, 'If my vacation aint this lit then I don't wanna go.'

Shocked, I checked Instagram and damn near shitted on myself. I had nearly 50,000 new followers. I was all over that motherfucker. There were all types of different variations of our pictures. Some with close ups to my smile, some with funny captions about girls taking dick by gun point.

Unsure of what to do, how to act, I simply stood there as mobs of people bumped and passed me by.

Whatsup God,

I can't believe this. Man I can't believe this.

Still stuck in place, I checked my e-mail and I had Film offers already.

'You ready to start shooting?"

"Hey do you have agent representation?"

"Would you be interested in auditioning?"

I smiled as I peered above.

Love Yo Family

I stood next to Mike as Whitney walked down the aisle and couldn't help but to smile. I tried to hide it. I know I was probably looking simple as hell. But this joy could not be contained. My nigga was getting married. He always said he'd tie the knot before 30 and he did it. Actually he did everything he ever said he would do. He deserves all the blessings God is sending him.

I'm not sure when my smile actually faded from my face but I'm pretty sure it had to be when I finally saw Erika. I stared aimlessly, lost in her beauty. Only acknowledging me for a brief moment, she smiled before focusing back to the wedding, something I failed to do. To take my eyes from her would be impossible. She glowed, a bright florescent light beamed around her. I still hadn't talked to her since the final night of the Play. I'd thought about calling once I got back from the trip but figured it'll be more romantic if the first time she saw me again I was in a tux.

Before long the wedding was over, Boo snapped a bunch of group photos as we headed inside, it was the moment we'd all been waiting for; the reception. I was ready to cut up, I'd been drinking since I'd woke up and was ready to celebrate.

After taking my seat alongside the Groomsman, Lee, KT and Jay, I watched as Mike and Whit slow danced before the D.J. cranked up the music and everyone stood to their feet. I was just about to make my way over to Erika before she beat me to the punch.

"Hey Movie star," said Erika as she walked over, dress fitting her to the T.

"I wish," I replied, attempting to hold in my glee.

"There you go, always tryna be humble. Boy, I saw all those offers you posted on Instagram that you've been receiving. You're lit."

"Yeah who would've thought a viral meme would do all this for me."

"Von, you're smarter than that. That meme isn't the reason you're where you are right now. You worked for this. The meme is just the opportunity. It would have come in another form if not Instagram."

"Damn. Why are you always right?"

"I don't know, I guess it's a gift," she replied jokingly. "But seriously, I've been praying for you. I'm so sorry to hear about your girl."

"Thanks. It's getting better day by day. All I can really do is move on with my life. I'll never forget her but like I said, I just gotta move on."

"Don't rush it though, give yourself time. I can't imagine how you're feeling."

"Trust me I won't rush, I'm taking my time with life now. I'm seeing things a lot clearer. I've kinda learned to accept death. It's a part of life. My loved ones spirits live on. I can't dwell on what life could have been if they were still here. This is how God wanted things. I only have one life and I'm focused on making every day count. I can't taint my experience by worrying and questioning things that I can't control."

"Von," Erika replied, shocked. "You've really grown. That's a beautiful way to look at things."

"Yeah, I was so focused on getting to where I am now that I was forgetting to live in the moment. I probably missed out on so much by moving too fast. I won't do that again."

"I know exactly what you mean, I've actually had to learn a similar lesson. I was so caught up in my work life, before finally after damn near having a mental breakdown, I thought to myself, why am I even doing this? What's the purpose?"

"There aint one! God gave us the Power to dictate our own life, it's up to us to arrange things in a way that make us comfortable," I followed.

"You're right. I wish I would have thought about it earlier in life. I really admire you."

"Thanks. Don't get it twisted though, this is new for me too. A new friend of mine taught me that sometimes you can be looking in the right direction but from the wrong angle."

"I think your friend is smart."

"Yeah," I agreed. "Made me realize life is pretty simple. A lot of times we look at strangers and compare ourselves to them. When in actuality that doesn't make any sense. God gives each individual a personal journey. Some long, some short, but each is precious in its own way."

"Boy let me find out you're a young Guru now," Erika replied, blushing, showcasing her dimples.

"Ay man," I said smiling. "I'm just a guy with an open mind trying to figure some things out. With all the game you kicked me back in the day its only right I drop a couple jewels on you." I said before pausing. "Ay you remember back in the day when you told me about following my intuition?"

"Yeah I remember that day, I told you it meant to follow your heart."

"Yep, that shit was life changing. Honestly that was some of the best advice I've ever gotten. It's basically the reason I'm where I am today."

"Well I'm glad I had such a profound effect on your life," she said, smiling. "You mind if I ask you a question?"

"Ask away," I replied.

"What is your heart telling you right now?"

200

"Well," I said as I stepped closer. "It's saying that after all these years I need to stop playing and tell you how I really feel about you."

"And how is that?" she asked as she stepped closer to me.

"I feel we were each other's blessing," I said as I inched closer. "You remember my new friend who's been giving me advice that I was just telling you about?"

"Yeah," she replied as she licked her lips.

"Well I was also told that there are no coincidences in life. There was a reason Mike introduced us and there's a reason we're standing here today. I ignored it in the past but not anymore, it's time-," I said before being interrupted.

"Yo my nigga thanks for inviting me to dis shit," interrupted Rell, he'd just been released from jail and was out on Bond. I'd invited him to the wedding. "Dis betta than any welcome home party I eva had. These hoes is sophisticated," he continued as he looked around. "I need me one of dem."

"Bro," I replied, annoyed.

"My bad, my bad," he apologized, looking over to Erika. "Sup I'm Rell, I'm Von's new managa. I'm not interruptin anythang am I?" he asked.

"No. I was just telling Von that I feel the same way he does," Erika replied, never taking her eyes from me.

"Oh shit. You must be Erika, this fool been talkin bout you all damn mornin. I like her," he said, looking over to me, nodding. "Real talk, gotta good lil vibe to her," he followed.

"I like her too," I said as Erika and I continued to stare off at one another.

"And I like you more," she replied.

"Well where I'm from when two people like each otha its only one thang for them to do," said Rell.

"Bro," I shouted.

"What?" he replied. "Nigga chill, I ain talkin bout nothin nasty. U'm talking about hittin the dance flo. I know you ain bouta let Mikes White ass co-workers steal all the shine," he said as he pointed over to the dance floor. There were about five White couples drunk dancing to the tune of their own drum.

"Well I've been told I have two left feet," I added. "But I know I can't be any worse than them. You mind?" I asked Erika as I stuck out my hand.

"It'll be my pleasure," she smiled.

We headed to the dance floor before I was stopped by Mike.

"Well looky here, do I need to tell the Pastor we're gonna need his services again?" he asked.

"Not quite yet," replied Erika.

"Well let me know, I think I can get yall a good deal," followed Mike. "But in the meantime come over here, we're about to take a little Bachelor Party reunion photo, who knows the next time we'll all see each other. It feels good to have all of you guys under the same roof again," he added as he pointed over to the guys. Everyone from the trip was standing together waiting on me as Boo held his camera.

"Bet. But can Erika join us?"

"You know it," Mike replied as we headed over. "Whitney's already over there."

"Ay Von, get in the middle with Mike and Whitney, we need this to be one of your famous pictures," yelled Uncle Pit.

"Bet," I said as I grabbed Erika by the hand before pulling her in close for the flick. We all smiled as Boo got in position.

"Perfect," shouted Boo, after looking at us through his lens. "On three, I want you to smile as if you had not a care in the world. 1,2,3!"

Whatsup God,

Thank you.

If you enjoyed American Dream make sure you spread the word.

If you purchased on Amazon or Kindle please leave a review.

If you're incarcerated please request to get this book and my other novels 'American Rap Star', 'American Maniac, 'Us Vs. Them', and my debut novel 'American Boy', in the building!

Thank you for the support. If you need to contact me:
Phone: 757-708-4890
Facebook: Kevin Brown
Instagram: __KevinBrown
Website:KevinBrownBooks.com

Made in the USA
Middletown, DE
12 February 2022

60864330R00116